Laughter and Early Sorrow and Other Stories

Brett Busang

Open Books

Published by Open Books

Copyright © 2017 by Brett Busang

Cover painting "Midnight Visitor" © 1988 by Brett Busang

ISBN-10: 0998427489 /ISBN-13: 978-0998427485

To Moms and Dads, without whom the follies of children cannot be conceived, imagined, or given free rein

Author's Note

These stories have been arranged, more or less, in the order in which they were written. Two of them have the same characters. The same people are mentioned in two other stories, but they appear in only one. (You'll see what I mean, though such coincidences don't really matter. All the stories are, however, set in, or originate from, the Memphis of my childhood and are rooted there. If there is a connecting thread, it is that and that only.)

Contents

Foreword

Almost everybody who was born in the post-agrarian period that might be separated by the two great wars that were, each in their separate ways, never supposed to happen, grew up in a place whose growing pains were as painfully obvious as the people in them. As downtowns yielded to the midward bulges that were reachable by the streetcar lines that are considered merely picturesque today, another march—toward a suburban Arcadia that was as ill-defined as it was irresistible—was on. To get there, you could neither walk nor run. The streetcars didn't go far enough. And the city limits, upon which limitations had been foolishly imposed, were expanding with a prodigality no one could have possibly anticipated (even if nobody seemed to think they were abnormally far away.)

It was into such a place that my parents moved, with me more physically in tow than my brother—who was of more recent vintage and unsteady on his pins. Our house was small, but serviceable; our neighbors forthcoming, but not so morbidly curious that they pried, and our world had expanded in one way and shrunken in another. We had the *Lebensraum* for which Hitler had reached too far just twenty years ago. The sky was as blue as it is said to be in heaven. And we were so adrift in space that we became the terrestrial astronauts that troubled Rod Serling so much, he had to write something about us every week for years.

Here the Main Streets of our grandparents were left to developers, who preferred parking lots to promenades. Here generously proportioned school buildings beckoned to a fertile population that would supply them so handily that, once a prototype was made, it could be endlessly re-produced. Here pastimes flourished as they never had before. And here the intersecting clothes-lines, the snoopy-looking TV antennae, and the subway fatigue that made New York City both emblem and eyesore could be moved into a den or backyard; mulched carelessly over; and left, more or less unconsciously, to its own devices.

Here mostly white people settled in as Ricky Nelson serenaded them, somewhat insipidly, from a tastefully abbreviated ducktail—which the "greaser" mentality had made dangerous. Here needs were synonymous with desires. And here a culture that was made possible by the received wisdom of Father Coughlin, Leo Durocher, and Lawrence Welk sat back, adjusted its goggles, and proceeded, with limitations that grew with every sack of fertilizer that guaranteed more perfect lawns, to have the time of its life.

It was here that I allegedly grew up and here (mostly) that I have roamed, from ball-field to abbreviated living-room to the topsy-turvy relations between hard reality and plausible delusion. I hope, in catching some of it, a pardonable license has been exercised; fair play has been acknowledged, if not precisely observed; and a sense of the small underbellies that often lurk beneath the bigger ones has become crudely, if only temporarily, visible.

Laughter and Early Sorrow

Sam and I would never have a hard time sneaking out of the backyard because of the way backyards were in those days, and perhaps still are. When, after World War Two, the builders came in and drew up lots, they decided that it wouldn't do to have a big yard out front and a dinky one in the back, for the garbage and such; so they pitched into it on a grand scale and provided a full acre for the homeowner of the future, who'd gotten a college education and had a longer horizon than his own mom and dad, whose center of gravity was in the cellar. (No cellars in these new houses either. Just crawl space enough for the centipedes.) But once a big yard was there, they had to put a fence around it. Fortunately, they built their fences not for sneaky people, but for the dogs the new residents would inevitably have and put out back. The fences were very good for holding dogs. The only way a dog could get out was to either dig under them or weaken them by the sort of head-butting not all dogs are willing to do unless they want to get out real bad. The dogs we had were diggers. We'd watch an emergent tunnel as Bowser or Marbles lay into the ground with forepaws that were controlled by strict cerebral protocols that allowed, not only for efficient digging, but for a moment's rest now and then. The hole got big real fast, the dog went underneath it, and we chased him around the next yard until we caught him and brought him back. On a couple of occasions, tragedy struck when a dog found the roadway, after which there was no stopping him—at least by us. The two dogs I lost during those years ran into Pontius Street, the big thoroughfare at the time, and were struck down before they could get across it. They were both alive when I found them, and expired shortly afterwards, disbelieving the fate life had dealt out to them. "Lark Becomes Tragedy" would read the headline in a canine-friendly newspaper.

For humans, these fences were a joke. You got a toehold and you helped yourself over them. In the case of the woven pine boards that connected each yard from the back—some developer's idea of a superior amenity—it was so easy that you had to create obstacles to make it interesting. We'd make rules about not scaling the fence except with one hand behind your back—or with no hands at all. Then we'd get the hang of it and try something more dangerous, like walking all the way across the yard on the soft rim of the fence itself. You could easily fall when you did this; it was therefore a more honorable way to get over. If you fell more than once, however, you were given a passport to the other side. We were not punitive in our methods, just appropriately rigorous, as befits children of a generation that had saved the world for democracy a second time.

Escape was not the problem during a summer's sleepover. One night I was at Sam's house and we were dozing in the backyard, underneath the scaly-bark tree Sam could climb and I couldn't. We planned to escape at two a.m., which would give us enough time to ride to "the site" within an hour and observe it for a while. Then we'd go in, look around for the desk that was apparently crammed with crinkly old documents whose monetary value could not, at present, be known, and then do what we had to do before it got light out and the jig would be up.

The problem was with Sam's dad, who had a habit of coming out and seeming to check on something in the utility shed—but was, of course, checking to see if we were still out there. Sam's dad favored "corporal punishment", a phrase meted out at school with a spine-tingling gravity. When I asked Sam what corporal punishment was—the image of a soldier with an oven-mitt being stuck in my mind—he said if I didn't know it, he wasn't about to tell me. Then he asked me whether I was born yesterday, what stupid-spores had taken over my mind, whose lousy batch of sperm had made me. I had no answer for these questions, being a slow thinker and somewhat incapable in matters of self-assessment.

So the oven-mitt imagery got re-enforced, and, when we saw Aldro, Sam's father, approach the tool-shed, I saw him as a lance corporal about to go into a room full of oven-mitts of various colors, sizes, and undistinguished workmanship. Sam was like that. He kept secrets from you in order to have a certain power, and therefore elevated status, in our body politic of two. I guess I could've just gone and looked it up, or asked my mom or dad, but that seemed weak somehow. The knowledge would be transmitted from the proper source when I was ready for it.

We really wanted these antique documents. We were about to subsidize a trip all the way down to Florida and knew we needed scratch to get there. Having arrived, we could, of course, live on the beach, but with any new lifestyle change, you really had to have backup. We figured these papers could get us up to a hundred dollars. That would set us up on the beach for a time period I wasn't prepared to quantify. It would, however, be long enough for us to be forgotten by parents, friends, teachers, and the police—should they take a keener interest in us than they took, according to Sam, in the average runaway. He said that runaways were so common that the statute of limitations on them was very short. The legalistic gravity of the word "statute", whooshed up with the dignified polysyllables that gave it extra stability, was enough to assure me that he, Sam, fully understood what we would be up against for a time and how we would be rewarded if we were successful.

Sam's dad kept on coming out there at half-hour intervals. When it got to be around two o'clock, we thought of calling the whole thing off. Aldro had come out at eleven-thirty, then midnight, but had staggered his next visit till after one. Maybe he'd given up. He was an old guy and, because it was a weekend, he slept in till about nine in the morning. He had to have his rest to piddle about in the yard. At fifty, he was a lot older than the dads I knew by name or reputation. He and Sam's mom had prudently waited till they'd had kids. Had waited till they got the house and the yard. Then waited, for good measure, a few years beyond that. The sort of caution that characterized a generation we put, in our spending habits as well as procreative enthusiasms, conveniently to rout, was passé to us. Yet it had made the world a better place and we were presumably, if not overtly, grateful.

"Maybe we should call this off," I said, thinking of the oven-mitts in Aldro's hand. My parents and Sam's had an arrangement. And while corporal punishment was something I only pretended to understand, it could be administered by either parent should the infraction be horrible enough to warrant it. There was no immunity here, even for me. That lack of immunity was suddenly a big concern. Aldro was not one to spare the rod—or mitt—if one was necessary. Sam said he didn't want to brag, but he had welts back there. I always said I believed him, for fear of having the welts produced. Not only did I not care to see him naked, but I thought if I had to see the welts into the bargain, I might be obliged, by some sort of esoteric solidarity, to acquire some of my own.

"*Aldro tires after midnight*," said Sam, imitating his mother, who liked culture and was always re-doing the house. She had Aldro build a whole new kitchen, which she furnished with homespun decorations and crudely made furniture. It occurred to me that the farmwives and prairie women who had made these things couldn't afford to have a second kitchen and felt badly for them. All that was left of them were a couple of knickknacks a lady who had never worked glanced at now and then and considered herself "artistic" for having done so. Thinking of these long-dead people and their straitened circumstances made me feel guilty, and a little sad.

All the more reason to want Sam to imitate her, which he did, but only when the mood struck him. I tried to egg him toward protracted routines, in which he had Margaret flush the toilet and say "Ah, how refreshing!" or—my favorite—tell Aldro, as she entered the bedroom with something flimsy on, not to "wave that thing at me, dear!" Most kids wouldn't readily imagine their parents having sex. Sam didn't seem to mind the concept at all. Or: he thought it so comical that it protected him against its crude and stark reality. I couldn't help myself. The image of airy Margaret, with her high-minded talk about period this and authentic that, sighting a tumescent organ tickled me to the point that I frittered away countless hours in English and Math trying not to think about Sam imitating her. Sometimes I had to admit defeat and go off by myself after the last bell rang and laugh till the tears streamed so prodigally, I didn't bother, whenever they got as far as my neck, to douse them as they followed gravity into my chest-area. In the midst of such a seizure, I walked home by an unfamiliar route so people wouldn't see me.

"I know Aldro," said Sam authoritatively. "One's his absolute limit."

"Aldro tires?" I asked, hoping to cue him.

"Ah, so refreshing!" was Sam's comeback. I collapsed into my sleeping-bag, unable to do anything for five minutes.

"Come on. Come on." Sam was suddenly nudging me with his foot from on high, as I rolled from side to side. "It's now or never."

I took a deep breath, had a final bout of hilarity, and got to my feet. Sam led me across the long yard, which Aldro would cut later on that day. Our bicycles were in a tricky spot: alongside the bus-sized kitchen Aldro had half-built himself, but hired a contractor for the finishing touches—which he could not properly visualize no matter how often his wife came at him with a magazine article and shook it. I did not understand the look on his face until somebody asked me to fix a table. When you sit at one, it doesn't seem very complicated. When one is wobbling and needs to be placemat-ready in a couple of hours, you might as well be asked to repair a flatscreen TV.

If somebody was in the kitchen, he or she could hear us. Aldro had caught us only once, when he'd turned off all the lights and waited in the dark, with the mitts on, and airy Margaret in the bedroom sleeping after having waved his tumescent organ away. (In my mind, she did this at least once every night.)

After seeing that the coast was clear, Sam waved me toward the bicycles, two dinky little Stingrays we had already outgrown, but were small enough, we rationalized, to get us into places no other bikes would. Once we got to them, we stopped. If Aldro came out, we could make a dash across the front of the house, jump the fence, and reclaim the sleeping-bag area before he could get close enough to start waving—yes, waving—the flashlight around. Sam was incredibly fast on his feet. The coaches at school were always trying to get him to run track, but he had such an aversion to all forms of competition that he managed to squeeze out of any formal commitment, any race that was actually *planned*. I'd make him run now and then just to show some of my athletic friends what a formidable talent he was. One time I even staged a meet after school. For some reason, Sam didn't mind the idea and casually whipped the field. I didn't ask him to show off after that.

Aldro *had* apparently tired after that last visit. As at school, however, it was hard for me not to think about Margaret flouncing out of the bathroom, so I stood very still trying to hold in the laughter while Sam went around front and checked. Aldro could be there at the front door with his flashlight, waiting. But as Sam came back and shook his head—and I swallowed hard against another pitching bout of hilarity—the heist began. As usual, Sam took off into the night and was nearly a block ahead of me by the time I got the kickstand into position and pushed off. After nearly colliding with the wrought-iron post that was said to hold up the carport, I managed to clear the driveway and achieve a cruising speed that was comparable to that of a lumbering animal amidst a svelte array of trimmer, faster quadrupeds who could hit the road running and not slow down until some guy in a safari outfit plugged them. Sam's incredible running style had been adapted to the sawed-off little bicycles we would not abandon; the best I could ever do was just keep him within sight. There were times, however, when I had to guess the course and try to ride along with him mentally. I had no idea why he'd want to maintain such a gratuitous lead; he'd eventually reach our destination and have to wait as I came poking in. Perhaps this was his competitive spirit lashing out in a perfectly non-competitive situation. Sam got there first and that was that. It was a two-man ritual that would be enacted, with certain technologically-oriented variations, endlessly.

The course was hard to manage until senses other than sight could serve you. I was often taken aback, as I entered a pocket of it where a stretch of lights had gone out over Station Road, at how dark total darkness could be. Half a mile past that, I happened to look up at a sky that was hard and domelike, as if it were designed by somebody who was trying to keep us all in. The stars twinkled dimly, and from a distance that did not make any sense to someone who measured out things by feet and yards. Light years: what were *they*? I sighted Sam over the brow of a distant hill and pedaled faster. We were going to a place out Pontius Street, which had an assortment of fast-food restaurants and failing appliance stores until it blacked out past a big hotel that had been built on that faraway site in a weak moment, when faith, rather than reason, was in control of men's investment strategies. It was, however, good to see it there, whenever, on a dry run, I could not see Sam, who was down the road about half a mile. I'd never confronted him about leaving me so far behind, but it got me panicky sometimes, like when you feel you know a place and all sorts of unfamiliar things crop up to unseat your believing self and put a vicious skeptic in its place. At such times your sense of the familiar gets skewed, and then somebody comes out from behind the bushes, or a parked car, and starts up with some ghoulish laughter. Or you *think* he will.

By the time I got to the big hotel, I was in a panicky condition, complicated by the fact that I couldn't stop thinking about Margaret refreshing herself. I had that funhouse feeling of being terrified, but mocked for being so, in which case there is no comfort at all. You can't rely on the terror because the mockery is getting to you even more. It's the most exquisite kind of torture imaginable. Here was Margaret saying how refreshed she was from sitting on the toilet on a collision course with the sense of existential abandonment that plagues lost mankind, condemning him to a life of pain and suffering without end. And there was Margaret again. And on and on and on.

Somebody was coming out of the hotel and getting into a big car, such as one saw on TV. A Buick or an Oldsmobile. He was all duded-up and glamorous, like he'd just stepped from one of those luxury car ads, and was about to go off and make more of them. His showroom-fresh car was nice and shiny, he stepped into it like a lord, and he drove off down a swooping driveway to the main road, burning rubber discreetly. I noted that he was driving toward Sam, whom I was following mentally, but whose physical existence had little meaning at that point. As I pedaled furiously, I imagined a scenario in which the man at the wheel, having sighted Sam on the road, slowed down so they would be moving alongside one another and suggested, in the dulcet tones of Laurence Olivier, that he should wait for a friend rather than "do this showy thing you're doing and leaving that poor fellow in the dust. For all you know," continued the noble Olivier, "this friend of yours could have a debilitating injury that might be hobbling him up. Be a good fellow and see what's the matter, why don't you?" And then Olivier picked up speed and drove off toward Germantown, where he would meet with people of noble birth and ancient lineage. And if such people weren't available, he could keep on driving.

After the big car had swooped down that long driveway, it got dark enough for me to hear the ghoulish howling that is always audible when you leave a large metropolitan area and go straight to the country—as you could then. At long last, I was able to forget about Margaret in the bathroom and feel like we were insignificant earthlings some super-race would come and enslave the following Monday. I called for Sam in the darkness. Which was not the thing to do. In absolute darkness there is a vacuum, into which infinite space comes and sits around like it has deed and title to the place. So if you say somebody's name in the dark, and into infinite space, it doesn't even echo. It happens inside of your own head, where it begets massive nuances and disempowering associations. But I knew the road and, while the only thing I could see was the yellow line that kept the bad traffic away from the good, I stayed the course and found myself near the place whose possible riches would enable us to skip town and live among fish-nets and sand-flies. Sam knew it better than I did. He'd eyed it hungrily from the road when I was playing baseball or doing homework. Sam was an indifferent student and threw like a girl. He had his fearless nature, his running, and his powers of mimicry. As well as the second sight that allowed him to function, and be sane, in the celestial stadium that was Pontius Street at three in the morning.

When I approached the site and found Sam down below it, between the railroad embankment and some low-lying bushes whose tiny thorns always surprised and disheartened me, I thought of Margaret and started giggling. Sam made a can-it sign, which I obeyed as best I could, and slipped down beside him, dragging the bike into the bushes. Which snagged it, of course.

"Just leave it," he said, alluding to my bicycle.

The sound of his voice, lowered to a stage whisper, startled me, coming, as it did, out of that vacuum.

I jumped. He jumped *me*, covering my mouth like people do when they ambush somebody and have a movie contract.

I squirmed without success, and was led to the vantage point we'd selected the last time we'd come out. I looked back at my bicycle, whose handlebars glinted in the moonlight—a visible thing that might lead someone to us. I pointed in that direction while Sam shook me off and continued to manhandle me. Well, it was no longer my problem. If the handlebars gave us away, so be it. Let Sam explain what we were doing to the cops, or to the FBI; we would have those priceless documents and there would be questions.

Our precious archive sat well off the road, behind somewhat denser foliage that was at least unbarbed. There was an old neon sign hanging over the gravel driveway that must've led people in pursuit of guilty pleasures to ugly little rooms without proper ventilation (let alone minty chocolates on each pillow.). Back in the day when there were cheap hotels, that's all the atmosphere you got. This had been one of them, but the old rooms had been sheared away, leaving a lonesome-looking outpost with no apparent owner or inhabitants.

After releasing me, Sam motioned me forward. Suddenly independent, I did as directed.

As he reached the gravel driveway, we saw a car approaching from Pontius and dove into the ditch off the shoulder of the road and hid there until it passed. We'd never run into anyone, but this was just the sort of place people on the run were always finding and hanging out in. *We* were doing it.

Once the car was out of sight, we ran to the door and pushed it open. It gave way with no sound and we were in.

It was the sort of place I had always loved. Tendrils from a long-standing morning-glory came snorkeling in from a casement window. An old desk piled with receipts, rubber stamps, and fountain pens sat underneath it. Its ornate character was out of step with a sleazy old place dedicated to unsavory trysts and illegal fornications. Moonlight seeped in from the window and made everything bluish, like a photograph in 3-D. Sam motioned for me to follow him. I crept behind with a sense of impending disclosure. This had to be The Place. I'd never been in there and couldn't know what it looked like—though he'd talked about it enough. He had fed my imagination with tales of a high-class mausoleum filled with forgotten things the like of which nobody had ever seen. And some of these things were redeemable for the cold hard cash that would allow us to live in Florida for the rest of our lives!

It was a bad time to be thinking of Margaret. I thought I'd gotten over her being refreshed by that bout at the toilet, but I remembered some of the other things Sam had her do and couldn't put them out of my mind. There was the one where she and Aldro are smoking cigarettes in bed. She turns to him and says, "That was the most sublime fucking we have ever done, my darling!" and rolls over with a peace that passeth understanding. I got to thinking of that one and it started to choke me so much I had to stagger out of the place and void the laughter that was in me.

The problem with me was that I didn't have any cool.

When I was with a bunch of other boys and they were telling lies about finding condoms in special drawers or subjecting a sanitary napkin to an all-out scrutiny that was lacking in neither scientific rigor nor pre-adolescent curiosity about form and function, I was the one to giggle. Even when I felt one of these giggles coming on, I couldn't stop it once it had a coy beginning in my throat and came up honking through the nose. Nobody who was doing bad stuff ever wanted me around because I'd ruin it by losing my cool. Sam was the only person left. He did daring things and would tolerate me watching or helping. I think he must've liked the control, just as he liked keeping secrets.

On the other hand, I disgusted him when I did something like what I was doing now. He had already threatened to give up on me if I didn't snatch self-control out of dawning hilarity. But whether fate is character, or vice versa, it was my fate never, ever, not to laugh or giggle when there was an opportunity for it. I'd be the one in class who kept giggling when everybody else had shut up. There was no stopping me.

Sam charged out of the place looking for me, like an angry father. I had taken myself away from the scene and was heaving my last beside a gas tank that had rusted so picturesquely that the rust seemed painted-on. Washers and dryers were there, along with a shopping cart from a local grocery store—and some milk-crates stamped with the name of a local dairy that had branched out into ice cream. I'd found an appliance graveyard on which I could spare nothing but a sense of shame. Normally, I'd want to commandeer choice specimens, or at least commune with them for a while.

Sam motioned for me to come along, like the father who couldn't be angry anymore because he'd seen everything.

I pointed to the place I'd relinquished, as if to say: "We're giving up?"

He marched us along, back to his bicycle, which was underneath the thorny bushes; and mine, which was on top. I noticed he was carrying something, but didn't think about it at the time. I was too ashamed to be observant. I couldn't even think of Margaret, whose unclad image had taken me to such heights of unreasoning appreciation. How did he come up with this stuff? And why did I have to think of it right then—just as we were closing in on the stash that would get us down to Florida for the Life of Riley forevermore?

Naturally, I didn't see Sam after the first leg of our journey home. Now that I knew the route better, it didn't matter as much. Nor did it seem to take as long to get back as it did to get out there.

We got back at about five o'clock—more than enough

time to get settled before the sun came up. There were a couple of unknowns, of course. It was possible that Aldro had gotten a second wind and come out with the flashlight after we'd gone. In which case he'd be sitting up for us, with the light in one hand and an oven-mitt in another. The idea of corporal punishment from a strange and possibly sadistic father began to upset me and I dawdled a bit on Station Road, where our old school was, hoping I might find something (other than returning to that house) to do.

But that was no good. If Sam were there with his father, I'd have to be there with him. I'd watch as he, Sam, got the fiercely unpartisan licks that were coming to him; and then assume the bent-over position to receive mine, with my absentee parents' blessing, for whom off-site corporal punishment—if it were seen as the appropriate means of rehabilitating me—was perfectly okay.

There were no lights on inside the house as I approached and hit the driveway, which slewed you up it if you were going too fast. I managed to remember this and slowed down before I could hit the family car. I dismounted, wheeled the bike over to the correct spot, parked it there, and waited for a moment just to make sure Aldro wasn't hiding somewhere in the darkness with his flashlight.

When I was satisfied that the coast was clear, I tiptoed across the backyard over to the sleeping-bag area and found Sam there, apparently dead to the world, with a box of something tucked underneath his arm. I said his name, then shook him a little. Nothing. The box was made of wood and had the name of a cigar-maker on it, with a statuesque woman playing on a harp. I looked at the woman for a moment and wondered what she'd say to her husband if he shook his thing at her and then thought of what Margaret did and, without trying at all, was curled up into a ball shaking with the kind of adrenalated laughter the trip should have drubbed out of me. Perhaps it was the sheer relief of having gotten back, as it were, without incident. Perhaps it was the phenomenon of laughter itself, which has a life of its own and plays itself out when it's good and ready. Perhaps it was more than that, or a combination of the two. I don't know. This time, however, the laughter had gotten all the way down into me and could only be pulled out by *doing*. Sam stirred after I had spread out a bit in the yard and was releasing jet-like spurts of it as I went. He came over to me and looked, as if I were something he would have to strike over the head for its own good. Then he realized that he had the box and hid it inside of his sleeping bag. I was trying to tell him, *I can't help it, I can't help it*, but couldn't utter a word. All I had to do was think of Margaret asleep there in the house and I'd sputter out a throaty something I'd never heard myself doing until that moment.

"What's wrong with you?" was all Sam said to me as he went to meet Aldro, who'd turned on the lights in the over-sized kitchen. He flipped on the light to the back porch as he came out, in a pair of baggy pants he'd obviously thrown over his pajamas. Here was Aldro with the oven-mitts who wouldn't stop shaking his thing and fucked sublimely. I wanted to say: *You know I'd think of these side-splitting images in my spare time and come up with them at the worst possible moment. You know I'm the first to giggle in class when there's absolute silence, with an absolute premium on shutting up, and with absolute ostracism as the result. You know me and yet you put these thoughts and images into my head!*

When Aldro came out I'd composed myself somewhat, but was still laughing. He and Sam studied me as if I were the sort of aberration they'd been warned about, but had not seen before and should approach with caution—or with a stick.

"What's wrong with him?" asked Aldro.

"I don't know. We were sleeping and he had this fit."

"A fit, huh?"

"He's been doing this for two solid hours."

Sam's reading of my situation was accompanied by the sort of head-shaking that occurs when the subject is pronounced hopelessly round-the-bend and is about to be taken away.

"Has he?"

"Ever since...maybe three."

"Three hours like this?"

"He generally tires easily," said Sam, for my benefit—which brought on another body-shaking volley. *Why was he doing this?* I would've stopped by now. But the sight of Aldro there shaking the flashlight at me—shaking anything—was enough to regenerate the whole *gestalt*.

"I don't think he'll hurt himself," said Aldro, who fucked sublimely.

"Nah, I wouldn't think so."

"You look after him, okay?"

"Sure, Dad."

"And try to get some sleep yourself. You're going to be very tired in the morning."

"I have. Gotten some sleep, I mean. The mosquitoes, they got me up first. It wasn't him."

"Well, goodnight."

"'Night, dad. See you tomorrow."

Having fucked sublimely all night.

I did stop after a while, and felt extremely tired afterwards. Margaret and her bathroom epiphany no longer stirred me; her pillow talk had no sway; her decorating prowess was merely pitiable. Sam was asleep, with the cigar box next to him. Sam was a very heavy sleeper as a rule, so I realized this was my chance to look inside of the box we'd both gone out to that strange and fascinating place to get. If the crinkly documents were there, we'd go to Florida at an opportune moment after school started and never come back.

Purged of the irresistible hold Margaret and Sam, her spin-doctor, had on me, I went over to look. The box was sitting on a patch of dew-spangled grass, well away from the sleeping bag—an easy trophy if there ever was one. I went over to it and looked inside for the crinkly documents that would save us from a life of tedium in the suburbs and found nothing but a scrap of paper that appeared to be torn from one of the spool-bound notebooks we did our lessons in. I reached in to get it, turned it over, and it said: "How refreshing!"

There was no laughter in me, only the fatigue that comes after a cathartic experience or a somehow disappointing one. Now that the sun was up, I decided to go home. I could come and get the things I'd left later on in the day.

And that's what I did, except that I took the scrap of paper and wove it through the spokes in Sam's front tire, like you did with baseball cards if you weren't serious about collecting them. I think it was the first time I was ever jaded—even if I didn't know what the word meant and might not have understood it if I did.

As I rode down the deserted streets and watched the sun brighten up all the fudgy areas I'd passed earlier on, I tried to think of Margaret again in the same way, couldn't, and nearly cried. Something powerful had lost its edge, forfeited meaning, taken the low road in and the high road out. I didn't want to go to Florida anymore; nor did I want to go home. I wanted to wander around for a while, all by myself, and enjoy the last few days of summer, when life is suspended and waiting: when you're expected to be someplace, but can let it ride for a day or two and not think about it.

Little Jo's Closet

Rick and Tommy lived across the street in a slightly bigger house to which an earlier, more visionary resident had added an extra wing. "Wing" isn't the right word exactly, but it'll have to do. Technically, it was a sort of annex. Can you be a wing *and* an annex? I have no better idea now than I did then.

For all its size, their house had a shut-in feeling—as opposed to mine, which was more open than it should have been. Honeybees, june-bugs and other flying insects were constantly chased around the house and squashed, mutilated, or humanely directed toward a more open area and allowed to exit. Why didn't we shut the door? Just didn't. In those pre-air-conditioned days, fresh—or even stale—air was all the air you got. The fans we put in strategic parts of the house were pleasant mockeries; they took the air and they swallowed it without moving it around very much. As mid-summer approached, there were no fans in the house. They'd all been purged.

Rick and Tommy's house didn't need airing out exactly—it just needed *air*. Yet it was a nice place to go summer afternoons if you wanted to cool down for a while. Their air conditioning—which, then as now, is to be distinguished from oxygen—came from a unit somebody stuck into an "annex" window. The unit dripped cold water like a salivating dog and emitted an unpleasant, boggy odor. Rick and Tommy's parents, known privately as "Little Jo" and "Darling Booty", served us refreshments on the super-hot days that drove us inside for a while. They were, however, so stingy with them that you had to learn, much too early in life, how to nurse a glass the way people do in a bar. They'd pour me one glass of Kool Aid and remove the pitcher the moment the red or blue liquid was done filling my cold metal cup. The pitcher was back in the fridge before I could think ahead far enough to ask for a refill.

There was an exaggerated formality in the way the mother, or "Little Jo", addressed me when I was over there. She would say, "I'm delighted to see you again. Won't you please come in?" She accompanied her words with a sinuous, gliding movement that made me visualize people at a tennis match—a lawn-tennis match. I wanted to speak some other language to her, a language with stately vowels and whispering consonants: a language that had all of the courtly grandeur of England or some other, better place. She probably knew she was lost on most of us, but she had *noblesse oblige* and could accept disappointing people and situations with grace and dignity. This was perhaps why her knowing children had re-named her "Little Jo." "Mrs. Shills", her wifely name, didn't suit her.

Her spirited elegance contrasted sorely with the lady who was married to the Cadillac guy down the block. *She* came out to greet her man in curlers. As the curlers bobbed on a head that was just moderately stable, she waved a cigarette at whoever might be passing by. The sloppy affection with which she kissed the guy who had brought in the bacon for another day was genuine, but it wouldn't get you many grace notes—as I remembered Dolores, our part-time maid, telling us—in heaven.

"Little Jo" wore a hairdo that was the latest in Suburban

Chic and could assume the air of a woman who was not only too good for everyone, but might stoop to smacking them if they got under her skin. She glided about the dark living-room and sunlight-deprived den with a dreamy intelligence that made me want to stop her and ask whether I could become her body-servant, whatever that was. Though she was extremely image-conscious, it came from deep within her: from a sense of personal distinction you're either born with or you're not. *Here, in a world no one but I can imagine, more interesting things happen.* She seemed destined for bigger things, yet she had somehow chosen for her field of dreams this bigger-than-average little house, this post-World War II subdivision, these children, and an older husband who had probably given her enough of the moon to convince her that she'd get the rest at some point in the future.

"Darling Booty" was not there a whole lot, but when he was, a pervasive gloom settled over everything. He was a big, square-jawed man cut in the mold of Douglas MacArthur. In an age that did not produce a lot of sissies, he was comfortably authoritative and neurosis-free. He dressed casually, in khakis and "Bing Crosby" sweaters, but walked around ramrod-straight, as if somebody would be grading him on his posture. Even when he sat down to eat a TV dinner, he could not relax into it. As he speared his pork-chop and ladled his cooked peas, he bent hardly at all. I asked Rick and Tommy what made him like that and they broke into a giggle-fit I thought wildly inappropriate. I kept on asking the question in different ways, but they couldn't stop giggling to answer it. "You've got to stop!" they told me. They seemed to get a big kick out of him being the way he was, yet when they were all in the same room Rick and Tommy didn't seem to know what to do. When "Darling Booty" walked by, they'd clear the way for him, more like courtiers than sons. Husband and wife shared an otherness, a sense of being apart somehow. I never saw them embrace, or try to kiss, Rick or Tommy. They seemed like distant equals, sharers of a space all of them owned together. If Tommy and Rick had told me they were paying on the gas bill, I wouldn't have been surprised. Theirs was like no other child-to-parent relationship I'd ever seen.

The Shills' didn't entertain at home, but went out on the town, resplendent in gown and tuxedo. When *we* did this, my parents might make me wear a tie and a blazer to go with it. They made my brother dress up too, but he didn't have to wear a tie because he was a year younger—which didn't make any sense to me, but seemed to satisfy *their* sense of justice and propriety. My parents wore the same kind of churchy things most people did: things they rarely wore at home: things they always put away carefully, or took to the dry cleaners, after each mortifying adventure.

Given the role-playing atmosphere they were in, it seemed a natural thing for Tommy and Rick to devise entertainments; they were born actors and could mimic people and animals without trying. But they were keenly interested in one kind of entertainment and that was any kind of entertainment that arose from their mother's languid pretensions, her movie-star attitudes, her gliding about the house without actually going anywhere. I thought I'd get them started one day when I was over there for a snack. I was looking at the newspaper and noticed something *she* had checked—some dress-up occasion that was going to be real big. I brought the paper to Rick, mincing, as I thought he would, and expecting him to go into one of his routines. But Rick grabbed the paper and said if I ever did something like that again, I wouldn't be allowed to come back. He didn't say I couldn't come back; he said I wouldn't be *allowed* to. I said I was sorry—said it lots and lots of times. This was the same Rick who, later on that day, ransacked his mother's closet and came out of it, so to speak, as the lady herself. He sashayed about the bedroom like some sort of beauty queen, with an imaginary cigarette holder and made-up lips that were pursed lubriciously. Compared to this jezebel, Marilyn Monroe was a decorous young lady who wore only as much makeup as the publicity office let her. I sat on the bed watching Tommy watch Rick. He seemed to be getting more out of this theatrical performance than the performer himself. He egged his brother on with compliments. "Oh, you're so beautiful, honey! Maybe you could do another dip for us now." And Rick would comply with another exhibition that topped the one before that. "Oh, what a dip that was! What a dip that was, darling!" Tommy exclaimed, shrieking in ecstasy. "'Little Jo' is feeling frisky today, I see. Oh, we all see that too well. Yes, too tooooo well!"

They could anticipate one another's thoughts. "You can hide nothing from me, dear," was something Tommy must've said to Rick ten times a day. It was fun to watch one of them act as if he'd been caught at something, then watch the other look scoldingly in his direction. They could time it out so nicely, Rick and Tommy, it looked like something you'd see on TV.

They knew *fashion* too! They could distinguish between the various stoles, wraps, and after-dinner gowns their mother had. As their long and delicate fingers rifled through them, they made well-informed decisions about how best to use them and commented respectfully on their design and workmanship. "Oh, this one feels nice now, doesn't it?" Tommy would say as Rick would hold it very gently, like something that was one-of-a-kind and not likely to appear on the earth ever again.

I had to remind myself that Rick and Tommy, at thirteen and fourteen respectively, were older than I was—but such sophistication in the matter of clothes seemed well-advanced even for your average adult. I couldn't, for example, imagine Beaver and Wally knowing so much in this area. Nor, perhaps, should I have.

To protect them against the ravages of light and insects, *she* kept all of her best clothes in plastic sleeves. "Little Jo" was fussy about her furs in particular. Why? Because they were so expensive. Ex-*pen*-sive, with the accent on the second syllable and the whole word ringing out as if this second syllable had a clapper. Rick would imitate the way his mother said this and go into one of his little drag-shows to illustrate. I watched Tommy watch Rick and felt shut out. "'Little Jo' has everything now, doesn't she?" said Rick, sashaying.

They rarely imitated their father. Only Tommy would risk trying on a big male voice, and it cracked somewhat. I remember him pronouncing, as his father, this heartfelt vow: "Whatever you want, my dear, is not only fine with me; it is essential to my happiness." Then he did some undulating movements in the hips. This I didn't get at all. But they weren't noticing me at this point. They were collapsed in each other's arms, swooning with laughter.

Lest anybody think that Rick and Tommy were rarefied creatures, hothouse plants, or Proustian ladyfingers, I would like to point out that they had another, fairly "normal" side to them as well. They could, in fact, display certain cruelties that could not be described as rarefied in any way. One day we were throwing a ball around and they decided to keep it from me. They threw it back and forth for a while and talked only to each other. "Hey," I said, "throw it to me." They pretended with seamless authority not to hear me and went on throwing. Then they vacated the front yard, which was for warm-ups, and went to the back, a place big enough for games. There they began to play against one another, with me looking on and occasionally reminding them that I was there and might want to join in at some point. Their playacting reached a new and insidious level when, out of the blue, one of them would fire the ball at me and hope I wouldn't be looking. It was fortunate that I was paying attention. Every time one of them threw at me, I caught the ball cleanly and threw it back as a way of proving I was still interested. Surely patience and good sportsmanship would win out. But they never let me in the game. I left the backyard at some point, crying, and didn't see them for two weeks.

When Rick came and knocked on my door, he had something in his hand, but didn't allude to it. It was one of those things he would undoubtedly show me later. It was his teaser. When he carried an object like this, I knew something had to be up.

"We've got something we think you'll want to see. Oh, yes. I think we do."

I wanted to address them shutting me out of the ballgame, but he, Rick, had obviously moved on. As I got to know them, I noticed how they lived entirely in the present. Whenever I caught myself remembering something we had all seen or done together, I refrained from mentioning it. The few times I'd brought up some good old rip we'd had, Rick and Tommy's faces assumed a mask-like ennui, they waited a beat or two, then they started chattering on about something they wanted to do now, or sometime in the near future. It was strange, not only being around aspiring drag-queens, but within a culture that had no good or bad times to fall back on.

"I don't know. I've got some things to do in the yard..."

"We'll help you with that. You've got to come over. We both want you to see something."

My mind flashed to earlier invitations, which often involved peep or drag shows in which one of them would dress up or talk about dressing up or make as if they might dress up just so they could keep dressing-up in the forefront of things.

"I need to go to the bathroom first."

I mentioned this outright because I didn't like to go to the bathroom in their house, which was technically the main bathroom, but had been commandeered by their mother. It was superabundant with frills and curlicues. Special soaps vied with a barrage of special masks and special clippers and special body conditioners to make it the most crowded and claustrophobic place outside of a steamer trunk or storage closet. Just being in there risked some special thing whose rehabilitation would be well beyond me. When I assumed the usual position in front of the toilet, I had to step on a pink rug whose nap was tousled, like a poodle gone haywire. It was creepy to have to pee standing on that rug and I hated doing it. I bent over the toilet seat so much that I couldn't stand comfortably. But I had to do it that way because, if I didn't, an errant drop might get on the rug, in which case I'd be in terrible trouble. It scared me to think of what the mother might to do to me, should she realize that I'd been in her private bathroom and committed a blasphemous act against her rug—with the best of rug-saving intentions.

Of course, this was the bathroom Rick always made me use, so whenever I knew I was going over there, I'd use my bathroom and not have to deal with my horror of the pink rug getting stained or sullied.

"You can use ours. I mean it, come on over right now—right this minute!"

"All right, I'm coming," I said, thinking of the pink rug.

How can you know when you're going to regret something? Or, rather, if you know you're going to regret something, how can you know *how much* you're going to regret it? I should have known things would escalate and refused to venture, not into No Man's Land—a place Rick and Tommy knew very well—but somewhere neither of them would be able to get out of without serious consequences.

However, when Rick was insistent he was virtually irresistible. He'd flash you his perfect teeth, run a small black comb through his excellent head of shiny black hair, and you'd find yourself going along. His voice and manner were perfect little units of seduction that propelled you in whatever direction he wanted you to go in. When he asked me to do something, it seemed almost a privilege to comply. The odd cruelty could be forgotten, slights of majestic proportions faded out of mind, a nasty bit of needling ceased, at that very moment, to sting as much as it had before—or at all. Here was a brave new day in a brave new world and here he was: my own personal guide!

"Okay, but...could I use *your* bathroom this time?"

"Any bathroom you want. Just get out of that Sunday parlor of yours and come on!"

When I entered the house, it seemed darker than usual. The funereal calm that overlay the floor-length drapes and Eisenhower-era TV was electric, as if there were a funeral actually going on somewhere inside the house. I felt like I was in a horror movie and was about to say: "Where are you taking me?"

Rick motioned for me to come to his parent's bedroom, which overlooked the backyard and was the most private area of the house. After Rick and Tommy's little drag-shows, you can bet they went over the area with a fine-tooth comb. What would that big man do if he'd discovered they were in there, let alone what they were doing?

"Come on. He's back here."

I followed Rick into the room itself, which I hadn't really noticed because of the entertainment that had always gone on in there. Now that I could see it clearly, I found its hollow chic revolted me. The bed was covered in pinkish satin; I'd noticed, while at some department store, that in certain kinds of light, satin appeared to move all by itself. Satin-shy, I circled the bed and wouldn't sit down on it; I didn't want anything to crawl up, or do funny things underneath, me. Yet it was not your usual bed and therefore commanded attention. The scallop-shaped headboard was painted in cream, with touches of gold-leaf on the outside. Out of the shell emerged two bathers in the nude. These nude bathers were painted in life-like colors, with real eyes, mouths and pudenda. They were somewhat idealized in conception, but the lifelike painting made them earthily real to me. I stared at both of them in equal fascination. The woman's lips were painted a hot pink, while the man's genitalia seemed out of proportion with the rest of him. (Why, I wondered, hadn't I noticed this before?) Had I been familiar with the Botticelli version, I would have quarreled not only with the man being there, but with the woman's pouting suggestiveness, which failed to capture fecund maiden—or any other unpolluted thing—quite spectacularly. Whoever had painted these figures had taken the original conception and transplanted it to a murkier place: to a strip club, say, and not the Vale of Creation; to Las Vegas and not an ocean-bed from which only gods and goddesses might spring. My mother had taken me to the Brooks Museum, where there were pictures of naked people, but none of them, as I remembered, were quite like this.

But this was not what Rick wanted me to see.

"Look, we found something way back in the closet," said Rick, trying to suppress a giggle. "We found something and wanted *you*...to see it."

Why me? I don't remember ever having asked them to see anything. Did I seem to enjoy their performances more than I let on?

Before I could ponder this question, Rick emerged behind the something he wanted me to see. This something was life-sized and wrapped up about as thoroughly as something you might want to use now and then *could* be wrapped. Tommy was trying to get through the multiple layers as a *maître d'* would, with bows that attempted to apologize for the delay; tense little smiles that indicated that he was trying very hard and would get this thing over and done with sooner than later. He'd seem to be finished, but get caught up in another layer. It wasn't working. There was just too much to get through.

"You'll want to see this," said Tommy, now standing beside the thing, which was only slightly taller than he was. Tommy was going to be the tall one in the family while Rick, well, he'd just have to get by on his charm.

"He certainly *will*," said Rick, starting to weary of all the layers.

As Tommy stripped away layer after layer, I began to develop an uneasy sense of what might be underneath them all. Were they wanting to show me some dead and forgotten person swaddled up in knots for centuries? Even if they could have gotten their hands on such an archaeological treasure, it didn't seem like they'd want to have it. Their interest was confined to living people—even if that interest was skewed a bit toward their mother.

Putting aside the more nuanced pacing that might have worked best with a third man on the job, they started to double-team their quarry, pulling and ripping until it was completely visible and standing before them.

Having liberated it, both Rick and Tommy ran away from the thing and stood on either side of me. They obviously wanted to see my reaction, which did not disappoint. For a moment there, I had no words. I just stared straight ahead, trying to get my bearings, taking myself in hand, reaching into parts of me that were heretofore unknown. Once I got to these parts, I might find some way to express the bizarrely transient feelings I experienced while contemplating this rubber siren, this humanlike thing, this almost-perfect likeness of Rick and Tommy's mother.

Whoever had designed her settled for near-nudity, a nudity mediated with little bits and pieces—a nudity all the more striking for being shy of absolute.

Rick couldn't stand it. He circled me as if I were some sort of slow-rising bread, a great big question in human form. "Well?" he said to me. "Well?" I let him do what he liked as I contemplated this startling creation and tried, mentally, to slow everything down. My head seemed to be whirring like the fan we had recently taken away from our dining-room, where it cooled down the meatloaf without contributing to one's overall comfort. When I was finally able to slow my head down, I realized that whoever had done the thing must have had intimate knowledge of The Missus. And whatever its editorial shortcomings, this lifelike creation provided the anatomy lesson few children ever get. I would see my mother dash from bathtub to bedroom, but in that momentary flash I discerned nothing anatomical—not in the strict sense of that word. It was just my mother speeded-up and, incidentally, unclad. You can't think about your mother naked anyway. Yet here was a "woman" who might tutor me firsthand, and I found myself taking slow and studious advantage of the opportunity.

I ultimately found the simulation too unreal. This was essentially student work. The student was talented enough, but he or she had a ways to go. The breasts were, for example, torpedo-shaped, and built—it seemed to me—according to false specifications. Magnetized to a faraway source, they pointed insistently in that direction. While I had not seen real breasts before, these just didn't seem right. Most living tissue lacks this sort of rigor. Being gravity-bound, relaxation seemed to be our bodies' most natural tendency. People tell you to stand up straight because your everyday inclination is to slump. A teacher in later years put the fear of God in me when she said I'd develop curvature of the spine because I slouched in my chair. She singled me out for spite; I looked around the room and saw a whole generation of slouchers before me. She did them all a great disservice by concentrating on me. If they have curvature of the spine today, it is entirely her fault. And mine, I suppose, for not telling them what I knew.

It wasn't just the breasts either. This new, inanimate Mrs. Shills had oversized lips that were painted in the most garish, super-octane color I'd ever seen outside of a bowling alley. To say they were red is to say the ocean is blue, all trees green, and every pumpkin orange. No language presently known to us can hint at such incandescent reality. They seemed to be on her, but not *of* her. They seemed to have powers denied body-parts—powers of flight and penetration; pre-emptive powers whereby one part could infect and overthrow another. Sensing this, I fought the urge to defend myself. If that red got on me, I'd never be able to get it off.

Finally, this new body was developed in a way Mrs. Shills' was not. She was a tight sort of character whereas this lady was soft and pliant. The matron who presided over pork-chops and cuts of salmon was not a hip-swinger. If her sculpted likeness walked, she'd verily bump and grind. I couldn't have articulated this, but I realized the sculpture was a fantasy creation meant to perhaps compensate for certain inadequacies (or run-down parts) either one, or both, parents wanted to be at their very best.

Knowing full well who "it" was, I asked anyway.

"Why, yes, it's 'Little Jo'! Were you expecting Doris Day?"

"I know what *I* think. I think 'Darling Booty' likes *her* better."

They must've seen this thing many times before, the way they were talking. This show was for me, not for them.

"He had her made after they got in a big fight," said Tommy, who went up to "her" and pinched her tummy. Below this tummy was something I made the little girl next door show me one time.

"What do you think of 'Little Jo'?" asked Rick.

"No, this is 'Little Jo's' swingin' sister," said Tommy, with a growl.

I had no idea what I thought of her except that she should probably go back into that closet fast. But Rick and Tommy would have been deflated if I'd said that, so I told them— meaning it—that it was really something.

"Oh, she's that all right," affirmed Rick.

Tommy didn't seem convinced.

"I don't think you like her."

I assured him that I did, flashing the smile I used for my yearbook picture.

"I like her," I said without conviction.

"He doesn't like her, Rick. Here we went to all this trouble and he doesn't like her."

"I do like her," I said again, but with more obvious elocution.

"I like her very much," I repeated. "I just had to study her...for a while."

"He needs to *study* her. I see," mocked Rick.

"I think we should, you know..." said Tommy, nudging an unseen person and winking slyly.

"I think we should 'you-know' right now. That's a Tom Terrific idea, pal!"

As if I'd called some sort of obscure and complicated bluff, they fell to stripping her down—and with a much-improved and workmanlike efficiency. They'd need that efficiency when it came to wrapping her back up.

They had everything off her before I could suggest that they hold that thought for a moment and sit tight. What's more: they had stripped down this obscene facsimile of their own mother in my presence and were acting as if I'd given them the cue. This was the secret of all showmen: do something outrageous and pretend your audience has been asking for it all along.

There was something less alluring about her totally naked. After the initial shock, I began to look at her with what may have struck Rick as a worldly expression. I was strangely unembarrassed, as if "she" was more "herself" this way. As if her absolutely naked self was the most essential thing about her and was the best possible expression of her personality. I was, in fact, "studying" her just as I said I'd been doing. If you took a picture of me, I might have been stroking my chin or looking for a notepad.

"Doesn't this boy have any gonads?"

Rick shrugged in disappointment. He had expected gonads. Then Tommy had an idea.

"Why don't you go up and touch them?"

By *them*, Rick meant the simulated breasts, which were greased, like a Channel swimmer, once they were out in the open. Unlike anything else on that body, these breasts, and their candied nipples, appeared *alive*. I will admit that I didn't care to touch them. What if my touch *awakened* them? Or, worse yet, awakened *me*? Best not to handle machinery you cannot—or should not—operate.

"That's okay. I can just look at them."

"He'll regret it, won't he?" insisted Rick

"No, I won't," I said.

"Come on. Just put your hand on one of them. See what they feel like."

Rick went around to the body and showed me by sort of palming one of the breasts, with his hand floating slightly above it. This old pro didn't care to dig into his work for fear of spoiling it for me. This was obviously the climactic moment in their charade and I didn't want to disappoint them, so after watching Rick, I motioned for him to step aside and approached the body myself. I stood before it, not in wild surmise, but with a performer's sense of waiting for the right moment. As I waited, Rick said: "Here he is. Now stand up and salute real nice!" Tommy topped him, saying: "This'll be a moment the three of you will never forget!"

When I got around to touching one of them, Rick and Tommy started howling. They bent double and writhed on the floor. They flat-out died, got up, and died again. They finished the sequence by kicking their legs up, as if they were giant bugs with roach spray all over them.

"We're gonna tell your mother!" spluttered Rick.

"He made a pass at 'Little Jo'!" wailed Tommy.

I did something at that moment I could not do at the Snowden Academy of Music, where I was routinely made to improvise on an accordion I could never learn to play by the book: I ran. I found the doorknob and hurled myself toward the living-room, whose gloominess momentarily deadened my senses. But, after hearing Rick and Tommy start to come after me, I managed to lurch through the front door and tore out of it toward my house, which, true to form, was open and waiting. They wouldn't have time to come and get me. They had, it seemed to me, a lot of cleaning up to do. And, of course, what if *they* decided to come home right then? There would be more hell to pay than in all of human transgression. Imagining the scene made house-watching irresistible.

I thought in days to come that had I not begun my vigil, the Shills would not have pulled into the driveway when they did. When you watch something, you seem to direct energy and activity to that place. Perhaps I had an unconscious desire to watch them pull in, get out, go into the house, and see that thing of theirs, denuded by their own children, standing somehow bigger than life in the middle of their bedroom. The most accomplished quick-change artist in the world couldn't have wrapped up that body and shuttled it from the middle of the bedroom into the velvet depths of "Little Jo's" closet in the time that was available to Rick and Tommy. As I watched, I noticed the curtains that kept the light out of the living-room switching this way and that. God only knew what was going on in there. But I was sitting tight. There was no reason for me to go over there and get into what was essentially a family kerfuffle. When my mother got home and asked me what I'd done that day, I said, "Oh, nothing." She accepted the answer readily and didn't ask again.

Some weeks later, Rick came over and asked whether I wanted to come out and throw the ball around. It was close to the new school year and there was an agreeable tension in the air born of fresh starts and new perspectives. He had a nice pre-school outfit on, which accentuated his excellent posture while drawing attention to his head, whose perfect symmetry made it seem bigger than it actually was. He was James Mason *fils* to his mother, *Madame de Carlo*. We went over to his front yard and started throwing from a short distance. When we got bored with that, we went out back and started throwing there. The old forest our little houses had, in part, displaced was forcefully present in the big pin oaks that stood in the adjacent yard. The sky poked in and out of the tree-tops there, with a pleasantly soothing effect, as if his, Rick's, back-yard was a man-sized terrarium and we protected wildlife. My yard had no trees out back and was good for sunbathing only. Try that in this yard and you'd get a pretty uneven tan.

"We're moving," said Rick.

"Moving?"

"To Ohio. It's where, uh, Dad's from. We're going back there."

"When?"

"Should be nice. I like the sound of it. O. High. O."

Okay, okay, so what happened?

"Cleveland's bigger than this place. I'm tired of it here anyway."

Did they find her in there, or were you able to get her back into the closet?

"Where's Tommy?"

"He's not feeling well."

What did they do to you? Could you just tell me that?

"How old are you?"

"Thirteen."

How are you getting along? Were you grounded? Are you still grounded?

"I'm going to be twelve in October."

"Tommy's fourteen. He'll be in his second year of junior high."

"Junior high."

"They have advanced math in junior high."

"I know."

"And nobody knows you."

"Yeah."

"My dad and mom never cared for Memphis."

I couldn't help but notice that he didn't say "Little Jo". Or "Darling Booty."

I followed Rick into the front yard where we threw a little bit more. It was more open there and you could see the sky full-out. The blue in it was braided with wispy white clouds that kept losing their shape as I watched them out of the one eye that wasn't studying Rick. His nice hair, his symmetrical features, and his small antic mouth looked pretty much the same way they had when he and his brother had goaded me into doing something I knew we'd never talk about.

The Great Walkout

"Just keep your eye on the ball, son," was all my dad, one of the two coaches on United Methodist, said before leaving me with a bat that was an ounce too big, with a barrel that was more suited to power than the sort of plunking I was good at. The pitcher, a hirsute fireballer named Giles Somebody was so obviously overage that, once he was allowed to suit up, nobody wanted to mention it. There was a general assumption that, if you contested his right to play this late in the game the entire league would close ranks against you in an all-out assault on fairness and morality. "Why didn't you say something earlier?" they would have said in unison. Even then, I thought it was an interesting position for a church league to take. There must've been other reasons for it, besides not wanting to be seen as a weenie, but they were never brought to light. The moral? If you wanted to sneak a ringer in, you could. And that's what Holy Cross, the only Catholic team in the league, had somehow done. The league played fifteen games; Holy Cross' record the previous summer had been a dismal 5 and 10—not bad enough to put them in the cellar, but they were nowhere near a competitive ranking and were painfully aware of it. (Our record had been 11 to 3, with one makeup game that wasn't played until after we'd won the title, but so what?) Holy Cross obviously wanted to close the gap this year and didn't mind fudging the rules to get it done. Overage players were not unknown in the league. We had a guy who was sixteen—but he wasn't much of a player to begin with. When it was found out, we could cut him without telling him the real reason. He went on to college and got his picture in the paper at some student rally. He was throwing something at the cops, whose chances of not being hit had increased exponentially.

Old Giles was seventeen years old—at the *outside*. He was probably asked not to ever remove his jersey because, if he did, body hair would spring out of him so prodigiously, it would have to be cut down on the spot. In a world where everybody had just begun to find a little peach-fuzz in places that might someday warrant a razor, he had a perennial five o'clock shadow, which made his complexion bluish below the eyes. His forehead was the only part of him that was hairless. But there wasn't much of that between over-bushy eyebrows and the brim of his adult-sized hat, whose "HC" looked newer and fancier than any of the others on the field. He'd pitched a no-hitter against the Jewish team the weekend before, and was about to steamroll over us. Keep your eye on the ball! This was all my dad could say to me when he knew chicanery was going on before his very eyes: knew, without using the perfect pitch he had for age and capability range that this long-armed hurler should not be participating in a church league for twelve and thirteen-year olds!

"Yeah, if I can see it," was my thought as Holy Cross ran to the field and started taking ground balls. The team itself wasn't much to look at. The third baseman had to take three grounders before he could get off a decent throw to first; the shortstop emitted an audible cry when a grounder took a bad hop and found one of the many soft areas on his torso. The second baseman was okay, but I couldn't imagine him standing in the way of a sliding runner and flipping the ball to first the way Julian Javier did. And the first baseman was another oversized clop-hopper who could probably reach the fence on a pitch that was grooved and slow enough, but was otherwise useless. He didn't bend for balls in the dirt—which he'd get a lot of with this infield—and seemed a bit of a showboat. When he stood alone at the bag, he preened in a way my puritanical baseball mind found highly objectionable. In two or three years, he'd shoot up to about six four and play basketball anyway. Here he was just biding his time.

But their coach didn't seem to mind. With every bobble, he shouted out vague, but mood-elevating platitudes. "Way to hustle, Bobby!" "Fire it right in there, son, you've got him!" "Nice throw, Reg!" To which this mostly untalented lot seemed neither to listen nor respond. The infield seemed, to me, like so many extras who had to shuffle onto a set because a crowd was needed, not because any of their individual contributions would be sought after or desired.

Same with the outfield. The coach hit shallow fly balls in order to speed things up. A well-hit fly would remain in the air long enough to shatter a player's confidence: he'd either overrun it, or allow it to fall ignominiously to his right or left. Then he'd miss the cutoff man, who ran all the way out to him as if the ball were in a special delivery package and could in no way be thrown. These were the kind of outfielders for whom running after a ball was an obscure and esoteric concept. If the ball was not hit directly to them, it just wasn't fair. A *fair* ball was a ball that reached you; all other balls were off the radar and not worthy of serious attention.

So that's it, I thought, smearing the handle with some dirt from foul territory. They were so confident in this pitching machine they probably recruited from some rowdy Sunday school class that they thought anybody who could jump into a uniform could play behind him. We wouldn't hit, so why bother with any real fielding?

Not a bad idea. It's not as if we were so sparkling. Yet part of our infield, with me at short and the prematurely wizened Sammy ("Sammydave") Davis on second, stood head and shoulders over theirs. But for a number of obscure and somewhat defensible reasons, it fell apart at either corner. Dyckman, at third, always stepped on the bag before he threw, on the not unreasonable assumption that there would always be other men on. When a ball was hit to him with *no* men on, it was our not unreasonable assumption that the runner would get to first because of the time lost during that meaningless pivot. Our first baseman was an amiable, but hard-working, stooge named Toby Slouch—a name he tried desperately to live down, but never would. Not untalented kids, these two, but very tormented people and not psychologically equipped to play the game. Toby tried so hard it was painful to watch. An athlete has to clear his mind in order to focus on whatever happens next—a thing that can never be known beforehand. Toby was the sort of guy who tried to rehearse every possible move before he made it. So when something did happen, he was in the midst of rehearsing for something else. "Just catch it!" With a guy who was always mentally rehearsing, this was no easy thing.

When we took infield, there were no second chances. "Play the ball," my dad exhorted, "don't let it play you." If it did happen to play us, however, we couldn't ask him or Mr. Greenfield to hit another one. That was it. "Everything counts," my dad also said, often right after he'd said the other thing. His harsh Calvinistic creed became our own. It allowed less for error than repentance. It was perfect, I guess, for church league, in which you were always repenting something.

Keep your eye on the ball. You can keep your eye on the

ball and still miss it. You can't, in fact, swing at something you can't see because there'd be no reason to swing. As this Giles took the mound, I began thinking about that expression and how stupid it was and why it had stuck around so long in a game that discarded everything that was ambiguous and lacked precision.

I momentarily forgot my pique as I watched a young man in his late teens ascend the mound and get ready to pitch to me. The ball was already in his glove, which no batter particularly likes. The more you can see the ball, the better off you feel. But when old Giles took it out of the air, he also took it out of circulation. When it came, it would come at me from one of four different places. But that wasn't the thing that frightened me. What frightened me was the expression on this man-child's face as his small round eyes found the catcher's mitt and homed in on it. It was as if the features had relaxed around these small round eyes, bunching up in a way that made them glitter. They were eyes squared, vision to the power of two, all-seeing eyes that saw even more when they were focused on a target. I saw this and I shuddered very quickly, hiding the shudder by stretching with the bat the way major leaguers do, and diving in the dirt. When in doubt, a baseball player should always dive in the dirt. Dirt is to baseball what turf is to a gallop. They mesh in a way two disparate elements rarely can.

My dad repeated the expression as I walked up to the batter's box and took the first pitch for a strike. I swung at the second and tipped it into the catcher's mitt. I was surprised that he held onto it. Must be coming in at about eighty-five miles an hour, which was close to twice the velocity any player on United Meth had ever seen. It was quite astonishing to watch—mesmerizing, in fact. It came in with a kind of buzz that was not unlike the last sound a housepainter might hear after he accidentally reaches into a wasp's nest under the eaves of a two-story house. The sound he hears before he jumps off the ladder and finds himself flailing at the air—his new, but temporary, element. Then there was the vicious trajectory of the ball, which started out ball-sized in the hand, but through some sort of phenomenological funny business became an ellipse, then a caplet, and finally a sliver of light—or, simply, antimatter. When it smacked into the glove, it raised a cloud of dust that had been camping out in the leather pocket unseen. The sound, when it hit, was like a slap, with an echo that stayed with you till the next pitch. Then there was old Giles' face, which turned, as he threw the ball, from mildly belligerent (the signal), to fiercely focused (the release) to godawfully smug (the call). I watched the umpire, who, in defiance of major league convention, stood behind the pitcher to afford a more comprehensive view of the entire field, click a second strike into his mechanical counter and bear down. *Not gonna strike out, not gonna strike out.* A strike-out would establish a dangerous, but understandable, precedent. It would also doom everybody else in the lineup. Statistically speaking, if the leadoff man doesn't get on in an average situation, no one else will either. But this was not an average situation. We were all facing a guy who was so terrifying he could have asked all of the fielders to clear off the diamond—and just pitch. I'd heard, from my dad, of old Walter Johnson doing that and found the idea intriguing and provocative. Such style and panache! But who wanted to be a victim of it?

With this passing thought, I took myself out of the batter's box and looked over to the bench, which was occupied with players my own age and younger, and flanked by the two coaches. The other coach, a Mr. Greenfield, nodded manfully toward me, as if to give me courage to take the third strike like a man. The rest of the players were curiously silent. First innings were generally raucous. Nobody was ready to play yet, and the nervous energy that came of divided intentions was raw and infectious. The bench razzed the pitcher, directing unsavory insults to various infielders while exaggerating the power of their man unconscionably. The pitcher always got the worst of it; he was taken to task for everything from a stupid uniform to a spastic windup to puny pitches that weren't fast enough to knock down a coke bottle at ten paces.

But there was none of that in the face of this strange and wicked ball they could all hear from the time it left the pitcher's hand till—not a second later—it smacked into the catcher's mitt like a hardball should, but never had in their soft and limited experience of the game.

The third pitch was a ball, which, if truth were known, cut the inside corner. Had the umpire been calling the game major-league style, I would've been called out on strikes. Old Giles seemed to know this and looked back at the umpire, who merely clicked in a ball. The next pitch was in the dirt and caromed off the backstop all the way to third base. After bobbling it, the kid at third threw the ball weakly back to the pitcher, who, removing his glove and pressing it between his left arm and ribcage, rubbed it the way major leaguers did, shook off a signal, and threw again.

This time the ball found the strike zone as if it were on an invisible track. The ball hissed like a heating valve that has things on its mind. There was an in-drawing of breath from the bench as it shot down the track toward the target in the middle of the plate. I saw the ball pretty well and swung. After the swing, a mass exhalation ensued, producing a sound somewhere between the aaaaah! you get when somebody cute comes onstage in a beauty pageant and the aaaaah! you make when you're finally off the hook and can hang your head and die. I sat down on the bench and said nothing. "I couldn't hit it either," whispered Sammydave who probably couldn't. But it was nice of him to say that. The next two batters were mowed down easily. The next thing I knew, everybody was in motion: Holy Cross was leaving the field while United Meth was taking it. My dad, who was careful not to show favoritism, took me aside for a moment and told me, as infield captain, to keep things tight. If they didn't score, they wouldn't win. Nice logic. But, of course, somebody always did score. And it would probably be them.

I liked extra innings and was hoping nobody would put any runs on the board, but, strangely enough, these bumbling fielders could hit. And when old Giles—who batted cleanup of course—strode off the bench, there was a distinct possibility that they would not only score, but score big enough to put the game out of reach. That's when Mr. Greenfield came out to confer with Thom McHugh, who was pitching for our team, and had been, as the announcers say, wild in the strike zone. From the way McHugh was shifting his feet on the mound, I surmised that the coach was calling for an intentional walk—a thing Thom McHugh had never done. Man oh man, I could almost hear McHugh—who was something of a hotshot—say: "Lemme pitch to him. Just once—just once, okay?" Then my dad came out to lend support to this unprecedented strategy. *They do it in the majors all the time*, he was probably trying to tell McHugh. *You walk the dangerous guy to get to the weak hitter. It's simple baseball strategy.* My dad was like that. He thought he could impress the impressionable with ironclad logic, when, in fact, it was best to appeal to raw emotion. McHugh had gotten mad at a call earlier in the season and turned on the umpire, who said he'd be thrown out of the game if he did that again. Coach Greenfield had come out to the mound and told him he'd never pitch to another batter if he sassed the umpire. McHugh turned docile and never looked at the umpire again. Whether they did that in the majors or not—which they did—was irrelevant; if *you* do it, you're out. It was a wise move to send Greenfield out there. My dad would've cited character flaws in players McHugh had never heard of, invoked a sense of fairness McHugh hadn't time to develop, and McHugh would've been thrown out of the game.

When Coach Greenfield left, McHugh seemed to be convinced. But he didn't throw that way. Old Giles stepped into the first pitch and hammered it into the gap between left and center. There being no fence, it rolled all the way uphill to the highest point of the small city park where we were playing and came to a stop underneath an ugly persimmon tree nobody had had the heart to cut down. Just beyond that point was Pontius Street, busy by the standards of the day, when a four-lane road (which it was) was considered heavy-duty. Nobody had ever hit one that far. But somebody had just come very close.

By the time the ball got to the infield, everybody was in. Four nothing. McHugh took the ball from Sammy, the second baseman, who patted him on the butt the way you did in the majors, and got the next man out on a blooper. But he was slapping his glove against his thigh real hard when he came in, and maybe even cussing a little under his breath, which you weren't supposed to do. But nobody said anything. Neither coach, in fact, even looked at him; they were probably doing a little fantasy cussing of their own.

Both teams settled down for the next three innings, with a predictable no-show for United Meth on the bases—but very little for Holy Cross either. McHugh got smart with old Giles and didn't give him much to hit. He even walked him the third time he came up. I was proud of him for that, in spite of an occasionally aching jealousy because he was the pitcher and I was not. I thought I should pitch all the time. But I was young then and didn't understand pitching rotation the way I came to.

In church league, you played seven innings, but I think everybody wanted this one to go on and on. There were rumors of old Giles maybe tiring out. "Make him pitch to you!" everybody was saying, with hopeful irrelevance. He didn't have to be made. He was pitching to everybody with such cruel and unnatural efficiency that only two of us had run up a full count on him. The mothers in the stands began to cheer for us—which they never did. They were there because it was another family occasion, with a similar social ranking to a drive-in movie or an evening's visit to one of those ice-cream parlors that had lots of those new and eccentric colors and flavors that weren't Neapolitan or chocolate.

"UN-I-TED...UN-I-TED!" went the cheer, as if it were an obnoxious thing to cheer for an individual player. Well, that was appropriate too, since nobody had distinguished himself very much. We had all hidden in a well of terror for the first innings, and mediocrity the rest. It was the sixth inning now and a sort of nervous excitement was in the air, inspired partly by the fact that the game would soon be over and everybody could go home to dinner; but partly by the genuine reality that was taking shape here: of a gallant Christian team facing this great behemoth and facing him off with dignity, if little else. I'd hear things from the bleachers between innings. The mothers were more candid and vocal than the dads. "How can they possibly think of letting a grown man out there like that?" "I know. Just look at him. He could be in college!" "Well, if he was smart enough."

For some reason, this gave me some measure of affirmation.

Faced with an unjust and intolerable situation, you didn't cave. Nor did you shut up. We weren't caving out there on the field, while our emotional support system was talking it up in the bleachers.

It was our turn up—my turn up, in fact. Score was still four zip, but we somehow felt like we were still in it. Old Giles had only gotten a hit that one time—the monster fly ball that had almost reached Pontius Street—and had done nothing but pitch those wicked cue-shots at us ever since. The coaches were in an awkward position. They didn't want to feed false hopes of victory, but they did want to affirm what their wives had: that we were doing well in a bad situation and should feel good about it. Even McHugh, who'd yielded that fateful hit, was in a nice groove. He'd only given up two base-runners since, and, in a surprising complement to his pitching, our fielding had also gone up a notch or two. Dyckman, at third, had whipped a nice one over to first on a two-hopper and had thrown the runner out even after touching the bag. For his part, Toby had scooped a few throws up out of the dirt, and seemed to do it spontaneously—that is to say, without some parallel scenario running on in his mind. Sammy had even turned a nice, unassisted double play, which drew ecstatic cheers, not only from our mothers, but from the mothers on the opposite team. "I can't believe he did that!" they were all saying. We couldn't either.

As we sat there in our baggy uniforms with the blue felt letters across our chests, Coach Greenfield said this: "No matter what happens, this is your finest hour. You may not win, but you've done a far better thing; you've shown us all what you're made of." We absorbed the Churchillian grandeur of these phrases with a sense of being humble strivers in a situation bigger than ourselves, just as the whole of England had during the Blitz. Or Sidney Carton in <u>A Tale of Two</u>

<u>Cities</u>. Then we were very quiet again, like we'd been during that first inning, when we were considering all the unhittable pitches we'd see over the course of a seven-inning game. My dad made a case for the kind of sportsmanship we were displaying; the teamwork he was proud to finally see (a perfectionist, he couldn't resist a dig even in the midst of a Major Moment); and, last but not least, the sense of this being one of the things we'll all remember for the rest of our lives. "I'm proud of you boys. Now let's go out there and get some runs!"

McHugh looked at me as if to say, "And he wants *them* too?"

But I was batting. I had no time to argue, rebut, or engage in idle speculation.

Perhaps old Giles will tire, I thought, as I watched him warm up—though I couldn't discern any deterioration in either form or content. Even his throwaway pitches were rockets. Yet he had to be somewhat overtaxed by a catcher who had to retrieve the ball so much, he couldn't even catch all the warm-up pitches. This can wreak havoc on one's rhythm. Bob Feller used to have all his pitches lined up in his head and released them in a prearranged order that depended on the batter staying in there with him. What if you ducked out for a while, had an itch, got dizzy? Maybe I could go up there and mess with him, get under his skin a little, throw his timing off so much he'd unravel emotionally. I had a vision of him getting real mad and throwing his oversized hat down on the rubber and then stomping on it, his unruly hair flying off in all directions. This was succeeded by another vision of parents, coaches, and players watching him have a psychotic episode, like Anthony Perkins had in the movie about Jim Piersall, in which a suddenly unhinged champion climbed all the way up the backstop and raved until he had nothing left and started to wilt and cry.

"Play ball!" said the umpire, who clicked the ball-and-strike counter and crouched down behind the pitcher. It was late in the day, with a golden light haloing the treetops and making the shadows long on the meadow-green field. Behind me, all the Methodist ladies were scrunched forward in their seats and were chanting my name: "JO-dy...JO-dy!" It was as if we were in a real game that might be written up in the papers. There would be a box score with our abbreviated names and our positions followed by the hits and runs we didn't make because of this ogre on the mound who bedeviled us with major league stuff he had no right to throw. On the five o'clock news, a former local standout might discuss some of the highlights with another good old golden boy in a blue blazer, who'd say: "Yep, that's one for the books all right."

I stepped into the box, seemingly ready to hit, but stepped out as old Giles took his gratuitous signal. "Time!" I called out. And Time stood still for a moment. I seemed to be able to do a lot of things while out of the box: take in the empty part of the outfield, where I pretended to think I might plunk one; look skyward, where I could see an ethereal landscape of fat faraway clouds and clear-eyed vapor; acknowledge the crowd, which was appreciative of my nonchalance. "Take your time. He's not goin' anywhere." Then my name again, rendered as a chant, which was very gratifying.

"Play ball!" said the umpire again, as I assumed my position in the batter's box and watched the first pitch—which did not catch either the inside or the outside corner, and was head-high. "Ball one," said the umpire, noting it on the counter. I took my practice swing and stepped in again. The bench had been in good razzing form for the past couple of innings, and it started on cue. "Hey, hey, pitcher man, can't hit a bottle, can't hit a can!" And so on, until all of the chants and catcalls assumed a collective identity, a fully mustered sound that broke with satisfying undulations and after-flourishes onto the field. For the first time during the entire game, old Giles looked our way. The look was baleful enough to effect a momentary lapse, but it ultimately made us reckless. It had the same effect as an irate teacher leaving the room: absolute quiet beforehand, which erupts into a wall of sound when she (most of the teachers were women back then) huffs past the door and makes a bee-line to the teacher's lounge. The teacher's lounge was a mythic place where, in reality, teachers probably commiserated with each other as best they could, being themselves in an intolerable situation that extended well beyond seven innings.

The second ball was, I think, a turning point because it was close enough to draw Holy Cross' coach from the bench for a little confab with the umpire. Arguments in church league were conducted behind closed doors. And if closed doors could not be found, they had to be simulated, with the two debating parties closing ranks on one another and trying not to raise their voices.

Yet church league and the majors had *this* in common: you didn't revoke a call unless there was some kind of overwhelming evidence—which could not be produced—or some strange and fluky incident—there were none—that might sway an umpire's decision. Under all other circumstances, a call was binding and could not be revoked. And this, of course, was one of them. The coach was out there because it was baseball etiquette to do so. It was a coach's way of saving face and preserving dignity.

Old Giles' next pitch was a blazing fastball right down the middle of the plate, which I didn't really have time to swing at for the same reason I hadn't before.

The count was now two and one—which was technically in my favor. I looked over to the bench for affirmation and got plenty of it. My dad was saying "Make him pitch to you, son. Make him pitch to you." Actually, his lips were saying it. The roar of the crowd—something I'd never heard from any batter's box before—was such that I could only read them. Coach Greenfield was looking abstractedly into the distance. He was a building contractor and was probably thinking of roofers who hadn't showed up that day, or supplies that had gone over-budget. He and my dad talked about such things after a game, or before Sunday school. His fine, sunburned face caught a few rays that could not reach my dad, who was about five six to Coach Greenfield's six two or three.

Mr. Greenfield looked like a coach should, even though my dad was more serious and thought long and hard about the subtleties of the game.

The last pitch I saw I drilled—being a lefthander who could do nothing else but swing late—between left and center for an inside-the-park homerun (the only kind in that league) that was, in terms of utility, not the best thing I could have done at the moment; but in terms of inspiration and morale, the only way to break the spell this great rude force had over us. As I rounded the bases, to the sort of ground-shaking bedlam I'd never experienced in my entire thirteen-year existence, I watched Giles remove his cap and brush his longish dark hair back over his forehead. If you watch cats, they'll lick themselves when they've done something stupid or embarrassing, like fall off the ledge of a table or become aware of chasing their own tails. They don't want you to know they know it. Pitchers have developed similar routines, particularly those who've been taken deep unexpectedly—and being taken deep is never expected. Few pitchers will do what they actually feel like doing, which is to inflict bodily harm on themselves, not just for yielding the homerun, but for being the sorry and worthless pieces of dung they are. If they did something like that, well, it just wouldn't be good for anybody. The grooming episode was old Giles' way of not only taking a break in the action, but marking a shift in attitude as well. He was showing he no longer saw things in the light of yore—which was just a few minutes ago—and was calling for a new regime: a whole new ballgame, as it were. After watching me receive the kudos that is always so mortifying to any pitcher, he turned around and directed the players as if they were a sort of orchestra. First he motioned to the kettledrum, the triangle and the tympani—the distant part of the orchestra that tinkled around in the distance, but waited for long periods of time for something to happen. This was the out-field, which he directed, with two bare hands, to sit down. Then to the brass and strings, which had more of a role, but were of no use to a soloist. He had them sit one at a time, with a hypnotic flick of the wrist: third, short, second, and, finally, first—who came closest to mounting a protest, but couldn't, in the end, force himself to do it because he really didn't care that much. Then old Giles faced home plate and made a welcoming gesture to the catcher, who returned it somewhat inelegantly, but with fair and reasonable intent: he would stay in the game because, in a solo act, you some-times need a page-turner or accompanist or some other cog to help the soloist achieve the perfection (or, in this case, near-perfection) everybody had come to see.

All this happened, of course, in the midst of the wild welcome I was getting as I ran around the bases, reached home, and came jumping up and down to my teammates, who slapped me on the back, chest, arms, face, neck, buttocks, with such all-out joy that I wouldn't feel anything till the next day, when I had a rash of tiny, knuckle-shaped bruises all over me ("Knew you could do it! You killed that sucker—killed it! Thatta way to keep your eye on it!")

It also happened to the accompaniment of a technical situation the Holy Cross coach came over to my father to talk about. I'd actually hit the ball out into Pontius Street, where nobody wanted to go chase it. The game ball we'd been using was theirs. Could we put ours into play now? My father obliged. When he turned back around, he noticed a field that was suddenly denuded, except for pitcher and catcher. He and the Holy Cross coach exchanged looks that said: "I think we've got a situation on our hands."

And then everybody saw what old Giles had done. The Holy Cross coach went from where he was standing next to my dad to the mound and said, "No, son, you can't do that" and motioned to the players to stand up, which they started to do until old Giles faced them again and had them sit back down. The coach did his little motion again and raised them, but old Giles went over his head a second time. Then we all heard him speak. "If you don't let me do this, I'm outta here forever. I don't pitch another pitch. I don't play on this lousy team again. I go to the showers and you won't see me in this spot another time and I mean it."

The two glared at each other until—wonder of wonders!— the Holy Cross coach left the field in the condition he'd found it in: with the entire Holy Cross team, sans battery, in a seated or recumbent (center, left field, and first base) position.

"Can he do that?" said Coach Greenfield to my father, echoing what we were all saying to each other on the bench.

"It's highly unusual, but I don't believe there's any rule against it," said my father, who was, in his way, relishing the unusual situation. A lifelong student of the game was watching sandlot history in the making.

"As long as they're on the field, I think it's perfectly proper," continued my dad, who popped those double p's in a way that must've caught his funny bone because he turned his head upward, as if to watch a non-existent airplane in the sky.

"But...what if somebody gets a hit?"

"I'd think we'd have a much better chance of winning," said my dad, on a roll.

So that was how it was. Jesse, the next batter, had not yet touched the ball. Theatrical as old Giles' move had been, it was not without a certain hard logic. I was the only player who'd hit the ball out of the infield. The only other contact that had been made was a weak pop fly and a dribbled grounder, which even Holy Cross' uninspired infield could manage. But it was still exciting and opened up a range of possibilities heretofore unknown. At this point, however, Giles spoke again to his mute and fallen orchestra. "If anybody hits one—not that anybody will—but if anybody does I don't want any of you to do anything. I'll field the ball. Do you understand? You do nothing. Nothing, understand?"

They all nodded, as the Holy Cross coach shook his head. If you know you're up against a madman, you let the madman play. I doubted whether Holy Cross would pitch him again, after this volatile and narcissistic stunt. In church league, you were out to learn teamwork. This was a sort of hijacking, which was anti-sportsmanship as well as anti-group, anti-teamwork, even anti-Church. Even if he shut us down, I couldn't imagine Holy Cross holding onto him. Even if we didn't touch the ball, as was likely.

But we did. Kind of amazing how you can turn on a dime and become a pack of dynamos even if you'd not shown any dynamism before. Jesse hit the first pitch up the middle and while Giles got to the ball quickly and ran it into third, where he tagged Jesse unnecessarily, having nobody in the field was suddenly not a good call. But old Giles would not hear of reversing his plan, and, after going 0 and 2 on Sammy, who batted third, he threw a pitch in the dirt, which shot to the backstop and caromed off it so hard that it swiveled back down the third base line to the shallow part of left field, near which the left fielder had been reclining, but sat up in anticipation of a rampaging Giles. Jesse ran under the ball to score run number two.

I thought I wanted to see old Giles mad, but I was mistaken. His former belligerence had been connected to a coolly competitive instinct. Any good athlete has to have a kind of warlike mind, which can circle the enemy for a while, but when it's time to strike there can be no hesitation. When either mechanism blows out, the athlete is doomed. He's either thinking too much or pushing too hard. And old Giles was now doing both. And we were all enjoying it to the hilt. Even the mothers seemed not to mind watching the inexorable destruction of a proud and lonely spirit happen in their midst. If he was so good, why was he falling to pieces like this? Maybe he didn't have the emotional maturity to play with people his own age and had to be here for psychological reasons. Perhaps that was why, as with Shakespearean characters whose tragic flaw dooms them, he'd been assigned to this team—which, in terms of his talent, would have been stupid not to take him. Yet somebody must have known that he was capable of such a thing and that somebody was probably feeling dreadfully, if invisibly, responsible.

The outcome, as anybody can probably tell by now, was ugly. He got it together enough to have the cleanup man tap one back to him, though he barely reached the bag before good old Toby Slouch—who could run when he wanted to—did. The fifth and sixth hitters walked and struck out, respectively, but the fifth, a painfully shy kid named Ed Estabrook, who played right field, managed to make it all the way around the bases because there was no one to stop him from stealing second, third, and, finally, home. The Holy Cross catcher lacked grace under fire and had become extremely nervous about base-runners, with which he'd not had to contend, and choked whenever somebody got on. In a reverse of the usual situation, Giles called him, the catcher, out to the mound for conferences. But he was not an effective psychologist, and far from chasing the fear of God out, he established Him there inside of the catcher completely and permanently. When Ed finally scored, the catcher could have tagged him out easily; the ball was right underneath him. But he wouldn't move to the right or left; so he just circled it like a dog chasing his own tail. When he finally found it, and held it up like some kind of embarrassing trophy, old Giles threw his glove to the mound with such unbridled fury that everybody froze. Not only that, but, as if to enact the fantasy I'd had, he stomped on it with the kind of savage glee certain diabolical characters in movies display before they start whooping madly. Yet he did not do that. Nor did he ascend a backstop that was barely taller than he was. He faced us, as if to say, well, you want to make something of it? Do you? And said: "You people have no idea...you have no IDEEEEUUUH!" He elongated the last word so that it might accommodate all of his disgust at himself, at a game that had gone terribly wrong, and at a malignant universe that had seen fit to humiliate him. "The only reason I'm here is 'cause they won't let me try out for the St. Louis Cardinals. They say I'm too young. But I'm not. I'm NOT!" Then he threw a searing line drive all the way to the sidewalk, from which it rolled out onto Pontius Street and then to the other side, where nobody could safely go. That was two balls out on Pontius in one game. Some more sandlot history for my dad.

But nobody was thinking history at the moment. Nobody was thinking anything. How could we? Nothing like this had ever happened in church league before. But then something else happened for which I could assign no reason then—and none now, really. The wives and mothers in the bleachers started it: rising one at a time and pulling away from him. It was the strangest thing I'd ever seen. It was as if everybody had seen enough of some unlikeable phenomenon and felt it was time to clear away from it because something really bad might happen if we stayed any longer. It was like an existential fire drill; we were using free choice to take ourselves out of a situation that had gotten so weird we didn't have a name for it. All we knew is that we'd had enough.

So we all drifted off. The mothers were saying, *Don't worry, we'll come back and get the cooler and things. Oh, nobody'll take them—they're church property!* When we'd pulled farther away down the cool length of the park, they started talking about him. *He was dangerous enough just throwing those pitches, but look at him now. I think he's downright crazy. Crazy as a bedbug. I feel sorry for him myself. Just look at him out there. Must've had some home life. It's how you're raised. Everything goes back to that. So sad!* Even my dad had no basic quarrel with our strategy. He and Coach Greenfield had taken the utility bag and had stuffed all the catcher's equipment and balls and bats into it as if they were the front men in some fast-disappearing caravan. And they were talking very close, like you're supposed to when you have "confidential matters" on your mind. My dad later told me, unconvincingly, that no game was worth what it was doing to that young man out there. I didn't believe him. I think he was as solemnly impressed, and then repulsed, as the rest of us. Some natural force had spewed out past conventional boundaries and had touched off a mass exodus of a sort that, when it does happen, can't really be planned. Somebody started to say something about those Catholics, but stopped. It wouldn't do to get into that now. When I looked back, old Giles was still on the mound. Holy Cross was in the process of skedaddling too.

The game was scored a forfeit, and we took the victory, which the Holy Cross coach didn't even bother to contest. I wished we'd been able to win clean, but it didn't really matter. We'd go to the playoffs (which we lost) even if Giles had skunked us. I also wished, for just a moment, that my home-run had been more of the centerpiece rather than just an exciting interval that led to the great and unanticipated climax people would talk about for years and years. But that's all right. I'll remember hitting that home-run for as long as I live.

I didn't turn out to be good enough to play baseball, and went into radio, where I do play-by-play for the sensational Triple-A club we've got in town. In fact, when I joined the church again in midlife, I ran into one of my old team-mates and he asked me whether I knew what became of that crazy pitcher at Holy Cross. I said, no, I didn't. I thought he might've popped up in baseball somewhere, but after that display of his, I wondered whether he had it in him to lose the way the rest of us did. In baseball, you lose mostly. Even a good batting average is based on you failing two out of three times. And if you look at pitchers who win three hundred games, most of them lose two hundred or more along the way. Baseball is one of the few games I know that is actually designed for losers, and if you couldn't live with that you couldn't play. "I wonder about him sometimes," said my old teammate as we left the church to find the fuel-efficient cars we'd parked blocks away. "Even after all these years, I wonder about him."

Summer Camp: a *Folie a Dix*

Camp life is different for everybody. I've known people for whom it was a largely idyllic experience not overwrought with pecking-order battles, as mine was—nor memorably full of intrigue. As mine would also be.

It started off on a wing and a prayer. I'd signed up, under the auspices of the Methodist church, to attend a YMCA camp in the impenetrable damps of the Ozarks. I was ten years old and no initiate. I was given to believe that my ultimate destination was wild and perhaps wonderful; surrounded by the kind of nature from which the awful and malignant had been savagely plucked. The activities would be wholesome, the people good, the weather seasonable. That's what I expected. The experience came to represent how no sunny expectation could ever be met in this world or perhaps any other.

The trip from a sun-drenched Memphis was not memorable. I did not want to be away from our home-team, the St. Louis Cardinals, who would win the pennant that year and go on to clinch the World Series against one of the doughtiest of Yankee line-ups. I didn't know that at the time and felt my presence at the radio was essential for both a winning attitude and play. I was wrong.

I was wrong about everything that year.

When I arrived, I was ushered into the Range-leader's office. It was suitably rustic. Character-building bromides hung on the wall behind an absent functionary's desk. Slogans like "Profanity may win the battle, but it loses the war," "Should right and wrong have two faces?", "A good mind and an evil heart can't—and won't!—be reconciled!" provided tutorials—in case they were missed in other places—that would induce the moral preparedness for which all summer camps were, with love for sinners as well as the insufferably pure-minded people who stayed home and read their Bibles, founded, maintained, and inflicted upon the rest of us. Or such was the understanding which brought our parents and protectors to the table, where our lives were raffled away for two weeks at a time.

"Find the trip all right?" asked the Range-leader, whose first-in-command status, as I would learn, was flexible.

"I think so."

"Good. We've got you assigned to a cabin. You'll like the boys there. Good, wholesome boys. I hear you're a ballplayer."

"I guess," I said in all due modesty. Wait till I showed him! Them! Everybody! I could throw a knuckleball such as no ten-year old kid had ever seen before. I could take out a man on second with one of those dirt-erupting slides that didn't occur outside of professional baseball. I could hit the ball pretty far too—though I shone at fielding. Oh, wait till they saw me reach to my left for a hard grounder, plant my feet firmly on the ground, and let loose a bullet that found the first baseman's glove before the runner was halfway into his stride! They'd remember me for as long as the game was played.

"No, I heard you were pretty good. Maybe we could round us up a team."

I wondered where the field was. He finally sensed that.

"Come over here," said the Range-leader, pointing past my head to a huge outfield surrounded by a little scab of dirt. I joined him at a window trimmed in log-parts and other leavings from field and forest. Rather fussy for a Range-leader's office, but it created an image. As I studied the small diamond, with its high outfield grass and pebble-rich infield, I thought more conclusively of how I would show them and imagined myself soaring high above second base for a diving catch they would not soon forget—assuming they could believe their eyes to begin with.

"Needs a little work. I guess you wouldn't mind performing groundskeeper chores for an hour or two."

"No sir!" I clamored back, eager to serve the camp that it might soon serve me.

"With an attitude like that, I'm sure you'll get along just fine," said the Range-leader, sizing me up as Someone Who Could Very Well Be Special.

Following this momentary lapse, he was all business: "You'll be in Cabin Number One. I'll walk you over there. Got everything?"

I hoisted my one suitcase and followed him to a clearing beyond which I could see a row of outbuildings with two windows and a central door. They had a crisp, barracks-like appearance.

"I'm sure you'll like it here. We've got an activities schedule I think an active boy like you will appreciate. Our cabins are ship-shape, as you can see. You will, of course, be part of that ship-shape order."

We were approaching Cabin Number One, which looked, as he said, ship-shape, if I understood what that meant. My dad, a Navy man during The Second War to End All Wars, used the word all the time. I would never ask him to explain a ruptured duck, however. I was soft on animals.

"You'll like your house-mates. Their places of origin might intrigue you. You'll be a city boy to them. Everybody's just gotten here, so we're all just settling in. Just remember: if you want to know something...just ask. You'll find that life's seekers are rarely turned away."

Near the threshold, the Range-leader stopped me and said: "All I would ask of you is that you be truthful. Is that understood?"

"Yessir."

"No matter what happens, I want you to feel comfortable with telling the truth."

"Yessir. I will."

"Okay, then. This is where you'll be staying for the next two weeks."

He opened the door on what I'd charitably describe as an open floor-plan. There was absolutely nothing in the cabin but floor-level beds and the bunks that were on top of them. Toward the left, there was a small table, at which two of my cabin-mates were sitting. They all stood up when I came in.

Introductions were made. The two kids who had been sitting down were Smitty and Irving. The others, shadowy figures who made a sluggish effort to be seen, were named Scott, Big Bruce, and Jerry. No last names were given, possibly under the assumption that kids liked the informality. I instantly forgot everybody's name as I was shown to my bed. I slipped my suitcase underneath it—something I would wish I hadn't done—and, for want of a more striking idea, I sat cross-legged on the stain-free blanket.

"You boys get acquainted. Canteen's at two, if you would like refreshments."

The Range-leader left through the screen-door, which he closed very softly, as if we all had some serious sleeping to do.

"Look. He's an Indian," said a wiry boy who might be trouble.

"Are you an Indian?"

"Me? Not that I know."

"Then why are you sitting that way?"

"It's comfortable."

"It's comfortable," said the wiry boy, trouble already.

"Leave him alone. I like Indians."

"Me too."

"He's not really an Indian. Are you?"

"No."

They continued to grill me. I was hoping the subject of baseball would come up so I might redeem the Indian fiasco and set the stage for some spectacular sandlot play.

But in came a formidable post-teenaged adult for whom all the others stood at attention. I was slow to rouse myself.

"Who's this?" he asked them of me.

"He's new. Just got here."

"You need to get up when I come in here."

I nodded.

"I didn't hear you."

"Okay."

"Still didn't hear you."

A nicer-seeming kid relayed the right answer through cupped hands. "Yessir," he said.

"Yessir," I repeated.

"That's better. Now I want you boys to go down to the water's edge and wait for me."

At this command, he left the cabin, slamming the screen door.

I assumed he meant swimming trunks and attempted to comply.

"Why are you doin' that?" said the wiry kid.

"I thought we were going down to the water."

"Did he say anything about swimmin' trunks?"

I shook my head.

"Unless he tells you to do something, you don't do it."

Who was *he*? I thought it was just us and the Range-leader.

"You don't mess with The Captain," added Trouble.

I nodded and followed the rest of them down a series of

steep, briar-cluttered paths toward the water that was one of the place's seminal attractions. There was a roped-off area within which I assumed it would be safe to swim. Beyond it was a treacherous-looking, lily-lousy water world that looked dark and forbidding; cold and deep.

The Captain soon joined us at water's edge.

"I want all of you to understand water safety procedures."

One boy shouted: "Check!"

"What is the first, and most important, of all water safety procedures?"

He would call on me.

I pointed to myself like he probably thought I would and looked instantly befuddled.

"You don't know, do you?"

I shook my head.

"All right. Who can tell me the correct answer?"

He pointed at a boy who looked like a human snake. He seemed to be coiled into himself. Whoever set him off would want to start running.

"When you're around water, you've got to be careful."

"What else?"

"Conscientious."

"What else?"

"You've got to check for snakes."

"Okay. But none of you have given me the first and most important thing a water-conscious person must do in order to ensure his safety as well as that of others."

Nobody seemed to know this first and most important thing. A few idle guesses rent the air. The Captain made no effort to conceal his contempt for such mass *naiveté*.

"None of you are apparently familiar with the first article of safety in the presence of an unknown, and possibly dangerous, body of water."

He looked toward us for confirmation; receiving nothing more than lowered heads and infantile mutterings, he kept going.

"All right, then, I will tell you sorry people what it is you need to know first and foremost. You need to stay out until given the signal by a person who has authority to tell you. And that person is me."

I let out a sigh of relief; at least you didn't have to go far to know something in this place. The other kids looked ashamed, like every man who should have known something at a timely moment, but did not.

"Now, listen. It is very important, given where you are, for all of you to know the rules. It can be dangerous here. People have been known to get hurt. Oh, yes! One of our own people almost drowned at that very spot. Last year. Yessir. He decided to go into the water unsupervised and he got the cramps. Yessir. The cramps. If you get the cramps, you are in trouble. If you get the cramps alone, you are up shit creek."

There was an attempt to suppress giggles, choke innocence down.

"Do you know how he survived?"

We shook our heads in unison. Trouble seemed to know all about this incident and was nodding his head as if it all made the most perfect sense to him. When the Captain revealed the correct answer, he nodded right along. "Why hide your light under a bushel?" he seemed to be saying. He was not the first young politician I'd encountered over the years; I knew the breed well. A two-faced liar par excellence, he became the ratter-out, yes-man, and double dealer the Captain had always wanted, but had never found among the milder yes-men it was his pleasure and privilege to rule. In addition to fighting skills that easily surpassed anyone else's, Trouble fast became a God-fearing dictatorship's civilian arm.

"He saved his life by floating. Yes, floating. He couldn't

move his arms, but he relaxed his body and went into the floating position. That's how he saved his own life. But I don't want any of you to have to do that. So what's the most important thing?"

"Stay out of the water unless a person in authority tells you to go in," we all said in imperfect unison. Unless The Captain knew what we were saying already, he couldn't have made out individual words from the stuttering conga-line that had assembled before him.

Without another word, The Captain left us all standing there.

When the kid I thought was called Irving started to move, the kid next to him shoved him back.

"We don't go until somebody in authority tells us."

Irving didn't like the shove and started to slouch. It was my very first image, at this particular place and time, of rebellion—an image I would see intermittently at best.

The Captain would not return that day. Rather than lurch away as authority-defying individuals, we crept back up to the cabin as one. Nobody said a lot. Learning the first principle of water safety had been a confounding sort of experience, the like of which we would start having at a somewhat more accelerated pace.

I dreamed that evening that I had dived into the water unattended and was being dragged down by some superior force that didn't have a face till it finished dragging me. The face was that of The Captain himself.

We all got to see him in the flesh as a bugle went off and we all formed a line in front of the cabin.

There was nothing about this kind of regimentation in the brochure. It talked about the wholesome, fun-filled, God-centered days we were going to have in the lap of nature, from whose goodness we would all suckle until it was time to go home. There was no talk of water safety or of lining up—or of what was about to transpire.

"I want you to all join me in a morning prayer," said The Captain who appeared among us quietly. He was got up in a sort of bastard uniform, with the attributes of both scout-master and school principal: khaki shorts underneath and a button-down shirt with tie above. When he stuck out his chest, however, he was impressive: as manly a fellow human as you might find in these parts. The Range-leader was, in fact, a little puny: the doting housewife of the kitchen to this assertive husband of lake and forest. He, the Captain, was in excellent voice that morning and was able to cleave God's rafters with the good fellowship of that day.

"I want You, O Lord, to bless all of these excellent young men in their endeavors today. I want You to crown their efforts with Your blessing. I want You to bless and keep them in Your bosom as they learn what God and nature, together and as one, have to teach them. Amen."

The Captain pivoted back to give us our instructions.

"On with your swimmin' trunks and meet me down by the edge of the water."

We were down there, suited up, so quick I was still half-woozy. Was there no breakfast?

"Now I want you boys to see the water as bountiful. I want you to see it as something that can give you as much as you put into it. It is a dangerous place only to those who misuse it, but a delightful haven for those who discover its secrets and put them to good use."

With that observation, he dove in and emerged at a little dock at least a hundred feet away. In so doing, he swam past the two-color ropes that defined the safe swimming area. Some of us were aghast. Could he do that? Apparently he could.

"Now, boys. I don't want you to swim all the way out here the way I did. Just dive in and tread water, okay? What I did was much too advanced for you now."

We all dove in almost at once and came up right away. I did not reckon on the incredible iciness of this wild water world. I had, in fact, never been anywhere near a spring-fed river—another highlight of the brochure. It was so cold, I gasped and swallowed water. I had to come up spitting and blowing like a starter whale. My struggle was not lost on Trouble, who swam over to me and dunked my head. Since I had not provided for this contingency, I didn't have quite enough breath to manage underwater. When I finally managed to break free of Trouble, I was so oxygen-deprived I could barely keep my head up. For the remainder of the time I was in the water, I just dogpaddled my way around. What Trouble had done to me was not lost on some of the others. They had gathered in a protective knot near the dock, where I joined them. They didn't seem to mind having a veteran in their midst and made room for me. I said nothing all the time we were out there listening to The Captain's monologues about what a richly rewarding environment the water was and how we'd expand our personalities once we confronted it head-on. It didn't seem odd that The Captain would want to dive into this water in his scoutmaster/principal outfit. It was just a little quirk, a super-manly sort of thing men like this must occasionally do to keep the image of superior manhood uppermost in our minds. The Range-leader couldn't have pulled something like this off. Clothes would never look as good on him as they did The Captain.

I didn't see Trouble until we got back to Cabin Number One. There he challenged me to a fight, which I refused, partly out of cowardice, but partly because I hadn't gotten my breath back. But refusing a fight was something you didn't do there, so everybody started to pick on me. Even Irving or Julius—or whatever his name was. I found he was Jewish, which was apparently a bad thing to be. I was being picked on by the high, the low, and the in-between. I would have to do something about that fairly soon.

Meanwhile, the canteen was a place where you could assuage the assaults to body and ego with the gooeyest of processed foods 1964 had to offer. You could insulate a spring-insulted gullet with the soda-maker's gaudiest confections. (My personal favorites were Rees' Strawberry and Barq's Cherry Cola.) You could manage your angst by means of a great, sugar-coated bonanza, led by the candy bar, but filled out with swirl-decorated baked goods that might send any attention deficit disorder—had one been diagnosed—into overdrive. All you had to do was sign a little slip and these wonderful elixirs and anodynes were yours.

It seemed that all bets were off in the canteen. Irving sat by me at the long, pencil-nicked picnic table that could accommodate ten or so. Scott took the opposite seat and Snake Boy took the end, as if he might need to run, or slither, off at any time.

"What you get?" asked Irving.

"Cherry."

"He's got her cherry," said the snaky kid, who snickered wildly at this one.

"Bet you don't know what a cherry is," said Trouble, who'd overheard and couldn't help himself. You never saw Trouble until he wanted you to see him. He was an excellent human embodiment of the name that seemed to fit him best. I would learn his real one and forget it almost right away.

"I...I don't know."

"He don't know what a cherry is," said Trouble to an audience he would have to enlighten personally; nobody else seemed to know what it was either.

"*You* know what a cherry is," he said to Scott, who nodded. What else could he do?

"See? He knows. Who doesn't know what a cherry is?" asked Trouble, addressing all of us. Since I was the only out-spoken innocent, everybody let that stand and said nothing.

"You wouldn't know what to do with it if it were right in front of you. I'm not sayin' anything except to say that *your* cherry is about all you're ready for right now."

And, for once, Trouble walked off without threatening—or executing—any sort of physical violence. He'd have to be reckoned with eventually. I was hoping against hope that it could be on the ball-field—an idea I immediately started to pitch to the others.

"Why don't we get up a little game?"

Everybody was agreeable, but when I went into the office to find the Range-leader, he wasn't there and the flunkey who was sitting at an adjacent table said he couldn't get into the baseball equipment without the Range-leader's approval.

"I'll give you my approval," I said, jokingly.

The flunkey ignored me.

After canteen I went out to the ball-field myself, game or no game. It wasn't bad in the least, with a sturdy-enough backstop, an infield in which bunion-size quartzite mingled with the native soil, and iron grooves into which starch-white bases might easily, if not inextricably, fit. With some discreet dirt-moving, a lime-bucket, and some adequate bases, I could get this thing into shape. I could make it *ship*-shape if it needed to look extra special. I reached down to taste the dirt, a prospector who would soon find pure gold. It was something I always did at an alien field: the first act of knowing.

"What are you doing?" asked a voice I knew. I turned around and was dumbfounded, but also profoundly unsur-prised, by the source. It was The Captain.

"Just checking it out."

"You're checking out the field?"

"Yessir."

"And how do you find it?"

"I...I like it."

"I'm so glad it meets with your approval."

I didn't understand such irony-steeped conversation and tried to get things back on track.

"Would it be possible, sir, to get up a game here?"

"And why do you ask that?"

"Because...I'd like to play. We all would."

"Your enthusiasm is infectious. How, after hearing you, wouldn't anybody wish to play the great game of baseball, which is hallowed throughout our land?"

How to respond to such a question? I wanted to play, here was a field, what was the problem? Ah. An authority figure who needed to sanction it.

"Can we...sir?"

"In good time perhaps."

"Sir, we would love to play here...if you would let us."

Such on-the-spot diplomacy was what the spin-doctor ordered. How could The Captain not relent under such genteel pressure? Not only could he, but he could harbor negative impressions not even the most skillful diplomacy might overcome.

"I don't like you, son. You have all the makings of a first-class snot. I'll bet you got a nice, big old Wilson outfielder's glove for Christmas. I'll bet you and your dad go out in the yard and play catch. I'll bet you've got two dogs and a Chevrolet in that teeny little slit known in suburbia as a carport."

This was a new tactic. I'd done everything he wanted. Why this?

"You probably think you're hot shit out here. Don't you?"

"No."

"Which means yes. Yes, you do think you're hot shit out there. I know you do, so there's no use in arguing."

I didn't say anything, which seemed the safest strategy around a suddenly Obtuse Authority that might continue to suck obeisance out of me.

"What was that? I didn't catch what you said."

"No, I don't."

"No always means yes to people like you. Don't try to fool me."

"No, it doesn't. And I'm not trying to fool you."

"Yes, it does, little man. There is no way in the world yes doesn't mean no when I say it does. And as to fooling me, that's a job you can't start early enough. You couldn't fool me if your life had been dedicated to fooling me from the day you were born."

I had no idea what to do. So I ran. I just ran past him to Cabin Number One, where Trouble was waiting for me.

Trouble was boxing champion of Cabin Number One—a title he'd held from the git-go and maintained effortlessly. He had the torso for it and the fast, jabbing reflexes that could unman you so quickly, you couldn't react. By the time you did, he was at you again.

He had lined up some intriguing match-ups, which would get us all through Fellowship Hour. During this hallowed period, we were supposed to recount passages from the Bible and marvel at both their literary style and rigorous morality. Yet the lion's share of our *fiction noir* fellowship at Cabin Number One consisted of getting our butts kicked by someone chosen especially for this office by Trouble, who fought just now and then, having proven himself enough to smother doubt and quash any hue-and-cry that might impugn an unearned supremacy.

"You. Wait over there," said Trouble to me.

Meanwhile, another kid was getting ready for that day's match.

The blinds had been lowered especially for the activity everybody was about to half-see. The gloom provided an atmosphere of secrecy no one who might attempt to impose sunnier conditions might penetrate.

"Three rounds. Man wins who stays on his feet," said Trouble to a hypothetical crowd.

"Got that?" he said to me.

My rival whaled into me without wasting much time. I'd never been hit like that before and found myself not wanting to be hit like that again.

"Get up...come on, get up!" growled Trouble at me.

I got up and was able to feint away from my opponent, the snaky kid whose coil-and-spring was very nasty indeed. But once he'd trotted out his best move, I found I could stay out of his way. It didn't look pretty, but it got the job done. Trouble didn't care for evasions; in order to ensure a *mano-a-mano* style, he made us stand closer together.

"I don't want any lunging. You stand there and you do it right—with none of that chickenshit stuff."

This was not good news. Having never fought, I couldn't ward off the pecking and the jabbing; the hitting and the flailing; the homing and the hurting. When Round One was over, I'd taken more hits. My face felt flushed and was burning. I visualized an orange-red backdrop, with blood-red flames licking around its base, and pepper-red people watching it, me, him, and whatever else might interest them. Well, it would be over soon enough.

But it wasn't. After Round Two, that wily bastard called innumerable time-outs. Time-outs every other second so that Snake could find his punch again and hit me squarely enough to draw more blood. I could taste it on my tongue.

Hell, I could taste blood all over my body. When you bleed, it seems like you're bloody everywhere. It wasn't the worst sensation in the world after you got used to it.

"Round Three...go!"

I think there must've been some pity in the heart of Snake because he didn't bear down so hard during this last round. He made his punches look convincing, but they landed poorly and inflicted no damage at all. It probably wasn't compassion for me, but his own personal rebellion against the strictures of a tyrant: his *cri de coeur* against oppression, not only of a minority (me), but of a talented professional who had to sully his reputation by pulling his punches with a pushover (also me.) Oh, well. At least I'd seen something good in human nature—which I hadn't seen much of since I'd gotten to the camp days before.

When it was over, and we shook hands, I was off the hook. Even while we swam. Trouble didn't take the trouble to try and drown me.

I thought of tending my wounds, but would have to do it privately. On the other hand, I didn't—couldn't—divulge the nature of the activity that had led to them to anyone who didn't know about it already. Occasionally, however, I would rub my face and notice that its formerly unaffected contours had been smashed about and yielded those uneven textures that alert medical personnel to a "situation." Additionally, the trauma one feels after getting beaten-up even in the more spontaneous arenas that are left to those who are not fortunate enough to know a Fellowship Hour or any other structured activity that can save them for the purely democratic experiences with which ordinary life abounds and for which we could all, when we got the hell out of there, expect to know again.

But Trouble—or somebody—had begun a private sport that would rock the foundations of my belief-system; that would cancel out whatever humankindness I might put on a private pedestal and worship; that would effectively bar me from the canteen forever.

After we finished swimming the next day and were let out to do whatever we wanted—as long as a suitable authority figure was nearby—I went over to the canteen and ordered the usual. After my order was filled, a crooked finger beckoned me to a little office.

"You're running on fumes. Did you know that?" asked a patient-faced little woman. She was the first female person I had seen there at the camp.

"I'm...what? "

"You don't know what that is, do you? Fiscal management. Mostly happens too late."

"Uh...no."

"I'm afraid you have only two dollars left in your account."

"Whaaa...? Let me see."

I went over the vertical slip of paper that had tallied up my transgressions before an honest, money-conscious body politic of one: her. Just a few days ago, the account stood at twenty-five dollars.

"I didn't get all this," I said.

"Well, someone did and it's showed up on your account."

"Someone...?"

"Yes, somebody has been ordering all kinds of things from your account. Would you have any idea who this person is?"

Of course I would—but he would kill me if I said as much.

"No, ma'am, I don't."

"You didn't order these things?"

"No, ma'am."

"Well, if you have no idea who might be ordering these things in your stead, I'm not sure what I can do for you."

"Probably nothing."

"Yes. Probably nothing."

Having not only seen that I had no physical resources, she was compelled to acknowledge the breadth of my fiscal intelligence. Indeed, she seemed rather eager to do so. But she said nothing to me about it and chose to regard it—charitably, I thought—as a more universal condition. If it happened to me, might it not happen to others?

"Amazing," she managed to say to herself, but, because we were in a place that had no competing soundscape, it was as audible as something she might have said to me directly, "how quickly they all catch on!"

Though I walked in dignity, I was actually stunned. Three days into the camp experience and I'd gotten dunked, beaten up, and bamboozled. What else might happen during the ten days that followed?

It was quiet for a whole week. The surreptitious boxing that went on in Cabin One was not my affair; it was conducted, under the auspices of the Cabin One Boxing Federation, by the strictest of rules and the most unscrupulous authority. If a certain amount of coercion re-enforced it, all to the good. A federation had to stay strong and keep going. If anybody wished to oppose its practice or philosophy, he'd have to fight. And since everybody had done that with just about an equal deficit of skill, matched by a certain raw talent for taking punches, there wasn't anything about The Federation anybody could really do.

The swimming was okay, now that everybody was used to the frigid water and could get along fairly well in spite of its sense-numbing temperature and sub-continental depths. I spent the last two dollars allotted me at the canteen and decided to close my account. By doing this, whoever was poaching would find that the teat was dry, the course of the river interrupted, the bounty choked off at the neck. I would most certainly feel the wrath of the perpetrator, and at a time of his own choosing.

And that is when I decided to run away. There had been no attempts to organize the baseball that might redeem and elevate me in the eyes of the bone-weary warriors who toiled under The Captain's iron rule on the one hand and Trouble's malignant authority on the other. To stay any longer was to invite further abuse; to chafe under a yoke that could not be overthrown; to lose whatever dignity might have stuck to battle-scarred limbs and shattered psyches.

The next thing that happened started out just fine. And it might have uplifted a grand social experiment that had been organized at the foot of the Ozark Mountains by a bunch of church pillars and sanctimonious, bible-crazed, free-booting liberals who didn't factor in the human urge for power and domination.

The Captain hadn't forgotten our conversation on the baseball diamond and had been putting together a sort of all-star team that would crush and humiliate me, a known hotshot who did not appreciate team spirit and was in favor of self-promotion and runaway narcissism instead. I'm not sure what I did to foster this reputation, but The Captain was a profound student of human behavior and had probably picked it up between the lines.

"Come to me, boy," said he as I marveled at this new phenomenon: unconditional dislike based upon steely hunches, uneducated assumptions, and malice aforethought. He had lured me just in time. I'd already wandered down the primrose path; my money was no good there anymore, so what else did I have to lose?

"I've got you a team. What position do you play?"

Before I answered, he'd put me down in the pitcher's slot.

To an as-yet unseen rabble, The Captain asked "Are ya'll ready?"

To which it answered, with a more than satisfactorily resounding: "Oh, yeah!"

This was the team I was going to defeat with on-the-corner fastballs and well-timed pitches to the head. And, of course, my infamous knuckleball, which no one here had yet seen or heard of. Here on the mound, I would redeem the various and sundry humiliations which had begun to occupy the very core of my existence. I was learning about the ways of the world. People who professed to be religious could, as I began to realize, become as balefully opportunistic as they could anywhere else. They could spot a sucker a mile off and they could home in on the kill—even if they could explain it all in scriptural terms. Biblical notions of kindness and tolerance were useful insofar as they went—but they clearly didn't go far enough. A peregrine falcon could well adhere to a superior sense of fair play, but when he's about to disembowel, dissect, and then distribute throughout his stomach that morning's field-mouse...why should he?

I recognized most of my opponents, who were taken from Cabins One and Two, with a sprinkling of a third cabin I'd not yet visited. I had a pretty good infield, but theirs...theirs was ravenous. They gobbled everything that was hit on the ground with such an implacable hunger that I could only watch in awe. They scooped the ball the way you were supposed to scoop it; they threw with their feet planted firmly on the ground, and their dirt-daubing gullets cried out the most soul-destroying obscenities I had ever heard on a baseball field. When we got up to hit, they caught everything and retired us after five pitches.

"Play ball!" shouted The Captain after I'd taken just two

or three practice tosses. I hadn't even worked out signals with my catcher, whom I didn't know, and whose special touch I'd have to get used to in the course of the game.

But things turned out well. I struck out the side without throwing too many balls and left the mound on a trot. My success was galling enough to draw a pebble from Trouble, who had to be somewhere. (I wouldn't spot him, along the third base-line, until the game was almost over—though I'd feel his pebbles throughout the game.)

Before the second inning, The Captain came out to the mound. He was wearing the silliest umpiring outfit I had ever seen—something that evoked handle-bar moustaches and long brass rails with spittoons underneath them. The anachronistic can thrive in disconnected places like Bible camps—and it is a mixed blessing, to be sure. The Range-leader was dressed up in the same way. I'd not seen them together till that moment. They looked good together, but not in a particularly good way.

Up to the fifth inning, play was tame. They were predictably brilliant in the field, while I was surprisingly effective on the mound. By the top of the sixth inning, the score was zip to zip.

I decided to really bear down and strike out the side for a morale-crushing blow to the enemy. But it was not to be. The first pitch I threw the batter picked up very nicely and lofted a line-drive double to left-field. I thought he might have an inside-the-park homerun, but my short-stop went way out past where any cutoff man should and relayed the throw into the catcher in the nick of time. I didn't deserve such heads-up thinking. But I think the guy was about fifteen. My very first ringer.

We got skunked that inning ourselves, so I had to bear down again, and yielded only a dribbler, which I muffed, but managed to recover and throw the batter out.

Then The Captain took center stage, as was his special habit and signal occupation.

"It appears that we have a cliffhanger on our hands. What shall we do? Call the game off?"

A chorus of no's ensued. From both sides.

"All right. I've been thinking about the most expedient course of action under the circumstances and I think I've got one. It is clear that the sides are evenly matched. Such parity is extremely rare at this level of play. I vote that the game be continued until one team scores!"

A hurrah went up at this uninspired decree. I was not being vocal that afternoon; whenever locked in a struggle for existence, a battle royal, a hard-fought contest between two near-equals, I just bore down and let the thing take its course. For all of The Captain's grandstanding, this was precisely what was to come.

The teams *were* so evenly matched that no run was scored till Inning Eleven, when I—yes, I!—was able to stroke a clean single to center-field. We now had one man on, with no outs. But hope died when the next batter grounded into a sure double play. Except: that the second basemen—usually a gluttonous eater of one-hoppers—bobbled the ball and could only get the lead runner. So we had a man on first with only one out. And then came Irving to the plate, a possible singles-hitter who had gone 0 for 4 that day. The opposite team razzed, but we stood behind him. Somebody started saying "The Hebe can hit...the Hebe can hit." In spite of my limited knowledge of offensive language as it applied to people who were apparently chosen for something, I repeated it myself. And, sure enough, the Hebe did hit, setting up our lead. Now there were men at the corners. If we didn't score under *these* circumstances, we might as well give up

At this critical juncture, The Captain came onto the field and said a new pitcher was going to ascend the mound and get them out of trouble, whereupon he himself started warming up.

That's no fair!" my team said *en masse*. Its persuasive timbre was not overwhelming.

I just looked. I'd learned something about Power and had become cynical. If you *could* be pitcher, you *would* be pitcher and that was that. There was no use complaining that somebody had stormed the palace, particularly if it stayed nice and clean.

He threw about eighty miles an hour—not an unhittable velocity if you were throwing from a major-league distance. But he wasn't and, because he wasn't, his incandescent pitches were largely invisible. The catcher had allowed one base-runner because he couldn't hold onto such quicksilver and let one of our strike-out victims advance to first. We had the bases loaded, but with no chance to hit—let alone see—the ball. Our best chance was snuffed by an authority figure who got his jollies dominating fellow humans a third his age.

I wouldn't get tired till Inning 13, when they took me for a couple of runs. We couldn't catch up under an onslaught of 80 MPH fastballs and died away like phantoms.

The Captain and his sunburnt irregulars had won and I got beat up that night, in a special edition of *Cabin One Presents*! After that, Trouble seemed to like me a whole lot better. (I had also recovered somewhat from our most recent encounter and marveled, not at any resilience of my own, but at a physiology that seems to be looking after us—even when nothing else is willing to do that job—independently.) In fact, between that final punch and the moment I left that goddamned quasi-Christian, character-destroying compound, Trouble would become almost friendly. I learned that friendliness could be a unilateral concept. I still feared and hated him and couldn't return the feeling.

I suppose it's strategically good to have friends like him, but, in the years to come, I've never felt comfortable with it. I have, in fact, thought that I should tell such people what jerks they are and just let them beat the crap out of me so that we might, forever afterwards, deal with one another like sworn enemies rather than nervous friends.

Problems still remained. What would I eat at the canteen, for one? For another, if I had to keep diving into that super-cold, spring-fed river, life would cease to have meaning for me. Perhaps I should run away now, thought I, sitting like a normal person on my bed late at night. There was still a week to go, but I was getting so frazzled that I wrote to my mother and asked her to send me aspirin. Other, more consciousness-eradicating medicines were not available to minors in those days. Even if I had known what hard drugs were, I would have been terrified, not only of the legal ramifications, but of the effects few protectors of public morals even knew about. If I were to ask a local television personality about the perils of cocaine—even if I'd known what cocaine was—he would have performed a double-take, said something about the irresponsible precocity of the very young, and told me, once we were safely offstage , to go home and forget about it. There was no roadmap for the sort of depravity our country would experience, with marijuana madness—which would temporarily supplant the fear of alcohol—some years later. For me, however, putting aspirin into play was a *cri de coeur* that ought to resonate. Being training-wheel Calvinists, we believed that, if you could take something, you should go right on taking it until stopped. If it didn't stop fast enough, greater and, possibly less reliable, reserves of strength and stamina would have to be called upon.

If any persecution exceeded those limits, it was all right to operate—as we would say a great many years later—outside the box. And among the cures that were available, geographical ones were the most tempting. And—until rolls were called and everybody else accounted for—the least detectable.

When I reached for my suitcase, it was not there. Trouble again, no doubt. He'd probably rifled the thing and strewn its contents onto the forest floor, through which a terrifying figure, Walkin' Charlie, rattled around with legendary impunity. I'll let somebody else tell you about him:

"When Walkin' Charlie comes in the night," said Bruce, following a bloodthirsty encounter between our coalition of the coerced, "he comes for the souls of little boys."

"I'm not a little boy," said Trouble.

"Me neither. I'm five foot seven—tall as my dad." This from little Scott, whose height didn't do him much good. Trouble had massacred him in the ring twice already. When the Range-leader asked him about his bruises, he said he'd bumped his head against the dock. Repeatedly.

"How did that happen?" asked the wizened counselor.

"I don't swim very well."

"If anybody goes out past the hour of twelve," our serial murderer consultant went on, "Walkin' Charlie'll be out there. Three boys have been lost to him so far. Three. Nobody knows where they are now. They simply vanished into the night. With *him*."

After elaborating at greater length about the murderous prowess of Walkin' Charlie ("I don't know if I should tell you this, but we have found body-parts out there. It is possible that these body parts are not human, but we haven't been able to determine that for sure!") our storyteller-in-residence flashed us a look that suggested he was suppressing the most fearful aspects of the Walkin' Charlie Experience and ceased—as if

he were an oracle who was being asked to work overtime—
talking. Most of us—whose sense of a dramatic conclusion
had been eaten away by elementary school teachers who had
ear-shattering bells to speak for them—had no idea that we'd
been abandoned. And like a party of stragglers whose sense
of confusion and betrayal was about, with the advent of a
night so cold, to worsen, we started to rise, shake it off—a
general strategy that applied to almost anything—and began
a sneaky pilgrimage. A few of us would get up, look to the
outside world as if it were one choice among many, and exit
the scene like tomcats who knew their place was in the alley,
but needed to be cool about it. Once outside, we had no idea,
because our activities had been so strictly regimented, what
to do. We were like cave-creatures who had been liberated
from the underground, but whose eyes were so accustomed
to the dark, we had no idea what we might do with anything
else. Lacking the perspective one presumably gets over time,
I couldn't articulate the feeling of there being a sort of gap
between what we'd been told camp would be like and how
it had, with a surprising relentlessness, evolved. I had envi-
sioned lazy laps around a concrete-sided pool; small creatures
that were ready, at a moment's notice, to land on a head
or shoulder; small rocks to throw at big ones; bird-calls to
identify from a field manual. For everyday fodder, the forest
would provide. Yet each day's initiative would be rewarded
by steaming chunks of red meat on which one might slather
barbecue sauce, which was popular nationwide, but of particular resonance in the South. But none of these momentary
visions, having slewed up from a sort of pastoral view of an
essentially hierarchical experience, materialized. I had neither
irony nor perspective, but a sneaking sense of what had been
promised as opposed to what was, without any sense of its
occupying a no-man's land of the psyche, being delivered.

So: I had Walkin' Charlie to face before I could get out to the highway and perhaps hitch a ride into the next town, where I might call my parents. They'd surely come and get me when they learned of the kind of place the camp really was. They wouldn't want their eldest son to be in an environment that would teach him the values of deceit and treachery; re-enforce the tawdry notion that violence and coercion were the most effective means of dealing with any potential adversary; that it was all right to steal something so long as the victim could not retaliate. If they knew these values were seeping into my system, they'd drive me back home in a hurry. Unless, of course, they were the very things I was sent to learn about.

Aside from the stolen suitcase—a fresh affront—I was getting the willies thinking that a Walkin' Charlie was out there; given my luck, he'd find me immediately and that would be the end of it. Victim #4 would go quietly into the night and certain extinction.

I decided to stay, but compromised by taking a walk up to the lodge, where I peeked into the windows. It was there I saw The Captain and our Range-leader locked in an embrace, the like of which I'd not seen before and didn't care to think about the following day, the day after that, or any of the other days I was there. I know what they were doing now, but at the time it didn't resonate with any of the experiences I'd had or known. Yet the image of the Captain's short shorts gathered at the knees has stuck with me.

One final humiliation occurred before the ghastly two-week period was over and it involved the dreaded spring-fed river, which I had grown to hate so much I had begun to dream of it drying up, with The Captain a great blue fish flopping around on its sun-blistered bottom. It was he who said we'd get adjusted to its numbing effects on our systems. Bull-hockey! When it's cold as that river is, you dress for it or don't go in.

This final event was the swim-meet, in which we all had to participate. I was going to do the relay with Bruce, who was a swimmer in the same sense that a person who is falling "flies." It is not that you are *in* the air or water, but *how* you are. Bruce was no gliding missile and that was that. An ignominious loss was a foregone conclusion.

"All right," said The Captain, who would be forever linked, in my mind, to our Range-leader in a way none of the other boys would become aware of, "I want all of you to do your best. The water is now your element and I think you've made tremendous progress. When you leave this place, you will take with you the formidable skills you have learned here out into the world. I am confident of that."

The relay was over quickly enough. Predictably, our team came in last. Fine. I wasn't bucking to be known as a swimmer anyway. I was, in fact, hoping we might be able to have a re-match out on the baseball diamond, possibly without The Captain. In fact, I had an idea about that; I would threaten to tell people about what I'd seen The Captain and the Range-leader doing that night if he, The Captain, didn't let us play. And if he decided to ascend the mound a second time, I'd spill it then.

But first things first.

"Defeat is not bitter," said The Captain after the race was over and we were pleasantly sunning ourselves on the dock, "if it can be redeemed."

Huh?

"This young man is a good ballplayer, but not the swimmer I'm sure he would like to be." This to me, who was perfectly content with his swimming.

He passed over Bruce, terrible swimmer and waterborne enigma. Why?

"I think he would like to redeem himself, wouldn't he?"

Everybody loudly concurred.

Oh, no. What vicious trap had he steered me into? Had he seen me watching *them* the night before? Was this a nefarious attempt to silence me? I would soon see.

"I want you, Jerry, and you"—here he pointed to me—"to do The Mile Swim. Right now. I will supervise the competition myself and swim alongside you."

The Mile Swim! This was something people talked about, but couldn't possibly think of doing, not in those treacherous waters with their black eddies and swirly rapids. They'd eat me alive after a few hundred yards. What might they do if a whole mile were available to them?

I raised my hand.

"I don't think I can swim a mile, sir."

"Then you'll have to drop out. I would, however, suggest you didn't."

This was as overt a threat as he needed to make. I rose to my feet and said I'd do it.

Jerry's face had clouded over a bit too. None of us had ever attempted this holy grail of a camp swimmer's shaky repertoire.

In the stomach-churning aftermath of my decision, panic seized me to the point of jellying my knees and making me gulp in a way I never had. The gulp started as an inaudible but agonizing clutch inside the throat followed by a system's failure that banished air from the lungs for a period that exceeded normal breathlessness. I fought the urge to sink down onto the deck and start crying. That would get me out of it maybe, but it would also get me much deeper in. Nobody had cried yet, in spite of a myriad of provocations. So I wouldn't either. Trouble was attempting in his own way to suppress an expression that, if gotten out of hand, might border on the absolutely horrific—an eye-searing portrait of human anguish. I couldn't conceal mine quite as well. Even the other kids were—dare I say it?—sympathetic. As we dove back into the water at the dock between The Captain, who would swim alongside of us, they stood at the edge of it trying to encourage us to go on. "You can do it...it's just a mile... come on, babe...it's baseball, think of it as extra innings. Extra innings, babe. Come on, babe. Extra innings!"

I didn't do too badly for about a quarter-mile, but sank into the water's dispiriting embrace shortly afterwards. Trouble and The Captain slipped ahead and were soon yards in front of me. I started taking on water. God, my lungs. They're going to collapse. When did I eat? Will I get cramps? You're not supposed to eat and swim.

Luckily, the camp's policy of swimming first and eating second saved me. As did my overdrafts at the canteen. I had nothing in my body but a cold and clammy sense of doom.

The course was out and back, so I got to see competitor and mentor swim by me before I reached the halfway mark. I couldn't believe I was still swimming. The great liquid trenches that were the river's stay to progress had totally overwhelmed me. How on earth did people swim in the ocean? Yet this river had a great brawling life of its own. Should we attempt to conquer it? Of course we should! Why? Because it was here—and because The Captain said we should.

The current would be with me after I made the turn. *They* were little bobbing specks in the distance, halfway between me and the dock. I was losing and would lose, but I might at least finish. There was my redemption: I'd finish. Perhaps that blond-headed fruit was right. Perhaps redemption of a highly personal and idiosyncratic stripe was at hand and I could ride to a Pyrrhic victory on that! By the time a cheerless numbness had set in, I had gotten close enough to be able to hear my name. The kids were actually cheering me, the underdog, on. What an incredible turnaround! Somebody else would win, but my tenacity and triumph would be celebrated.

I saw them hit the dock, The Captain easily, Trouble without any sense of joy at all. Winning had taken everything he had. It was the first thing he'd done fair and square, but one had to admit that he did it. Perhaps this would be a lesson to him. He might not have to bully so much in order to get his way in life. On the other hand, a legitimate victory might merely embolden his criminal sense and liven up antisocial tendencies that had just found their groove. Is character destiny—or do the same damned people just keep getting lucky over and over?

It took me a great while to get to the dock. By the time I got there, the cheering that had bolstered my spirit had waned, everybody was sitting around the way people do in a waiting room, and a sense of anti-climax was most palpably in the air.

I hoisted myself up on the dock and just lay there, fried by the superhuman effort that had kept me above water and, eons after the victors had come splashing in, home free. I was hoping that everybody would get a second wind and herald my arrival with some sort of spirit-soothing racket. But nobody made a sound.

When I woke up later on in the day, there was silence. And solitude. I took one final plunge into the steely-cold water and dog-paddled my way back to the shore. It might have been late, it might have been early; I didn't care. Hell, Walkin' Charlie might've been lying in wait for me. If he had, I would have asked him how he wanted to flay me, which side might have appealed to him most, and helped him look for the proper instrument—should the forest be able to provide it—and let him kill me with it. Unless it is rendered into a horror story, or allowed to stray into the kinds of low-percentage catastrophes that used to play so well on the evening news, life doesn't give us spine-tingling incidents and harrowing conclusions. It deals out its pain-pricks one little pinch at a time. It delights in deferring trouble so that, when it happens, it is fearfully memorable. It is never so bad as when it withholds the worst it can do. So that we may live in dread. So that we may patiently suffer. So that all of our pleasures are pucker-faced and our occasional triumphs are more likely to chatter their teeth than open a mouth so wide, all we see is a roaring tunnel.

That evening, the camp counselors gave a little concert. One guy strummed bar-chords on a small oar; another had made a Swiss Army Knife serve as a mike; the rhythm section consisted of a drum set made of a galvanized tin bucket, banged with a wooden spoon.

> *You get a nickel*
> *I'll get a dime*
> *We gonna find some really fine wine.*
> *Gimme wine wine wine*
> *Gimme wine wine wine*
> *Gimme wine wine wine*
> *Wine wine wine wine wine wine wine!*

This paean to alcoholic obsession went over extremely well, giving good Christian people an opportunity to let their hair down. The Captain got into the act with a tender ballad that was one of Elvis' signature hits. He'd fudged the words a bit, but the tune was still there.

> *Love me tender*
> *Love me sweet*
> *Love me all the time*
> *Make me your*
> *Love-slave now—*

Look, I've made a rhyme!

We didn't know he could sing too! He was *musical*. Surprise, surprise!

The Range-leader had to stick to his social standing and sang something inspirational. He and The Captain exchanged looks I hoped nobody else would notice. (I had noticed them signaling one another with tie-moves and belt-buckle preenings. Was I the only one?)

When it was over, I asked The Captain whether we might have a re-match. He said he'd think about it, then went over to our peerless leader and patted him on the butt.

The next day I walked into the Range-leader's hutch and told him I wanted to pack it in.

"Is there anything about the experience you're dissatisfied with?" he asked with profound *naïveté*. He sat around in an office; how could he know what was going on?

"No. I just wanna go home."

"But surely there's a reason. There's always a reason."

Interesting view for a man of faith.

"No. I'm just homesick."

"A lot of boys are homesick, son."

No, they weren't. This place was a natural lodge for most of them. Trouble could stay here until he had to go out and get a job somewhere—and perhaps he'd just forget about that and become a Lifetime Resident. The Captain had to be in a place like this in order to assert his natural, or unnatural, authority in a structured setting. Everybody else, more or less power-deprived, was now used to it. The most winning adaptation strategy was surrender. We'd all mastered it and had discovered a sort of powerful unity therein. This was a lousy situation, but we'd learned to love it—just as people in

America had also learned, with the help of Dr. Strangelove, to Love the Bomb. It was, of course, the perfect situation for those who were either born with the power, could achieve it through mauling, or had it thrust upon 'em by means of close and nurturing contact with the already-powerful.

"Could I call my mom and dad?"

The Range-leader folded his hands in a way that suggested silent communion with the Lord. It was from such profound connections that his counseling style had evolved.

"I don't want to make you stay if you don't want to. But I think those who do learn the most."

He was right about that. If I stayed through to the end, I'd probably learn how to kill somebody and cover it up. I thought I'd put that off for a while.

My mom must've heard something in my voice—the subtext that lay beneath mere words, vibrating a sense of calamity into them.

"Are you okay?" she asked me, with that combination of genuine concern and salvation-is-just-around-the-corner cheerfulness that can be frustratingly neutralizing.

More in the interest of Truth rather than the residual terrors that accompanied the life-at-camp imagery that flitted through my brain as if I were yearbook-processing and wanted to seize on to something that had made it worthwhile, I said: "Yeah, mom. I'm fine. It's been great."

"Okay. You just didn't sound very sure."

"Oh, I am. Very sure. Very sure indeed."

I wasn't an "indeed" sort of person, but found that I could easily become one.

"Okay, then. Okay."

After that second okay—which re-established the sense of comfort and certainty I had momentarily usurped—she said they'd come to get me over the weekend, when my father got back from his business trip.

The weekend? Might as well stay. The weekend was when it was over.

"I guess your mom told you what I've been trying to tell you."

I couldn't take issue with the man The Captain was straddling through the window that evening.

When I walked through the door of Cabin One, however, I was greeted with a surprise. As I cleared the door, Trouble came up from behind me and threw me to the floor.

"Wrestling match...wrestling match!" went the shout.

I couldn't bother anymore. I just let him pin me and went back to my bed. Such peaceful non-resistance was anti-climactic and had turned people inside out. It seemed everybody was tired of being a victim. People weren't so inhuman after all.

"I want to go home," said Scott.

The Snake stated his aversion to the place in no uncertain terms, followed by similar professions. In disillusionment, we had achieved unity.

Only Trouble maintained his sense of man-handling authority—though he departed from his vow of silence to call me a baby. I just nodded. Perhaps I was a baby. Perhaps infantile resistance was as much as I might expect of myself.

The rest of the week passed largely without incident. Bruce got stung by a wasp and was treated by the Range-leader himself. The fights had become so routine, only half of us bothered to watch. I even did one to show that the spirit of the kill could be activated if I wanted it to be—which I didn't. When my opponent's punches came thick and fast, I didn't even block them. I also think their aim had, in the interest of a waning season's lassitude, deteriorated somewhat. I was there for the asking, but they didn't particularly care. In the eye of a storm,

I had achieved perfect serenity.

Trouble wanted to hatch a plan to raid the canteen, but nobody would join him. We were a bunch of lapsed Christians who were sadder but wiser—and very, very tired.

That last night, we talked of what we were going to do back home.

"I'm gonna go get my bike," said Irving of a bicycle he'd lent out to a friend. Irving was okay. Luckily, he could also fight. The rumblings of anti-Semitism that had broken out early on were smothered by him personally.

"I'm not gonna do anything but eat," said Scott, who had lost weight. He didn't like hot cereal, which was the breakfast of choice among camping Christians. He had also turned out to like the water and became an enthusiastic swimmer. He was the only one among us who could do a back-flip off the deck.

Trouble broke into this valedictory mood with a disconcerting ferocity.

"You know what you were here for. You were here to get conditioned to real life. Real life is like this. I know. My dad told me. He was in the Navy—the United States Navy! Nobody was tougher than him. They used to make you jump from the top of a ship into the ocean. Some people got broken legs doing that. You had to be tough to be in the Navy. And my dad was the toughest."

Following this peroration, Trouble lost his standing completely, not because of the content of his words, but because he started crying after uttering them. Trouble crying. I had seen everything now. I found myself forgiving him for the overdrafts. Maybe he needed the candy more than I did.

Before our parents showed up, the Range-leader stood us out in front of the office and harangued us.

"You came here two weeks ago as boys. You are still boys, but I think you know more of what it takes to *become* a man than most people your age do. You've learned teamwork, you've learned cooperation, and you've learned community. These are things you'll take with you for the rest of your life. I'm proud of each and every one of you."

He and The Captain exchanged the fleetingest of glances, followed, on The Captain's part, by a visible wink.

When my dad came—my mother had to stay home to look after my brother, who'd caught whatever it was that was going around—he shook the Range-leader's hand and asked him how I'd done.

"Fine," said the Range-leader. "He turned out to be one of our better swimmers."

"Good," said my dad, who mussed my hair.

"He's a good little ballplayer too," said The Captain, who was also hanging around to see everybody off. I started to look wide-eyed at the man's brazen hypocrisy, but the sadder-but-wiser me took over and shrugged his shoulders.

I watched some of the other kids with their parents. Trouble had a little sister, who looked, alongside him, undersized and embarrassed. Such a frail creature had no chance—unless her frailty might protect her. I could only hope Trouble would find his better nature before taking her spirit and laying waste to it.

I studied the two for a moment until I saw her give him a kick to the shins, which made him hop into the backseat on one leg. I had not seen Trouble in anything other than a position of relaxed and arrogant supremacy—except for those anomalous tears—since I'd arrived at the camp. I discreetly applauded this fantastic turnaround and waved at Trouble as he and his little sister were driven away.

Everybody else was gone in short order, as if the place had satisfied every possible human need and didn't require backward glances. We were the last to go. My dad wanted to look at the ball-field.

"Needs some work." He was alluding to the pebbles.

"I wasn't able to do much with it."

"You'd need to drag it," said he, in his Damage Assessment mode.

"We only played a couple of times. We swam a lot," I said, understating our activity schedule magnificently.

"Look at the rocks out there. You could take a grounder right up in the kisser. One bad hop and it's all over, mister."

"It played all right," I said, remembering The Captain and his gratuitous victory.

"I guess you don't know what the Cardinals are doing."

"No," I said, galvanized as I hadn't been in two weeks.

"Are they ever on a tear! Even Maxvill's hitting. Maxvill! Those weak-hitting short-stops'll surprise you."

At this revelation, we walked to the car and got in.

"Where's your suitcase?" asked my dad.

"Got stolen."

"Stolen?"

"Yeah. It's what goes on around here."

My dad adjusted to this surprising development surprisingly. He would have slipped a disc at home. *What do you mean it got stolen? I'm going to that counselor and I'm getting some answers right now!*

"Well, the stuff wasn't irreplaceable. Did you have a good time?"

These last two sentences proved that my dad hadn't a clue about anything.

Except when he mentioned a nick that had survived the surreptitious care I was providing the wounds and gashes whose half-lives had fortunately been as short as I wanted them to be.

"I see you didn't back away from a curve," he said, glancing at a boo-boo that hadn't quite let go.

"Oh, yeah," I said, touching it in the way people have always done with things they're used to, but are brand-new to everybody else.

"Oh, yeah," I said a second time, as if to corroborate his vision of a clumsy batter rather than a sitting duck.

"I had a great time, Dad. Thanks."

"Maybe you'll want to come back next year."

"Maybe. You say Maxvill got a hit?"

"*A* hit! Three-for-four yesterday. You know what they should do with that baseball? They should mount it up for him and give it to him on a platter. And when the Cardinals clinch the deal, I'll betcha they will!"

We drove back through countryside so breathtaking that even my under-developed aesthetic was roused. In all of my years on the planet, the sun had never shone more brightly, foliage had never been more translucent, and the natural noises— as opposed to civilization's quiet shudder—that came and went were vaguely musical, as if nature was a chorus that, even if the slightest attention were given to it, could soothe and spirit and activate the soul. Yet as I drank it all in, my thoughts went back to baseball. The Cardinals would be playing later on; if we were close enough, we could catch them on the radio, with Jack Buck doing the plays and Dizzy Dean the perennial color man honking it up behind him. I thought about their exciting run for the pennant as we drove past picture-perfect little hamlets with their one Esso Station either detached from, or symbiotically connected to, a little grocery store with a tomato stand out front. I thought about what might happen during the remainder of the season with a sense of pleasurable anticipation I'd not entertained in two full weeks. Flood and Brock chasing down fly balls at the warning track; White at first base scooping short throws out of the dirt; Gibson and McCarver, baseball's most formidable battery, polishing off National League batters like a well-oiled machine. And now Maxvill—who could stop time with his glove—going three for four! Nothing like the triumph of an underdog to balance out the predictable force of life's heavy hitters. He'd probably never do it again, but it didn't matter. The miracle was that he'd done it at all. And it looked like he was sweeping everybody else right up with him!

You Listen at Your Own Peril: a Minor Morality Tale

Most victims of a confidence trick eventually get wise. Yet the power of psychological insulation can be overwhelming, in which case the learning curve is barely perceptible. This is the sort of learning curve the trickster loves best, but rarely finds in a world of faster and faster learners. Most people get wise halfway through the second time a flim-flam occurs and find a way to excuse themselves. I was an unusual victim in that I knew all along, but the scamming was being conducted so masterfully that I couldn't tear myself away from it; I wanted to watch it unfold, study its fascinating permutations, and know, in full, how a person could do it. I found I could experience moral indignation at the fact that I was being scammed, but also a breathless, even awestruck, admiration for the scammer—who was at the top of his game and therefore not to be denied. You know how you can't keep your eyes off of something you know is bad—or at least not morally elevating, socially redeeming, or even pretty to look at? Well, that's what happened to me. And now, after nearly fifty years have passed, I can finally talk about it.

It happened in a movie theatre during that wonderful, rootless summer of my eleventh year, when my parents dumped me—after a feverish prayer—at my grandmother's house and just left. Three hundred miles would separate me from good behavior, stern responsibility, and structured activity for two full weeks! What on earth would I do first?

Time was not structured at my grandmother's. An inveterate house-cleaner who made the place all lemony for me and my grandfather, she provided whatever structure there needed to be. My grandfather wasn't very useful except as an obstructionist—a job he took seriously enough, though he let the work come to him. His second job as chronicler of ages past he performed ably, if sneakily. He came up on you and started talking before you could fight him off. He knew that nobody would resist a needy old man; thus, anyone was a potential audience—unless that anyone possessed the sort of hearing military people want for national security. I protected myself by sneaking out at an early hour and left my progress through the world to chance. To fate. To a sudden urge to follow a road I'd never traveled. Or to the more familiar attraction of another road I knew entirely by heart and could walk even if all the lights were busted out and I had to go by touch.

On this particular day, I walked out of the door onto the porch and decided to sit on the swing for a while. This was not strategically intelligent. Yet I was the sort of lazy person who didn't care much for sitting and thought I should learn to do it. My grandparents' house had a great many staging-areas for quiet conversation—the only lasting remnant of the companionable lifestyle people were always talking about, but which I never saw. Around there, you were expected to *do* something—even if, as in my grandfather's case, it might take on an unorthodox form. He'd been an accountant in his earlier days, but could no longer work with numbers. He'd give you some money and hope it wasn't too much or too little. When my grandmother sent him out shopping, she gave him the exact amount of money he would spend, with a list of all the items pinned to the lining of his jacket. It would come out right most of the time. And when it didn't, the grocery gave him credit—which she would deal with later on. Throughout his working life, he'd written inspirational columns for the local newspaper. His subjects were taken from the great, rumbling sermons he no doubt heard as a young man and had adapted to a meandering sensibility. He said that thrift had a good mind while penury was its stupid cousin. He prophesied that the decent man would go to heaven before the good man because the good man always needed to stay longer to prove himself. He let everyone know that it was all right to take a drink now and then, but if God were bartending, how much do you think He'd give you? He weighed in on the wages of Sin, the love of Virtue, the vanity of Talent, and the house arrest Guilt set aside for the leisurely sinner. For the sage and sententious things no human being had ever expressed so well in prose, he trotted out his rhyming dictionary and came up with some real head-bangers. He wrote the following under the influence of winter:

> *O misty-eyed Autumn, which gets in our blood*
> *And bids us pick the apple, and not saw our wood;*
> *It ends with a sorrow, when the sly hoarfrost kills*
> *Not just our harvest, but piles high the bills!*

> *Worse yet is the smooth-furrowed, virgin-pure snow,*
> *Which wipes our sins clean row upon row;*
> *It buries our secrets for an icicle-hung hour,*
> *But yields them back in a March-livened bower.*

> *Thou winter, which keep'st thy counsel so well—*
> *Please keep the secrets cunning April will tell!*

I ran across this, and other, poems when I was fooling around in the basement, among piles of old newspapers and other junk. The sun-yellowed newsprint had a crumbly texture you could touch only once. And while I left the poetry intact, I managed to scuttle more useful smatterings of knowledge and hearsay without trying. Amidst the ornate clutter I'd come to see first, the newspapers were not much of a find. I was far more interested in an old clock whose tarnished-gold fittings I thought stupendously elegant. Every time I saw it, I knew there was better stuff in the world than the tawdry leftovers I had. But there were more newspapers than anything else, so my attention went to them. I extracted a less crumbly one from the middle of a knee-high accumulation and found my grandfather's meditation on the upsurge in local birth rates; I thought it stern and fair, if a bit starchy. The date on the newspaper was June 16, 1927.

> *You mothers who in maidenhead saw the breath*
> *Of morn upon your gentle brows: Fight death*
> *Not with increase, but with a greater plenty,*
> *A finer issue—a yet more lasting bounty*
>
> *Whose fair and smiling visage looks to thee*
> *And saith: "Strength is in Love and grace in Chastity!"*

A more recent, WWII-era paper ran these pithy couplets:

> *When we're weary-seeming and feel our fire is lost*
> *When we're topsy-turvy and tempest-tossed;*
> *When there's nothing to do (maybe) but throw in the towel;*
> *Exchange the lyre for the jew's harp; and bright gold for*
> *a trowel;*
> *When we have no anchor in God; nor even hot breath*

> *from the devil;*
> *When there's no balm for our soul, nor straight line for*
> *our level:*
> *We can take heart in what's firm and foretasted—*
> *Be it hardship or heart's-ease, or the base-runner wasted;*
> *It is from these hard lessons we know we are strong,*
> *We have only what's ours, as we stumble along.*
>
> *We have only what's ours as we stumble along;*
> *We're just lowly clay which scours not long!*

This last gave me a sudden urge I'd never had before. I wanted to write a poem myself! Yet rather than invent my own lines, I decided that I would garble his and create fresh material that way. After some hours and joyless pacing, I came up with this:

> *When the fire's so hot, it's roasted our gut*
> *And we can't keep the flames from licking our butt—*
> *We better find God—or a hose—real fast*
> *'Cause we'll never be able to sit on our ass!*

Irked by the journeyman's tone, I attempted another. I began to toy around with alliteration and other coy devices. I now realized that, in poetry, it was the expression, and not necessarily the subject, that made for quality and character.

> *Pray, ladies, spread not thy legs the way you do*
> *As a Playboy bunny or a Penthouse shrew;*
> *Keep everything buttoned because it goes without saying*
> *That if you lose your shirt, you won't get it back praying.*

I didn't particularly like the judgmental tone of the thing, but it had so overtaxed my capacity to rhyme that I could not come up with the singing couplet that might suggest other possibilities. Yet I was poet enough to see that, should I tack it on, the overall feeling might be lost. So I just left it as it was. I'd wanted to retain my grandfather's morality, but update it a little. I felt that I had succeeded more or less and filed my poem away with the others, hoping that, in some distant day, my halting effort would be read along with my grandfather's and seen as comparative literature.

Remembering the secret work I'd done, as well as the various fruits of *his* imagination, I sat and waited for my grandfather, whom I generally tried to avoid. I was, at long last, in the mood for a story.

After I began to get fidgety enough to consider other options, my grandfather came out and started talking. When he sat down next to me, I noticed his leathery skin, which had dark spots in some places and pale ones in others. Though I'd asked, he would never tell me how his skin had gotten like that.

ME: Can I touch it?

GRANDFATHER: Why would you want to do that?

ME: I don't know.

GRANDFATHER: Well, if you don't know, how can I tell you anything?

I will never be able to think about the content of the story he told me without visualizing that skin, which seemed to slosh up and down his wrist without anatomical bobby-pins to keep it in place. Will *my* skin ever look like that? From the look of it now, it'll probably take no more than a year or two.

The story was about his brother, who'd gone off to a neighboring town to look for somebody who'd skipped school and run away from the farm. These were rural people, so there were always farms in their stories: farmy people and farmy incidents which, often as not, had to do with dying gruesomely or living the sort of hardscrabble life I, a city boy, couldn't possibly imagine. (The implication was that I was too soft to endure such a life, which was very possibly correct.)

"You'll understand that Lymon was not familiar with the area so he couldn't come back even if he wanted to. So you know what happened?"

"Nossir."

"Well, he got on this boat and went up to Paducah, where he got into some trouble. They had to come git him in the jail."

"Really?"

"Yessir. The jail. He'd gone and got himself in trouble because he didn't have any money for a hotel room and was just roaming the streets. He was brought in for vagrancy."

"Oh," I said, with a limited understanding.

"You know what a vagrant is. It's someone who's just roaming around. Did you know there used to be pigs on this very street?"

"Pigs? Here?"

"Well, how do you think the street got cleaned?"

"Dunno."

"Young man, streets don't clean themselves."

"I know that."

"Pigs did it in those days and they did it better than we do. If there weren't so much traffic, I'd say put the pigs back on the street. Look at that trash out there. It makes me very perturbed to see it. Do you understand?"

"Yes sir."

"Just so you do."

I would come to realize that my grandfather had no taste for the direct tale, but was a born meanderer who, if he came up short in one section, made up for it by developing the next minutely and conscientiously.

"So when Lymon came and got him out, he took him back to the farm, where he made a huge mess of things because he was a city boy like you and didn't know how to work with his hands."

At this pointed observation, my grandfather looked at his hands, then at mine, as if to draw a comparison. I looked up at the window over the swing and saw his "Notary Public" sticker. With the authority of his office there above him, I felt at a slight disadvantage. *I can't work with my hands. If somebody had taught me, I might. I'd gladly work with my hands if I knew how. But I don't! How am I gonna do something I don't know how to do? Would you tell me that?*

"Nossir, people don't work with their hands anymore. Why, when I was your age, I could fix bicycles, I could fix buckboards, I could go out to the barn and shoe a horse in five minutes. Five minutes and that horse could trot away and not worry about a thing. What the average boy could do then would shame a president. Yes, shame a president!"

I looked duly alarmed at the state of boyhood in our country. But he'd already switched gears and was back in the tale.

"He couldn't do anything, but he could charm the ladies. Oh, he could charm the ladies all right. And when it came time for him to marry the one he was charming up the most, he skipped town again. Skipped town and was never heard from in this our life."

"I'm sorry."

"Sorry? Nobody was sorry about him leaving except my sister Caroline, who was so heartbroken we had to force-feed her after seven days in her room. I think if I saw that man today, I'd run after him. Old as I am, I'd run after him and I'd just throw myself at him. Well, only God can know who among the righteous and the wicked, when at a crossroads, will come to Him or be damned!"

My grandfather had the storyteller's gift of satisfying you only up to a point. His exit strategy—so essential to the art—was brutally calibrated to make you thirst for more. If you didn't say "Is that all", he hadn't done his job. And so, in honest thralldom, I said it.

"No, that isn't all," he said, and left for the lemony fragrance I'd abandoned.

With his conscious chicanery ringing in my ears, I leapt out of the porch-swing and started walking. Fate was pushing me in a direction I knew hardly at all, down a fairly busy street with houses that had a pushed-in look to them. Though it was a hot summer day, their curtains were pulled incongruously back, not in cooperation—as my open-aired grandmother's were—but in defiance of the soaring temperatures and generally muggy situation. Their yards had the lackluster appearance of the sidewalks in front of them, and were wide and weedy. There were no flowers and hardly any sense of comfort or amenity. The broken-shuttered, fallen-clapboarded feel of their facades seemed to express the run-down, complicated lives inside of them. These houses were nothing like the ones I was used to in Memphis, where all but the most unsavory yards were crew-cut and every car idled underneath a carport that was as essential to a house's design and character as its living-room or kitchen.

And then a voice. "Hey, c'mere!"

"Me?"

"C'mere!"

Boys are often literal-minded people and, even in the midst of planned rebellions, follow directions gladly. And so I did.

When I got to the side of the street the voice was on, I followed it to the inside of one of those houses that had struck me, from a distance, as unsavory.

I learned, upon entering, that it was possible for at least one of them to be more unsavory inside than out. Yet the voice was telling me to sit down and be comfortable. *Did I want something. A glass of water maybe? No, I'm fine. How about a little beer? Beer? No, I'm fine! Sure you don't want any? That's what I'm drinkin'. Hey, but each to his own. Never force a good man to do anything, that's what I say.*

While the voice withdrew, I studied the room I was in. I'd never seen anything quite like it. Two measly blocks away you were in a completely different culture. My grandmother would be appalled. *I* was appalled, and I lacked her fifty-odd years of worrying over antimacassars. Where, I wonder, was that slightly earthy smell coming from? And all these newspapers and magazines: shouldn't someone have put them away somewhere? My grandfather would have gone to hell before he tossed a newspaper aside after he was done with it.

"There you are!" said the voice, now a person, now a boy possibly a few years older than I was. He looked like the place he was in: earthy and unkempt. They unconsciously blended, the two of them, to become a sort of living monument to the slovenly and uncaring.

"I was lookin' for somethin' to do today. Nobody's home, so I can do whatever I want. Not that I don't do that anyway."

This is when I should have found a way out. I had never heard anybody so young profess to be master of his own fate and I must admit I wanted to hear more. But then he approached me, leaning, as if he were circling a marvel and sizing it up.

"Just a minute. You don't seem...you're from somewhere else, aren't you?"

"Yes," I repeated, as if by rote, "I'm from somewhere else."

"I knew it! It's obvious from the way you speak. You have a

sense of... refinement about you. I could see that right away."

His somewhat orotund way of speaking struck me as unusual, as if it were a kind of sparkle misapplied to an old stick, or a shiny something that had been run over so many times that its essential character could not survive.

He sat down with his beer-can and opened it in a way that suggested a certain familiarity with the ritual.

"Sure you don't want any? There's plenty in there."

"No."

He slapped himself suddenly, like the impeccable host who's failed in his duty.

"I said I'd get you some water. Could you possibly forgive me?"

With this bid for lenience, he grabbed my forearm and squeezed it.

"I'll forgive you," I said, eager to make allowances.

"Thank you. Just water?"

"Yes. Water. Nothing else."

I had not yet sat down. I didn't want to disrupt the general disorder by sitting down on something I might want to tidy first. I was also attempting to dodge, in my person, the earthy smell that could be rising up off of these surfaces or drifting in from elsewhere and collapsing onto them. I wanted nothing to do with that earthy smell. It was repellent to nostrils that had just sniffed lemony-freshness; anathema to a paper-straightening sensibility I didn't even know I had. Instinct told me that the best way to deal with it was to stand pat and be ready to run if I had to. I complied with my instinct to the very letter.

He came back in with a large, streaky-looking glass full of what appeared, on top, to be water. Some sort of oily sediment roiled at the bottom. I took the glass and sipped it.

"Not real thirsty, I guess," he said, obviously disappointed.

I took the hint and started gulping. Some of the oily sediment touched my lips. I recoiled unobtrusively and fought the urge to wipe them. I set the glass down on a sort of coffee-table that had three good legs. The other, marginally functional, leg had been grafted onto it with an expedient sense of surgical nicety and looked temporary at best. It was the bum leg no self-respecting coffee-table ought to have and fit in perfectly.

"Hey, I've got an idea. Let's go to a movie. Wonder what's playing?"

He rifled through one of the newspapers that were splayed out on the available furniture, stirring up the earthy smell, and read off some titles, vetoing them as he read.

"Here's one," he said of one I'd already seen at the drive-in, and stood up. He was taller than I was and stoutish. His skin was very white, with a tan-line that was cut off at the wrist, like a mature man with an office job. His hair was slicked back over his head, but couldn't be disciplined in places, where it crashed and burned off into weedy clumps and degenerate sandbars. While he was not a healthy specimen in the all-American way, there was a rude energy that burned outward from his skin and, like the earthy smell, radiated into you. I was fascinated by the frank force of him and would have probably done anything and gone anywhere he suggested—within reason, of course. I had a six o'clock curfew and never missed it.

I am grateful now that his mind ran along legal channels. He could have said: "Let's hijack that car" and I would have helped him do it. It was one of those things you did on impulse or not at all.

Conventional authority figures rarely mesmerized me, though they were fearsome enough to compel obedience. This fellow's charisma was such that it took every rule-book, torched it with a kind of panache that was as powerful as the flames themselves, and kept right on moving.

"Hey, and you know what? We can meet my girl."

He dashed (for him) out of the room and came back with a nice checkered shirt, which made him suddenly dapper. I looked bland in my solid-white T whose label was always migrating outward. I wouldn't know it had done that until somebody came and flipped it back. Of the two of us, he was most definitely the one to watch.

"She'll like you. She likes men with class. Hey, you might steal her out from under me."

With this hopeful observation, he jabbed me with an obscene emphasis. I was doubly excited: by the prospect of seeing her as well as taking her away. What a day this was shaping up to be!

"We're gonna meet her at the-ayter. Come on."

For someone of his size and disposition, he sure could walk! A single stride took him ten feet away from me. The ratio of my steps to his was at least two to one—and almost twice that when he got excited. After a few long-striding blocks, we got to the small downtown, distinguished from the residential part by its relative bustle. The sidewalk was overcrowded with men in suits and overalls. Young women in ankle-length dresses cut a wide and knowing swath around them. Some of the men looked; others tried very hard not to.

"That's what I'm talkin' about! See those babes! Wait till you see Diana!"

I looked around, as if I might.

"She'll meet us over there. Come on."

We walked another block or two, past stores that sold gift items only and other stores that offered a liberal selection of house-wares, farm implements, and "notions." Unlike the suburban-style outlets I was accustomed to, these stores were strung along in a sort of wobbly unity based on easy access and walk-in convenience. Cars were parked, not alongside of them, but diagonally. Some of the cars were very old, with headlights that bugged out and chrome that had lost its capacity to reflect anything other than its lowly condition. Only a few of them looked like my dad's car, which was sleek and low—also for easy access and walk-in convenience. Because he was a traveling salesman, he had to have a nice new car to drive around in. It didn't look like that many of the people in this area needed cars like that.

"'M'onna get me a T-Bird someday. Back-seat has extra room for you-know-what!"

To accentuate this point, he dug his elbow deep into my chest-area. I coughed out my recognition and concentrated on breath-control. It seemed crucially important to be matching strides with this walking paragon, who had blustered into a high gear and stuck with it. The theatre *had* to be very close now! I was fortunately correct in this assumption. He stopped abruptly at a corner, like a cavalry leader who's just set eyes on a good campsite. I was able to stop just behind him, a fresh recruit who gamely follows.

"We better go in here and get refreshments. I hate that movie candy. Tastes like something in grandmama's hope-chest."

After peeking down his shirt-front with a bemused expression, and then pretending to have found something edible there, he bolted, with me following six steps behind, into a Rexall and laid in a bagful of Mars Bars, Three Musketeers, Zero's, and some local stuff that was wrapped in wax paper.

The theatre happened to be next-door. He paid for both of us, tossing me a look that said "Think nothing of it!", and we fizzled into the lobby, where they were selling that lousy candy. The smell of popcorn filled the air. There were no air conditioners then—or none here, at any rate. The blade-hurled breath of a small electric fan tousled our hair as we exited the lobby. He made a hacking sound as we cleared the double doors.

"Popcorn *smells* good, don't it? But it's like eatin' sawdust. Come on. She's down in front."

He strode down into the darkened theatre with a prairie-dog's sense of the best and quickest hideaway, slipping into a short row of seats off to the right. Sure enough, she was there and waiting.

"Hel-lo!" she cried to him provocatively.

She wasn't immediately visible, but she didn't need to be. The sultry purr of that voice was so unmistakably lubricious that it did something to me way down below the knees, which buckled somewhat, but were able to right themselves so that I could sit down. Once I did that, her silhouette, which the silver screen outlined as if it were creating a kind of three-dimensional universe of its own, was indissolubly classic, if a little raggedy-edged. Her hair seemed to be tousled, as if it were showing the bedhead condition it would undoubtedly assume, and preferably with me. A somewhat aquiline nose, coarsened by the effects of something that may have been more frighteningly mature for my comprehension, was slyly noticeable, and a chin that lifted her face up and away from me and toward the goings-on in front of her, showed less moral character perhaps than the drybrush of creation, which hovered there as I watched.

"Hey, honey," he purred back to her, opening the big brown bag full of goodies.

"Who's this?" she asked, pointing to me. I'd settled in behind them.

"This is a suave and sophisticated man from out of town. If he steals you, it's not my doin'"

She gave me a very brief look, which was not at all satisfied with his description, and settled in next to him.

"He probably has a bag of tricks I haven't even thought about," he said to her, driving home his point. I shrugged. Such talent called for a becoming modesty.

"Just don't let him get near you. He'll preach you a sermon that'll have your panties off on this floor!"

She laughed, but didn't look at me. Her eyes were already stuck on him.

When the movie came on, they snuggled close together and started eating out of that enormous bag. She had an appetite that easily matched his. The cartoon wasn't over before they'd made a little pile of the wrappers on the aisle seat, which he'd abandoned to be to the right of her—clearly not the advantageous position I had behind her. I knew this because he kept affirming it to me—though he certainly had the jump on me in terms of an overall seduction strategy. That is to say, he was a whole lot closer to her in the real, and not the potential, sense. And that seemed—at least in these early stages—a pretty good place for him to be.

Though the movie was action-packed and star-studded, I found I was more interested in watching them. Watching was not, however, what I was supposed to be doing. I had come there—as I had been assured—to participate in something. Yet I found that, as the movie progressed, I was still just watching. I would be brought up short from time to time by their mutual appetite for all the candy, which they ate with hard-chomping, peanut-spitting enthusiasm. I was able to tally up the candy-wrappers because I would periodically scoot up and let him make another observation about the amorous progress I was making with Diana, whose hand had disappeared down his shirt-front. His hand was meanwhile grazing in similar areas on hers. Sometimes he'd look back at me suggestively, as if to signal that she was just warming up with him, but his own amorous progress was so one-sided that somebody as "sophisticated" as I was might begin to notice that the jig was up between me and Diana.

He eventually ceased to tout my superior prowess, partly because he was exercising his so abundantly, but partly because he seemed disappointed. Perhaps I hadn't understood the game. Perhaps I was expected to leap in somehow and offer a better plan.

As the movie ground to its comparatively unexciting conclusion, he and his Diana were so obsessively involved that I could make an ignominious escape without attracting their attention. I knew he would not look back at that point and say that he was just a poor boy trying to make eyes at a movie star (or some such blather) because he had to know I knew that he'd taken me for a great, ego-deflating ride I'd not want to think about with him (or her) anywhere near me. So as the screen couple fused cinematically above them, I scooted out of the place and went back to the big house in the middle of town, where I had some leftovers out of the fridge, and went back to the porch-swing to think about my next assault on the unknown.

"There you are!" said my grandfather, who'd been out in the front yard with his push-mower. Tautened by red suspenders, his immaculate shirt-front stuck to his bony chest. He wheezed a little bit, but was otherwise in decent fettle. He was not the sort of man to stop and chat when he was working, but there was unfinished business between us.

Where've you been? I wanted to finish my story."

"Downtown."

"What fer?"

"Nothing. Just walking."

"That's all right, I guess."

"I guess."

"Want to finish up for me out there? I'd do it myself, but look at me! I'm soaked already. This is going to be one hot summer!"

"Sure. I'll do it."

"You know how to use it, don't you? It's not one of those electric ones. You've got to push it one way and one way only."

"I know. You let me use it last time. "

"I did, huh? Well, maybe I did at that."

"I'll do better this time."

He wiped his neck with a handkerchief he'd been spreading out on his lap. It had some initials stitched into it and was starch-white.

"You know how the story ended, don't you?"

"No, I don't."

"This is what happened. They found him in Ohio and they brought him back to see the bride. In the time he'd gone, she found somebody else and they got married. Still are married. But when they brought him over, they didn't tell him. They just sat and waited till he found out for himself. I think he ran back to Ohio that day. Yessir, I think he *ran* back."

When he was done wiping, he re-folded the handkerchief and put it in his back pocket.

"You know what the moral is, don't you?"

"Nossir, I don't."

"The moral is that vanity is God's way of taking us down a peg."

I knew, from an experience that was as fresh as the mulch he'd put down in the yard, that more than he would possibly understand, though you don't interrupt a seasoned storyteller with superfluous knowledge or irrelevant redemptions.

"He thought she'd wait for him forever, but she got over him and married the next one come along. And, you know, they're married even unto this day. This very day they're still married and they've been pretty happy, I'd say. Went through the Depression together, just as we did, but we all got through it, didn't we?"

"Yessir, you did."

"Just don't think of yourself as being indispensable. There's always somebody else. You remember that. There's always somebody besides yourself."

I spent the rest of the day with the push-mower, making sure I'd mastered it so that, when dinner came around, I could have something of my own to say for a change. I'd been listening way too much that day and was real tired of it.

Moment Musicale

Accordion fever swept across Memphis, Tennessee in the early 1960's. And it made perfect sense. The Mouseketeers gave us kids who were talented beyond their years. The Ted Mack Variety Hour trotted out crooning children and Mickey Rooneyish hoofers-to-be. In this new, water-sprinkled era, kids were not necessarily expected to fill up their idle hours with chores. They could be done any old time, or not at all. Kids were, for the first time in history, the center of attention. Children who were seen and not heard were embarrassingly passé and unfit for the New Era. The time was therefore ripe for activities that catered to a juveno-centric universe and your benignly unscrupulous entrepreneur was there to cash in on it.

That is where the New Accordion came in. Somebody had come up with the idea that vast numbers of children would throw away their cap pistols if they could be tempted with the color and romance of a more sparkling persuasion. The accordion academy was created to provide that color and romance, but with a solid structure that would channel their fidgeting and discipline their minds. Its founders were seasoned musicians who wanted nothing more than to nurture talent. And its salesmen were sincerely committed to a Better World.

To that end, well-spoken young men descended upon

our raw-contoured suburbs carrying booklets and brochures. Adorable children in the throes of accordion mania adorned their pages, along with testimonials from delighted parents. "I can't believe what the wonder of music has done to my Samuel's confidence!" raved a homemaker from Whitehaven. "Your program has been a godsend," crowed a doctor's wife way out in Germantown. When the literature failed to capture the accordion's allure, a *real* instrument was produced and the prospective accordionist encouraged to hold it in his lap and squeeze it. "It won't bite you, but it *will* talk back," prompted the salesman.

Seeing the Real Thing, parents would think: "Oh, what a great opportunity for Johnny to become musical!" without realizing that Johnny might graduate from accordions to the The Village People. The Mom was, of course, more patently enthusiastic, while Dad performed calculations in his head. The early Sixties was a period of unprecedented prosperity, but men, and some women, still earned their money and weren't going to throw it away on just anything.

"Squeeze it out. That's right. All the way out. Now squeeze it in and press on some of the keys."

"What keys?"

"Come on, son. You know what keys are."

So the kid pressed on the keys and out came a veritable symphony—a gentle chaos, a self-made orchestra. This is what the salesman had been relying on. If the pitch didn't work, the kids wouldn't be able to resist themselves as music-makers in embryo.

"Wow!"

"Isn't it something?"

"It sure is!"

Moments later, the salesman would be invited into the kitchen to work out the details.

A great many of us were undone by these well-spoken young men who descended upon us during those post-McCarthy years. People weren't suspicious of strangers anymore and had decided there was nothing wrong with a two-piece bathing-suit as long as the girl was chaperoned. No longer a solider, Elvis Presley provided the nation's soundtrack. My dad could sing "Nuthin' But a Houndog" as well as any Pennsylvania-born appliance salesman.

The tale I wish to tell begins during my second year of accordion thralldom.

But first: I want to make it very clear that I was not a good musician; nor would I ever become one. But I had a compensating sensibility that allowed me to get away with murder on the keyboard for as long as I was considered useful to my fellow accordionists. I was the patsy who could not be exposed, humiliated, drummed out. Why? I had that unquantifiable thing called *flair*. Whenever we did our yearly concerts, the band-leader always put me right out front. I could hold a smile longer than Miss America and I had the consummate liar's capacity for pretending to know a song I could just barely hum.

If I had any favorite years, these first two would surely qualify.

From my privileged coign of vantage, a terrible third year was unimaginable and took me utterly by surprise. If I had just known, I would have found a way to fade out quietly. But I did not—could not—know and came, smiling from ear to ear, to my own funeral.

During its peak years, The Fussell Academy of Music had registered as many as five hundred of us. We took private lessons there and were left to the mercies of a cheerfully sadistic band-leader at least once a week—twice and even three times for the truly gifted. It was not unusual for moms and dads to spend weeknights driving kids to lessons and band-practices.

Location was not the academy's strong suit. Parents commiserated with one another about the long drive, the lost hours, the damned hole-in-the wall where they stewed and waited. "Why'd they put it way out here?" you'd hear them asking as they braced themselves for the drive home. "Guess it's cheap." "Not for us, it isn't." "Well, what is?"

To get to the Fussell Academy of Music, *we* had to cut a wide swath through the south of town, which took, in that pre-expressway era, as much as half an hour. My father threw the massive accordion-case into the back seat and muscled the two-toned Chevy down the driveway into the street, taking care, as he eased it down, to watch for passersby. The dire possibility of young life abruptly terminated haunted him. One precipitous slide was all it took. The remedy? Eternal vigilance. "See anybody?" he asked. "Coast is clear" was my invariable answer. "Gotta look twice," he insisted, which I did. "Nobody in sight," said I, after that second look.

Some years ago, a five-year old had been killed in an adjacent driveway. My father wasn't about to let that happen on his watch. He hadn't roamed The Pacific Theatre to come back and slaughter his own. He needn't have worried so much; there weren't many five-year olds mucking about the neighborhood at eight o'clock in the morning. In this first decade of television dominance, most were inside watching cartoons.

My father was a genuinely conscientious driver who loathed "fresh" attitudes about safety on the road. "These people"—by which he meant his adopted countrymen of the South—"have no sense of what happens when you get into one of these things. It changes you. Having such power means you've got to be *more* careful, not less".

I didn't see what he meant, but it was too costly, in terms of overall passenger strategy, not to agree.

"Uh-huh."

"You'll learn soon enough. That's another thing. I've always thought they should increase the legal driving age around here—*especially* around here!"

As he eased into traffic, he proceeded to observe bungled turns and lackadaisical signaling. In his moral universe, there were lousy drivers and lousy drivers-*to-be*. Once you got behind the wheel of a car, you lost any claim to human feeling, let alone adequate reflexes.

"Guy's half-asleep. Take a nap, why doncha? Guess you didn't see what that one did."

I wasn't attuned to the nuances of the road. We were moving forward and that was enough for me.

"You'd think they'd test these people," he would say. Then, as if to corroborate a home truth: "Yeah, you'd *think*!"

There were no shortcuts to the Fussell Academy, so, after he settled in at the wheel, my dad left all the other drivers to their private confusion. He was a salesman of electrical do-dads, with city-wide connections that spooled out into regional affiliates; these proliferated into great national networks of astounding complexity. All the big offices were in New York, but lesser outposts were scattered around the nation. At these, he picked up his supplies, his catalogues, and whatever scuttlebutt he needed to survive. "See this?" he asked me once, offering me a hank of electrical wire. "This can power a baseball diamond. This one little cord." He left it with me, as if to say: "I give you Creation. Now be careful with it." His object lessons were always the same: he'd offer me something, make a pronouncement over it, and walk away.

We stopped now and then at a kind of business lounge, where a guy could pop in anytime he felt like it and do nothing at all. The sleek Bayridge Building was the biggest of these "lounges", with its burping water cooler and meandering hallways. Next in line was The Artesian Exchange, named for the city aquifer—a source of pride to this day. City Builders was the most dismal hole I'd ever been in and was a personal favorite.

As we drove, the City of Memphis got beautiful for a while, with its wide traffic lanes, its unspoiled lawns, its wall-to-wall magnolias. It had been voted the nation's most beautiful and here, in its sprawling mid-section, that particular honor seemed plausible. Yet the beautiful city would soon give way to a seedier underbelly, and this was where things got interesting. Even at my age, the suburbs had begun to pall. There wasn't much in them but a drab and unproductive stability, which doesn't mean a whole lot to kids who don't understand the nature of security—which they themselves don't provide. I wanted glamour, dissolution, danger. And the farther we got into the city, the more these things seemed possible. I was keenly interested in anything that overturned the suburban aesthetic, with its relentless right angles and freshly paved roadways. You could watch this older, rawer city go by and imagine the cops chasing people through it. That was the kind of place I wanted to be in—so long as I could come home at the end of the day.

The great Sears and Roebuck tower, standing like a great citadel over the tiny, man-sized houses in its midst, roused my pilgrim soul. It was Urban Glamour Writ Large. Its strategic location was the secret to its effectiveness. We didn't see it until we shot out of the leafy Parkways and approached the final leg of our journey. And there it was: Shangri-la, El Dorado, The Taj Mahal! We had already passed another beloved site—an eccentric dwelling somebody had decided to Mediterraneanize with pink stucco walls and something called a gazebo. I found the word infectious. *Gazebo*. It had a gazebo.

"Could we stop?" I asked. I wanted to gaze at this monstrous creation for a few moments. I'd been drawing pictures of the pyramids and the great Sears and Roebuck tower struck me as a worthy parallel.

"We don't have time."

"We've got fifteen minutes."

"You saw it already. You see it every week. You'll see it again next Saturday."

"Can't we? Just this one time?"

"You know, I like Cincinnati, but I don't go there any old time I want."

"Okay," I said, unable to supply a comeback.

If the matchboxes he collected, and brought to us, were any indication, he went to Cincinnati quite a lot. From these matchboxes, I knew where some of the nation's best second-rate hotels were. They had names like the Foxborough, the McDuggan, Chevy Plaza. They were mostly tall, square-cut buildings in the seedy Manhattan mold—even if they were in places like Des Moines, Iowa and Little Rock, Arkansas.

He relented and moved into the left lane for the slight hairpin turn that would take us into the heart of the surrounding neighborhood.

"All right, but just for a few minutes."

Somebody with a Mississippi license plate cut him off as he was about to make his move.

"Did you see that? Mississippi. They come here from Mississippi. And they all find *me*. I have a mind to…maybe someday."

We pulled into a side-street. Behind it was an alley that was gravel-paved in the middle and weedy at its perimeter. On either side of it a poverty-stricken cluster of outbuildings leaned. Things were not tidy here, as they were in my neighborhood, in which emphatic lawn ornaments and fussy yardwork were aesthetic lightning-rods. In the alley, man's delinquent nature was here to stay. An alley was a quirky, desolate sort of place nobody expected to look good. In that every nook and cranny around our house was patrolled with a fine-toothed comb, it was strangely liberated here—an alternate universe of unpainted clapboards and half-assed repairs. Our values would have prescribed a Project in which paintbrushes and shovels had everything presentable-looking in an afternoon. Wasn't gonna happen here and I felt sinfully glad of it.

The street itself was filled with medium-sized houses chock-full of stimulating details like paste-on shutters and white-washed tires. (These were sunk into the ground and served as planters.) Swing-around porches provided refuge from the sun. Cast-iron jockeys painted in what was politely known as "blackface" stood by a driveway to greet you. (In that day and time, political correctness consisted in voting for the candidate that looked best on TV. If you chafed at the notion of injustice, you let it eat away at you from the inside.) Some front yards had sundials while others settled with a cleaner-cut look than their neighbors. There was nobody out, but it was still early. I could hear Bugs Bunny wise-cracking from living-rooms and bedroom windows. One of the drawbacks of a Saturday morning lesson was the implicit sacrifice of morning cartoons: those same cartoons that kept driveway-bound children out of harm's way.

"Thanks, dad. I really appreciate it."

"That's all right. Haven't stretched my legs all week."

We got out of the car and walked toward the great monolith and stared at it.

"They've got one in Chicago that makes this one look like a toy skyscraper. That's right: a toy skyscraper you could hold in your very own hands!"

"I'd like to see that!" I gushed.

"Maybe you will someday," he said. "Maybe you will."

We finished the drive without a hitch. No Mississippian-Errant was sent by an angry god to spoil this final spurt, this journey's end. I was glad of it. At this stage of the drive, my father could get volatile.

The Fussell Academy of Music occupied an entire one-story building on Jackson Avenue. It was easy to find a parking-space on Jackson because Jackson was not jumpin'. It was one of those streets that functioned as a thruway to Downtown and, if that wasn't good enough, West Memphis, Arkansas, where the dog-track was and betting had free rein. Jackson Street's businesses were small-time and, from all appearances, vacant. The thrift-store that stood opposite the academy set the economic and moral tone of the area. You bought give-away things there—a swindle customers no doubt considered while they were waiting in line.

The academy itself was like the burrow of a small animal, protected somehow from the milieu around it by tinted windows on the one hand and the sense of a sacred mission on the other. It exuded Purpose and Propriety. The musical adaptations of its founder, a man with a vaguely Hawaiian name, were displayed in long glassed-in cases toward the front, where you purchased sheet-music for various assignments. He'd show up unannounced, in a dapper-looking suit, and fondle the receipts. People would form little knots and point his fine-spun hair out to each other. ("Just like silk! How does he keep it like that?") I didn't care to witness such idolatry and preferred to imagine those people reacting to my presence—as it might manifest itself some years later—in this way. Nor did I like his style. It was more than a tad overcooked, everything tucked in just right and no creases; he might have been a gigolo as recently as 1947. Yet when he deigned to nod to me that one time, I nearly swooned with its heady magic. *He noticed me! He noticed me! The man whose face is on the sheet music noticed me!* I had to stop for a moment and coax my heart to stop pounding. Would he say a little something the next time? Or would my sub-par performances in those little rooms where I fretted and dithered filter back to him? Defiler of a musical temple, I was not then, nor would ever be, worthy of any nod again.

I went straight to the little room that seemed to be an afterthought, waving, like a deckhand on the Titanic, to my father. I was able to suspend the dread reality of my week's effort until that very moment, when it dawned on me that I had practiced no more than twenty minutes per day, and mostly on things I knew already. I was working on an accordion symphony designed to create an eerie mood as explorers descended into the earth with nothing but a flashlight and a few day's rations. It was a stirring thing, though it changed every time I played it. No point in writing any of it down. The chords were too complicated. Nor did I appreciate musical structure enough to realize that you needed a beginning, middle, and an end. I had a longish middle movement dead to rights. The rest would have to wait until I was old enough to re-shape good raw material into something both exciting and coherent. I would not, alas, cobble together my symphony's disparate chatter. Which is just as well. Its rambling character would have been out-of-synch with the minimalist tendencies of that era.

I went in and got ready. The room smelled as it always did: of that peculiar essence of trapped instruments suddenly and brutally aired; of collective guilt and fear; and of the man who most frequently occupied it: Mr. Hunsecker, a person so old I knew, for a fact, that he was going to die in my presence. During the time we had together, I struggled, by means of subtle kicks and rising inflections, to keep him alive. Every time we both came out of that room, I considered the experience, if not the lesson itself, a great success. I never told my parents that I became a life-support specialist every time I took a lesson. If the secret were out, he'd flip forward into an open grave.

"Well, hello, young man," said Mr. Hunsecker. "I see we're ready to play this morning."

I had strapped the enormous instrument to my person and was sitting in my hard little chair when he came through the door and closed it behind him. Other lessons were in progress. Notes spilled from keyboards fellow players had worn out with dedicated practice. When they heard me, they would pause for a moment, smile knowingly, and pronounce my name. They *knew* who made those sparsely tentative sounds. I was the notorious slacker who lived by flair alone.

"Well, what did we learn this week?"

"Uh...I didn't work real hard on the assignment."

"Tsk, tsk, tsk," said the old man. "I wonder why you ever come here."

I did too.

"Well, let's begin. You do know what page it's on."

I did. "The Carnival of Venice" was the geographical center of the accordion songbook it was every second-year student's task to get through. Some of the most diligent musicians were in the middle of Songbook Number Three. Number Three! These fast-playing wonders showed up at band practice, opening their cases with an aplomb that defied their years and mine while pulling out a spit-polished instrument that might play a polka all by itself. They seemed supernaturally capable, bright beyond their years, poised like lions assured of their kill. I think it was amusing for them to tolerate me, an untalented stooge whose pathetic attempts at synchronicity they loved to expose by stopping, during band practice, well into a tune so that everyone could hear me squeak and gibber.

"The Big Show's coming up."

It was! Every year the entire academy, separated into cadres based on age and capability, gave a whopping concert. Parents, grandparents, and long-suffering siblings showed up in crashing droves and applauded like mad—no, like parents and grandparents—when the collective wheezing was done. I loved it because of the performing aspect of the thing. I couldn't play, but I sure looked good in a clip-on tie!

"I know."

"You're to play a solo this year."

"WHAT?"

"Yes. Your name was selected."

But...why?"

"I frankly don't know," said Mr. Hunsecker, with a candor that was very rare for him. To give him his due, he was a plodding and patient instructor who had geared his expectations farther toward the bottom than he was used to. My dismal tweetings tested his endurance while putting him fast to sleep. He was probably as shocked to hear of my special distinction as I was.

I repeated my question: "But why?"

"Possibly because you have shown a capacity for public performance."

"Oh."

"There would be no other reason that I would know of."

"Oh."

"Why don't we skip the lesson and try to prepare you for your solo? Tell me. What is your very best piece?"

"I don't know."

I did know. I just wanted nothing to do with playing that piece, or any piece, in public. Though confidence may flourish in a solitary setting—which was provided by the room in which my father's catalogues and electrical specimens were kept on shelves that buckled sometimes and tottered the rest—it crashes and burns when under the scrutiny of millions. (Millions might be described as that indefinable number that surpasses that of a familiar gathering. Which it would have here. A classroom was one thing, but an auditorium quite another.)

"Come, come. When you doodle around with pieces you know already, what do you most often play?"

"Uh...'Lady of Spain', I guess."

"Ah, yes. That old chestnut."

"Hmmmm?" I was not yet aware of the cliché—or any cliché, for that matter.

"Wanna hear it?"

With "Lady of Spain" I felt supremely confident. I played that piece with such pyrotechnical skill that the Overachievers at band practice sat and studied me without shame. If we'd finished and had a few moments to spare, they'd sit me up on the bandstand and have me play it. I now realize that they enjoyed watching a kind of idiot savant, capable of stunning musicality as long as it could be confined and focused; it did not have to stray; and no actual thought or effort were involved. I was born to play "Lady of Spain," everybody knew it, and just let it happen.

Every time I got a chance to play "Lady of Spain", I became a different person. I sat erect in my chair, my fingers lolling at the keys. I swept the room with a look that said "You're not going to believe what you're about to hear!" and started, first at a slower tempo than was called for; then with an awakening sense of the music's intoxication; and finally, with a shower of crashing chords so thrilling that people dumped their instruments, shot up out of their chairs, and started beating their hands together. With the room's febrile energy directed at my person, I felt serenely happy—a man who had *arrived*, even if he had no place to go afterwards.

When the applause died down, I stood up, a grandee still, and acknowledged the sweetly rolling thunder with a secret smile: the smile of a person who'd peaked and knew it.

As I was putting my instrument away, I allowed my fellow bandsmen to file past me, a marvel come rudely to life. Then, at the next practice, I was back to being me again, the least competent accordionist in Fusell Academy history and a sort of esoteric joke among the *real* musicians. I could not read music, I could not follow any beat, I could not understand why I was there and what I was doing. I was so completely out of my element, I provided an object lesson for the rest of them. As they watched me flounder, they could think: "There but for the graces of talent and discipline, there go I."

Why did they keep me?

Because I could play "Lady of Spain" like a gypsy. There could be no other reason in heaven, on earth, or anyplace in between.

I played it for Mr. Hunsecker cold, but it didn't matter. After the first few notes, I was absolutely on fire. When I was done, he shook his head in a manner that was nearly identical to the band-leader's, who watched me off to the side, as if I were a fascinating sociological phenomenon she might expose to the world someday. She didn't applaud like the rest. She was too much of a pro for that. She could attempt objectivity, but my "Lady of Spain" overwhelmed all comers. It was a force of nature and that was that.

"You are a strangely gifted young man," said Mr. Hunsecker, shaking his head. "You shouldn't be able to do this, but I have just seen it with my own eyes and you undoubtedly have done it. In all my years as a teacher, I have never known anyone as musical as you are on the one hand, and as slow to learn on the other."

Mr. Hunsecker was never so alert as when he marveled at

my split personality. Good! That meant he would last another lesson. I knew I'd be able to cruise right on through when he stood up, adjusted his glasses, pinched the two little places the glasses had pinched already, then let the glasses fall to his white-shirted chest. This was his longevity position. Whenever he assumed it, I knew I was home-free!

"Should I play that?" I asked Mr. Hunsecker, who was still overawed.

"I don't think there's time to learn anything else. But we should at least attempt 'Carnival of Venice' while you're here."

There were exactly thirteen minutes left in the lesson. I knew I could keep him awake—and alive—if I stopped very frequently and created audible diversions. The music stand, which made a hard, metallic noise whenever it was touched, was the perfect vehicle for these.

So as my "Carnival of Venice" crept along, ministering to Mr. Hunsecker's drowsy spirit, I was able to jar him up by means of a constant dribbling, hammering, and scratching as I presumably adjusted the sheet music—which needed no adjusting since I was never able to get through the entire piece.

"Try that again," he said, nearly comatose.

WHAM! went the music stand, which had an immediate, life-giving effect.

"Oh, would you play that passage a second time?"

When he started to lapse again, I dropped the sheet music down onto the little trough, which was made to hold book-length scores.

"That was better. Why don't we hear the whole thing now?"

And as he drifted off a third time, I took the cast-iron base of the thing and let it wobble. When it was about to fall, I righted it, but the sheet-music cascaded to the floor.

"Well, maybe you *could* learn it. Maybe you could," he opined, tilting his head downward towards his wristwatch. "All right.

I think we're done. Yes, we are! Is your father with us today?"

A gratuitous question, since I could neither drive myself to the lesson nor pay for it.

But I said, yes, he was just out waiting in the car. Or tooling around the neighborhood. I could never figure out what he did while I was taking my lesson, and didn't ask.

"Hello, there!" said Mr. Hunsecker, whose smart bolo tie seemed louder outside of the practice room. A natty dresser who worked with an elegantly subdued palette, my father never failed to notice, and deplore, Mr. Hunsecker's color-sense. As his other faculties had deteriorated, Mr. Hunsecker's feel for shouting primaries was alive and well. During our time together, he introduced chirrupy notes of coral-pink and sherbet yellow that, once in the light of day, could make your teeth stand on end.

"Glad to see you, sir. How's he doing?"

"Coming along. On that note, so to say, I have good news for you. Your son has been selected to play a solo in this year's concert."

"A solo, eh? How 'bout that?" said my dad, resisting the urge to chuck me. Though not the delicate type, I hated to get side-swiped by any super-masculine paw that needed the fat part of an arm or butt to smack. I could take it all right; I just didn't care for the strangely seedy intimacy, the sure and ready sense that children's body-parts could be probed or patted—even a pudgy little face might be pinched so hard that color would desert the insulted area for a while. In an era that had banished pedophilia to the backrooms of polite conversation, it seemed to rage in these odd little places.

"Yes. He has achieved a certain distinction for his rendering of 'Lady of Spain'."

"Yes, I've heard that a few times myself," replied my father with a sardonic nod in my direction. I always finished my anemic practices with it, as if to prove I'd learned something over a two-year period that had made sparkling musicians of a few, and competent ones of almost everybody else.

"I think we're going to go with that, though he is making progress with other pieces."

"Do what you know best," said my dad.

"Yes, I think reliability should carry the day."

"Are you excited?" asked my dad, as we took in an uninspiring part of town. A gaggle of gaunt-looking houses leaned against one another at an intersection that included a package store and a steeple somebody had set, in dead earnest, on top of a former grocery. A hand-painted sign identified it as "The Apostolic Congregation of the Holy Redeemer." (Balcomb Phillips, Pastor was written underneath it.) Here master and servant were given appropriate billing.

"I guess."

"Be positive. Not everybody gets to solo."

"I guess."

"Nervous?"

"No."

"No?"

"Nuh-uh."

I was telling the truth. I could play "Lady of Spain" in my sleep. I was, however, experiencing something I never had: shame at my facility; disgust at my powers of concentration; extreme disappointment at my inability to take on fresh challenges that might increase my range—or not retard what I had already.

For the first time in my entire life, I spent two hours of a perfectly glorious Saturday afternoon practicing on "Carnival of Venice." When I was done, I played "Lady of Spain" at a flight-of-the-bumblebee tempo. Tortured soul that I was, I still enjoyed rattling through it.

There was no pretense at the Fusell Academy that I should learn anything else for the Big Concert. At band practice, I was brought up to play "Lady of Spain" two times, once because that's what I did and the second time because people still couldn't believe it. It was the only practice-session I was allowed—or that was considered necessary.

I was to join the band for the opening number, then walk out to the middle of the stage, wait till a baby spot found me, and play my rousing number. For the first time in my life, I experienced a sort of group feeling, a sense of strength and unity that made me want to do for *Them*. And so I would— but then what?

That was a question I put completely out of my mind.

During our last lesson, Mr. Hunsecker was about as demonstrative as he'd ever been. I ceased thinking about keeping him alive for the whole time.

"Are you ready for the Big Day?"

"I think so," I said serenely.

"Not nervous?"

"Nope."

"Not even a little?"

"Not really."

"You are an extraordinary young man. I have never known anybody to be so skilled within such small parameters. Well, let's play your number and do it with real feeling this time."

I was offended. As if *real feeling* had ever been absent! *That's what lent power and majesty to the thing!* When I played, I was at one with the culture, ethos, and intuitive spirit of that song. Every time I made its unassuming note-clusters come alive, I experienced afresh its pulsating glamour, its infectious melody, its hand-clapping *élan*.

And so, borne along toward a legendary place that acted

135

first and thought later; took its pleasures when it wanted; and seethed with a blood-red spirit, I began. When I was done, the old man was on his feet mopping his brow.

"My, my, my," he said. "My, my, my."

At that moment, The Founder came through the door. A Great Man was suddenly among us.

"I wanted to peek in on our little prodigy. How are you, my son?"

"I'm...fi...okay...good."

"I've been listening at the door. It's rare when somebody of your age catches the *spirit* of something."

"Yes, it is," affirmed Mr. Hunsecker, still mopping.

"Notes on a page, that's all we musicians get. It is up to the artist to divine their secret, to understand their power, and to provoke the response the composer had in mind."

"Shall I have him play something else for you?"

"No, no. I just wanted to come in and see for myself. Who knows? Someday this young man's name may be synonymous with our instrument."

After throwing these delusions up on the wall, The Great Man addressed me personally. "Someday, young man, you could be the very face of The Accordian."

"Oh, I doubt that," said Mr. Hunsecker, not unkindly. He was speaking a truth with which two thirds of the people in the room absolutely agreed.

"Ye of little faith. I started out very late for someone who's made music his professional career. But I really wanted to play. Just like this young fellow. One may learn the notes, but desire is in the heart alone. And this young man's got it."

"Thank you," I said.

"Oh, why not?" said the The Founder, showing his reckless side. "Let's hear him play something else."

"Well, all right. What shall it be?" asked Mr. Hunsecker

doubtfully.

Rather than let Mr. Hunsecker choose, I pulled out "The Little Brown Jug," my second-best piece. It wasn't a stunner, but when I played it, I felt irrepressibly gay (in the old sense of that word,) a cad and a bounder, a man after your heart and everybody else's. Once I settled in, I could have been an old-timey musician playing at a provincial tavern. I saw Mr. Hunsecker deflate a bit, but in an earthbound sort of way. He wasn't going to die as long as I was in the room with him.

"More spirit than accuracy, but a diamond-in-the-rough is a diamond still," said The Founder, with a pat on Mr. Hunsecker's arm. It seemed that whenever two men were in a room together, one had to chuck, hit, or slap the other.

"Well, carry on, young man. I expect you to be a great hit at The Concert."

Mr. Hunsecker had called it a Show; He'd called it a Concert. In that single choice of words lay the essential difference in their personalities. As one had become a leader, the other had fallen into the second rank and would possibly die in a small, acoustically-tiled room with a music stand and a metronome.

When the Great Man had closed the door and evaporated from the space entirely, Mr. Hunsecker turned toward me and said this: "You know what you have, son? You have moxie. And moxie...well, it's more important to have that than almost anything. It's certainly more important than having talent. Not that you don't have it. It's just strangely incomplete."

I didn't see either man before the Big Concert, which was held, every year, at the gigantic Ellis Auditorium—a distant citadel that stood at the foot of the Mississippi River. It was so big, we were all issued name tags and given explicit instructions about meeting back up with one's parents after it was all over. By the time the "concert" began, most of these name-tags had gotten lost somewhere. As any professional performer knows, you can't keep any slap-on thing anywhere near you in the heat of the moment. And in this way—if in no other—we were professional musicians.

Ellis Auditorium was a Memphis landmark, a sort of legendary place comparable, in local minds, to Radio City or the Grand Ole Opry. It was the home of the symphony. Broadway plays were performed there. Significant unveilings and announcements occurred on the auditorium's main-stage. It was redolent of larger possibilities. You could imagine a Toscanini coming through its doors, followed by an entourage chattering in Italian. It was possible to conceive of the great tenors of the world hopping into limousines from the backstage alley. Its spellbinding grandeur tugged at your emotions as no mere architectural marvel could. Its buff-colored brick, its high, Italianate arches, its long and stately presence got under your skin and stayed with you. A city that had been founded on cotton and hardwood had made it, but wasn't entirely comfortable there. The ill-fitting tuxedos and hundred-mile stares of its devotees made a hash of its gilded stage and mere figureheads of its performers. No matter. Its dignity belonged, not necessarily to Memphis, but to the world. Great people came here from the outside to perform. But, on occasion, the great Ellis Auditorium could also play host to lesser, local talent and be equally gracious.

Before we drove the 10-mile distance, I removed a pair of special cuff-links and sat with them for a while. They had been owned by some anonymous person with an obviously superior sense of style and panache. Neither my mother nor father understood how I could draw strength and serenity from such things, but they let me keep them—and sit with them as the need arose. I can't explain it to this day, but they steadied me as nothing else could against possible jitters and unexpected *contretemps*. On the other hand, I wasn't particularly nervous. Audiences were not people. They were a collective energy field that lacked the individual voices that could tell you how good or lousy you were; whether your fly was open; who shone and who didn't. Audiences were a static force that encouraged and embraced whatever was happening onstage. They were the benignly appraising relative who knows nothing of your faults and just wishes you well because you're your mother or father's son. They can boo a performance now and then, but boos are an aberration. Audiences come to love; they come to hear and see a performer's best self; they wait for magic moments and spectacular convergences. Of all of mankind's gatherings, audiences are the most easily enraptured and slow to critique. I knew this and wasn't much concerned on their account.

I was, however, beginning to think about something that had occurred to me after my solo appearance was announced. I had begun to feel meanly, as if I had done something wrong, or a little bit less than I should. All the way to the auditorium, I looked gloomily out at the city as it passed: from the tidy lawns of our Easterly enclave to the estate-sized green-belts of Walnut Grove. I caught none of the glamour, promise or fantastical allure of a place I would temporarily possess. It seemed as if the tawdry outskirts of Downtown, with its pawnshops and flea-bags and parking-lots, were the *real city*. People arguing and gesticulating, neon flashing, trash unceremoniously dumped: these were the real milestones, these the landmarks that spoke to me as we drove the last few miles toward the foot of the river.

"There it is!" exclaimed my mother from the front seat. "Aren't you excited?"

"Yes'm," I said, still mired in guilt and loathing.

"You don't sound it," said my Dad, who tried to study me through the rearview mirror. They had a mumbled conference and separated.

"I know something you might want to do afterwards."

I knew what they were intimating. We'd passed an ice-cream parlor that dealt in things largely unknown to a Memphis audience. Chocolate, vanilla, and Neapolitan were the least of its treasures. In addition to these, a whole gamut of exotic colors and palate-enriching flavors were available to whoever cared to stroll in and ask for them.

"Would you like that?" chimed my father.

"I guess so."

"He guesses so."

"Is there anything wrong, honey?" asked my mother sweetly.

"No."

"Butterflies," said my dad.

"Nervous?" she asked.

"No."

"Then what is it?"

"It's...I don't know...I can't explain it."

"Well, it'll be over before too long, thank God."

"Shhh."

"I'm not talking about you, sport. I mean all those other bands we have to sit through."

"But they're really good," I said, meaning it sincerely.

"Of course they are. I was just trying to say that, when you're done, it just won't be as interesting."

"But it will be. All I know is one song. That's it. When I play with the band, I fake it. Just watch. You'll be able to see. I can just play 'Lady of Spain'."

"Well, even if that were true, you can do it better than anybody else."

They had another muttered conference.

"If you don't want to do anything afterwards, that's fine. We'll just come home and watch a movie."

The first band consisted of the fewest, and youngest, kids. They played a very catchy, but easy melody and retired from the stage mostly without incident. The applause was scattered, strained, considerate. A terrified ten-year old had wandered from his chair toward a gaping audience, buggy-eyed with stage-fright. One of the younger instructors had to come out to escort him away. His legs locked halfway through the forced march and he had to be lifted up from his armpits and whisked offstage. People were too horrified to react—and too relieved to do anything but hope the next act brought no conspicuous casualties.

When our band came on, we got a rather different light-ing-scheme: a hot pink and Mediterranean blue wash that found the hollows in our faces and drained the patchy color out of them completely. It stoked fragile emotions. It opened wide the personal differences between us. It made a sham of the professional decorum with which we marched toward our chairs and sat down in them as an ensemble. More impor-tantly, it sapped our collective will to shine. When we started, at a cue given the brightest among us from the wings, we were not quite in synch and must've sounded as well-played music does to a drunk. When a drunk says "Speed it up!" you know you're keeping good time.

Our act was rewarded with loud, but perfunctory applause, the audience trying much too hard to appreciate a lackluster performance. I lingered as everybody else stood up and filed, as we had at rehearsal, offstage. It was a good exodus, per-formed with more brio than the piece itself.

There was no chair for me in the middle of the stage, so I went back, got mine, and set it there. I guess the feeling was: if I needed one, I could just grab it.

Once I was immobilized, I let the baby spot find me. A startling transformation took place then and there, a complete

141

severance of Myself from Them, a trembling reaction that was not exclusively physical. For the first time that day, I was nervous. Unable to conceive of sitting still while my mouth was going dry, I got up and moved away from the spot-light. It pursued me, but I kept on moving. Looking toward the offstage area, I noticed The Founder motioning me to stay put. His palm-flat hands pushed from midriff to floor, as if pantomiming a massage. When the spot cornered me, I knew I'd better calm down. I could already hear mimeographed programs rustling. I hazarded a look at the front row and saw a young matron trying to stifle an anxiety attack, possibly on my behalf. Then somebody came out and put a microphone in front of me. I took that as a signal to speak into it and said, "Ladies and gentlemen, I have come here before you to play an old-time favorite. It is called 'Lady of Spain' and it is the only song I know how to play.'

Admitting my profound singularity freed me; I could now do what I was there to do.

Without bothering to get comfortable, I unleashed the magic other band-members knew intimately, but to which no larger audience was yet privy. As I sailed through an imaginary Spain, I felt a legitimate musician, if in a very small and limited way. I stood up to play the last thrilling passage, bringing the number to a close with the arm-overhead, pointy-fingered salute of the flamenco dancer's. As I knew it would, the crowd went absolutely wild, coming to its feet as one and applauding with the ecstasy of the redeemed. Individual voices began to ask, tentatively at first, but with a swelling and, alas, unmistakable audibility, for an encore. "Encore!" they started to shout. "Encore...encore!" Didn't they hear what I had told them? I knew one song. ONE SONG. I could play this one song as well as anyone, but after it was over, I had nothing. I tried fleeing the stage, but the audience clapped so hard and with such undisguised gratitude (few had come seeking actual entertainment) that, after looking toward the wings and seeing The Founder there egging me on, I returned to the place I had occupied, seconds ago, in triumph, but would no doubt leave this next time in utter disgrace. I found the dying man's courage and stepped up to the microphone.

"Ladies and gentlemen, you are very kind. For an encore, I will do the ever-popular 'Carnival of Venice.'"

As I composed myself, Mr. Hunsecker emerged from the face-stew backstage and began shaking his head, whether at me or at my choice of music I couldn't tell. But I was not in the mood for nay-saying and disposed of him with smirk. When the executioner presents a righteous man with a blindfold, the righteous man tells him what he can do with it. Yet my last thought, before I started plunking out the tune, was that I might succeed in killing the old man here after having spent so much time and effort keeping him alive at the Academy.

As we swung into the driveway at the ice-cream store, my dad took me aside and said: "Hey, I'm proud of you. After all, you told 'em."

"Yes, I did."

"Well," said my mother, "I'll never forget the crowd going wild over you. The other part, well, you did say."

"Sure did."

I should mention that The Founder didn't bother to acknowledge me as I came offstage. He looked like people in the movies do when they're about to say: "And don't you dare show your face in my house again!" Mr. Hunsecker was oddly self-possessed. He no doubt felt vindicated. Yet he was no monster and I'm sure he didn't enjoy watching me stumble through another crowd-pleaser almost any other student could have played far better. At the next lesson, he said: "Well, my son, you did tell them what to expect. I think that shows an extraordinary honesty." He wore a bright-yellow tie with a little hand-painted dog in the middle, which my father couldn't look at. "If he wants to be seen at night, he's all set," said he.

My disgrace left me glumly isolated; the other band-members now feared to associate with me. The source of contagion must be eschewed lest others catch and spread it. At times, I felt as if I'd let them down. I could have found a better way. A performance isn't necessarily about how good you are; it is about illusion. And in the interest of preserving this illusion, it had been necessary to overlook my out-of-kilter excellence, my song-specific flair. Whether I'd emphasized it or not, I failed the moment and, consequently, the event itself. Perhaps honesty is not always the best policy. There might well be something in assuming that white lies live in the minds of other people—as in a baseball player's ability to hit a home run even if he can't get the ball to dribble past first base—even if they aren't very good for you in the long run. A perfect emcee is not the person anybody remembers. It's the act that fails and the dying fall that runs roughshod over the Perfect Moment.

I left the accordion after that third year, partly because I could never live down the The Founder's disappointment, but also because it began to take way too much energy to keep Mr. Hunsecker alive. I tried to learn a few extra tunes because you should always have an ace-in-the-hole when you need one—even if you may never know how, or when, to play it.

Year of the Falling Santa

When the car the hit the road, my brother and I were already asleep. My father had put together this complicated deck for us to sleep on, which afforded both of us room enough if we were absolutely still. I was a cruel person and would shove my brother out of the way whenever his body spilled over an invisible divide that was no wider than a piece of wet string and happened to touch mine. He was an infuriatingly docile little brother whose hero worship and little-brother shyness were completely lost on me. He'd poked his ear with one of those pre-childproof Q-tips, which, if you weren't careful, you could jab down in there and break something. After the accident, his life was defined by the injury the Q-tip, or, rather, childish probing with a blunt instrument, had caused. I'll bet you there's a class action suit in there somewhere; he couldn't have been the only one.

Almost everything was more dangerous than it is today, though to hear Kentucky people tell of it, you couldn't walk more than a yard in any direction without getting whacked with something. Whenever we went there, I always sought assurance in the matter of lockjaw, which you could get by stepping on almost anything at a farm—though the classic "rusty nail" was trotted out as a first line of defense—or, rather, casualty. Because of its evocative nature, it had a kind of flaw-less pedigree and went right into production at the onset of any vacation, whether one had been scheduled or not. Still the same, such were the terrors of rural life, almost anything would do. "If I step on a rock, will I get it?" "Depends on the rock," somebody would say. That was not what I wanted to hear.

The trip generally took about seven hours, up through the State of Tennessee into Kentucky blue-grass, or just a few counties shy of it. I lived in Lexington, the center of blue-grass culture, many years later and the little coal-fired towns and dankly luminous villages we passed on the way to our middle-sized destination were similar to the ones around there, except they looked meaner and uglier to me as a young adult.

We had to set out late because there wasn't a lot of vacation time in those days and my dad wasn't so well-established that he could just play hooky for a while and hope they'd want him back whenever he happened to show up again. The Sixties were like the Fifties until people started squawking about civil rights more audibly than they'd done before. Or maybe it was just The Beatles.

Anyhow, there wasn't a lot of slacking in those days—if you wanted to work. And most people seemed to want to well enough. The world was no longer innocent, but a lot of people were, particularly about such antiquated concepts as "showing up on time," "pulling your own weight," "looking out for your neighbor." These days, people who want to be innocent have to work at it.

We were not just Kentucky-bound, but Christmas-feverish. It was the first time my brother and I were going to visit our grandparents for the Big Holiday—or at least the first time I was old enough to appreciate what we were there to do. We'd been summer visitors—relatives from Down South who rolled in for half the month of July, though my father would leave early on to get back to work.

The summer vacations we would have there did not involve a lot of structure. When my brother got to be a little older, we'd leave the old house in the morning and return at dusk. Breakfast and dinner were sit-down meals and attendance was, by and large, compulsory. But after a few days you could start skipping out if you wanted to. Come home hungry in the night and my grandmother would get you some leftovers out of the fridge or make you a sandwich. Being there in the summer was delightfully laissez-faire. When you got back home, people clamped down on you again; you had to re-gain your vacation-style freedoms an inch at a time, if at all.

I can't remember anything about the early part of the drive, except rolling into a town or village and listening, out of the deep and pleasant trance that comes to the mobile sleeper, as my dad fueled up the car. My dad's driving chores—considerable even to him—went unacknowledged, though he had his revenge when he drove off to work all by himself, leaving my mother, brother, and I in Kentucky without a car. It didn't phase me a bit, since I didn't need to go around shopping. It probably didn't hurt my mother much either, since she hadn't learned to drive yet and had done without a car before her marriage. Anyway, she had backup with her two older sisters, who drove snappy little things without much regard for legal niceties. It was just getting to be necessary to drive everywhere, but people could do without a car and not feel deprived. I know that's difficult to imagine now, but it was true. We could walk to the store where we lived in Memphis, though you can't now—not because the places aren't close enough, but because the traffic will kill you before you get there.

It was a sort of heroic drive for my father, who sat behind the wheel for a living, even if he kept, for the most part, to a manageable radius. He worked as a salesman for various electrical supply companies and, when he left on business trips, the back seat was generally heaped with three-ring binders full of product catalogues. There were gaudy ones and plain ones; catalogues that made some small attempt at personality and catalogues that didn't bother. Graybar Electric was one of the latter, though there was nothing wrong, in a technical sense, with its catalogues. You could look through them and, if you were a builder or engineer, you could pretty much find whatever you wanted. The layman, however, could get glassy-eyed very quickly. I preferred the samples of color-coded wire; the breaker switches you could pop into the On and Off position; the small abstract sculptures that belonged to a loose confederation of objects denoted "conduit." If I heard that word once, I heard it a million times. No other word passed my father's lips with such a hopeful fluency. I can't hear it—though it doesn't come up very often these days—without time-traveling to that small house we all lived in: my father pacing, my mother listening, and me wondering why I had nothing better to do when it was so nice outside.

My father prided himself on his driving and was consequently intolerant of fellow motorists, particularly Southern ones. As a Pennsylvanian, he not only had a state's reputation to maintain, but a deeply personal aversion to an arbitrary driving etiquette that seemed to make up its rules rather than follow pre-existing ones. If you wanted to make a turn in Memphis, you just did it. My father railed at such devious spontaneity. It lacked courtesy, which was the foundation of decent social behavior. "Discourteous" was the second most-overused word of my childhood.

At night, driving wasn't so bad, except the two-lane roads that traversed the State of Tennessee and continued on into Kentucky could be dangerous. All you had was that great yellow divide, which separated northbound and southbound traffic. It was the thinnest of barriers, the riskiest of social contracts, the scariest of places to be when it was raining—or whenever the sun sank low enough to be visible below the visor you could pull down to protect your eyesight.

Yet night was better for driving long distances because there wasn't as much traffic after it got so late that the people who might have gone to sleep at the wheel got to where they wanted to go and the people who were afraid of it knew how to drink coffee. On the particular night we set out from our little three-bedroom house on a street developers had carved out of an old-growth forest only Chickasaw Indians had known before us, visibility was perfect until early morning, when it turned misty. When my dad stopped off at the first little town, he was cheerful still. He poked his head into mine and asked whether I needed to go to the little boy's room. I stirred, but said no. "Sure?" he asked. "It's gonna be a while." I was sure. My brother slept through it all. Not a peep from my mother, who didn't seem to care much for these trips and studied the road.

Cheer dissolved at the little breakfast-place we knew from other visits. A futurist-style logo, done up in neon cubes and cylinders, spelled out its name ("Tower Restaurant") as well as its enduring claim to popularity: "Waffles Served Twenty-Four Hours a Day." When we drove up, it was already—or still—packed.

I liked going there, but I don't remember any of those syrup-drenched meals being happy. This one was no different. Mom and Dad were pretending not to be speaking about something, I couldn't make up my mind about what I wanted, but I wouldn't let my little brother order because I didn't want him to make up his mind first.

"You can't have that," I said to whatever he was attempting to ask for.

"He can have whatever he wants," said my mother, who

wouldn't like me until we got on the road again.

"What should I get?" I kept asking, though there were only waffles. Such rapid-fire questioning guaranteed that my brother wouldn't get a word in edgewise. I wince at such pre-emptive behavior today, though it still comes out in conversations that are insufficiently apocalyptic on the subject of global warming.

"Let your brother order, please."

"Let me go first. I want...waffles."

"He wants waffles," answered my mother as if this were breaking news. She had an excellent sense of irony, which is foreign to the child mind.

"I said that," I pointed out to her and everyone.

Rather than speak, my brother pointed to a stack of waffles that had been appetizingly obscured with what I called—and thought very funny—"waffle-juice," or maple syrup.

"I want that too," I said.

"Good. You've already ordered it."

She was right; I had nothing.

This was my father's cue to get up for a moment, then go somewhere—often to no apparent purpose. He was always Going Somewhere when we were out. On this occasion, he may have been looking for someplace where he could scream into the Kentucky Outback and not be heard except by the kitchen help. By the time we'd gotten to this gleaming outpost in the night, it was three or four a. m.

"Why don't you tell us what time it is?" suggested my mother to me.

"I don't want to," said I, as cranky and unavailable a person as that ninety-year old sitting over there with an unhappy caretaker of a second cousin.

My mother's teaching instincts had been engaged in reviewing the minute hand and the second hand for me and she wanted to go over them while we were in a place with clock-faces galore. Just as we mastered the nuances of time-keeping, my father got back from wherever he'd gone. As he sat down, the waffles came.

My brother got his first, then I got mine, followed by mom and dad.

A quadrant of mine had been slathered in butter, which I detested.

"I can't eat this!" I said. My brother had already started on his. From the few words he was able to get in edgewise, my brother's was the Voice of Reason, Moderation, and Community Spirit. It remained largely unheard because mine was the Voice of Instant Self-Gratification and Eternal One-Upmanship.

"What's wrong now?" asked my dad, who expected things to get worse once a downhill trend began.

"Oh, he just doesn't like butter."

"Here, just do this," said my dad, spooning off the offending pat, which had pooled at its base and infected my waffle.

"Oooooo, I can't eat that."

"Then don't," said my dad, for whom things had already worsened.

"It's all right. You don't have to eat that piece," said my mother, who had accepted ruination, to me.

"Okay," I said, eager to get started on the rest of the waffle, which was as tall as my forehead and tantalizingly vaporous. If I'd thought to pause between gaping mouthfuls, I might have smelled some of the "wheaty goodness" that was always coming from a stack or bowl.

"Do you want me to cut yours?" This was directed to my brother, whose inclination to swallow his waffle whole had to be moderated somewhat.

"Here, I'll just cut this into little-bitty pieces for you," said my mother, suiting action to word. Unaccountably, my brother started crying, which he only did when his ear-problem acted up. Oh, no, I thought. Not now. Not *here*! The last time it had acted up, things had gotten ugly. Not being a heroic sort, I left the scene as my father bent over him with a small plastic tub into which his nosebleed cascaded interminably. My mother had gone quiet, the non-combatant who sees into a war's grisly future. Fortunately, my brother was not a crybaby—a word that applies to the production of gratuitous tears—and pulled himself together after swallowing one of the infinitesimal bites my mother had cut, using both knife and fork, for him. For insurance, my mother poured on more syrup, which came in a nice, jolly little container, with a nickel-coated handle that allowed the experienced user flow-control.

My father was about to say something like "What now?" when my brother started to cry in earnest. He managed to stifle it when he saw the tender look my mother had composed for him. In those years, she tried very hard to arrest conflict and mediate between father and sons. She had a much better handle on diffusing situations than my father—who was often their source—ever would. My brother would not have been assured by the expression my father had composed as a means to discourage private suffering. Yet he knew more than anybody else that, once we were out of the restaurant, it would be a straight, two-hour shot to the town of Owensboro. If this wasn't a mood picker-upper, nothing in our sleep-deprived world could be.

All things considered, it was a fairly good meal. I had forgotten about the damage the butter had done, my brother became a lifelong waffle-lover, and both Mom and Dad were able to sit through the latter part of it in an amiable silence punctuated by half-muttered questions about whether anybody was likely to be up or who would sleep where when we got to the house.

It was still dark when we pulled up in front of a rangy bungalow whose prow-like form was appealingly sinister. Because it wasn't dangerous to be walking at night, the streets were illuminated with no more than a barely adequate number of street-lamps, which put out less than the ones I was used to. A gentle mist was falling. The grass smelled damp, the pebbly sidewalk was slippery, the concrete steps that led to the house caught the porch-light and shot eye-searing gleams through the mist.

They were up, as my mother had predicted back at the restaurant. My grandmother ran out and embraced me first, then my brother, then my mother, then, with a slight hesitation, my father too. This ritual done and over with, we all went in to discuss which rooms were ready, when the bathroom might optimally serve visitors, and how we would all sleep in the next day.

"How was your trip?" asked my grandmother to me personally. She seemed to know what everybody else was going to say. My brother was half-asleep and was not seen as wanting to weigh in on this subject. "I don't know," I said. "It was okay." I think my grandmother was always waiting for me to say interesting things. I must have disappointed her with my mundane preoccupation with the material world, expressed with the uninspired commentary of the average mind. My mother supplemented my bland offering with the observation that we'd had waffles this morning. I nodded assent. At this point, my grandmother had given up on me.

She was a tiny lady, shrunken in the way old people seemed to get, but she could bustle around all day and still be up and doing long after the dinner dishes were on the drying-rack and the leftovers put in snap-lidded, pre-Tupperware containers I could never open. Because of her constant ministrations, there wasn't an unclean surface in the entire house. When I was there, I cleaned up after myself. I was honoring a domestic Ideal she had nurtured along since before the turn of the century. When you visited my grandmother, you didn't spit in the face of The Past.

When she embraced me, she smelled like talcum powder and some other extremely sanitary thing. Strangely enough, I don't remember her ever washing her hands.

Granddad sat on the couch, sleeping. He was very lean, with features that were unusually free of the countrified malice I would occasionally observe in people around there. He wore khaki-colored pants held up with suspenders. When people on Wall Street began to wear suspenders again, I saw my grandfather in every stockbroker, though I could not follow him into the boardrooms they occupied; nor discern the frenzy to buy or sell. Both he and my grandmother were, for want of a better word, refined people. She had a collection of china from all of the United States' capitols, which was displayed on a wide-fronted credenza opposite the big dining table. A lot of old ladies had similar stuff, but it was never so well-dusted. Even the fancy-lace thingy underneath it did not exhibit the usual wear-and-tear. It was starch-white and did not appear to attract dust or any other thing that roved and settled.

When we filed past him, Granddad snapped to attention momentarily, then drifted back to sleep. Even in repose, he was on his guard against possible incursions from the outside world. He'd lost everything during The Depression and couldn't rest easily since then.

"How about if you fellas go to your bedroom?" asked my father as he waved us toward the hallway.

"I've made up a room for them," said my grandmother, waving him through.

"That's good. We thought these kids might have to sleep on the couch."

I felt a sudden tightening of the throat at that possibility, which my father had presented in the way of joshing. He was a redoubtable mood-changer. His journey from the sullen to the sun-reflecting was marked internally and not visible to the naked eye. He went sad on you, he went glad on you, and you just had to hope that, at the end of the day, the glad might have a fractional superiority.

"They won't have to sleep on that old drafty couch," said my mother.

"No, they won't!" answered my grandmother triumphantly. Granddad was there anyway. We couldn't sleep around him, could we? My father allowed for this fundamental precept and made a sharp right into the room he and my mother occupied. The drive was over and even he might want to sleep in.

We were led into the nearest bedroom—the place we always stayed—and were asleep in minutes. As I drifted away, I heard my mother say something about how the house smelled so good. My dad couldn't agree more. It not only smelled good; it smelled heavenly. He never used words like this; he was obviously glad not to be driving anymore.

We all slept in that morning—with the exception of my grandmother, who didn't appear to need any more sleep than a pigeon. By the time I opened my eyes on a new day, the great small house I hadn't slept in since the summer was filled with daylight. Christmas would roll around in two days. Meanwhile, it was great to be there. I yawned with an exaggerated moaning and stretching.

"Want any eggs for breakfast?" asked my mother through the door.

For the moment, I didn't know what eggs were.

"You'd better say. She's cooking them right now."

I said yes and looked over to my brother, who was still sleeping. I nudged him and he rolled over. Since the ear operation, he slept more and moved slowly. It drove me, a hyperactive kid, absolutely crazy.

"Want eggs?" I asked him, the Total Sleeper.

Nothing.

"How 'bout some frog-legs?"

No answer to that either.

Then I started tickling him. He resisted unsuccessfully as I poked and jabbed ribs and stomach.

"Did you say eggs?" he asked through laughter-induced tears.

He had heard. Then again, he had learned to pay attention. He made straight-A's, to my C's and B's. When you get hurt, you develop compensating abilities.

I told him there weren't any eggs left and ran to the kitchen. He wasn't going to be sure about any eggs unless he came in there himself. He needed my cruelty in order to stay alive.

There were two tables at my grandmother's house: the dining-room table, which was long and formal; and the kitchen table, which was generally reserved for breakfast. From it wafted the rich and aromatic smells of coffee—which my parents never drank at home—and hot cereal, a cheerful, wheaty exhalation that steamed up the place very wholesomely. A fried-egg smell circulated among these others, for a kind of triple threat to the senses. Breakfast at home was much more expedient, if rather dull. A bowl of cereal, pieces of buttered toast, a stack of waffles that came out of a waffle-maker that got too hot too quickly and left the waffle-ridges black. Here you had a nice sit-down experience that felt much too civilized and was therefore uncomfortable for about fifteen minutes. But with an efficient grandmother serving you stuff, you fell right into it. Before the first breakfast was over, I was already a champion giver of orders, as well as an eager runner of table-to-refrigerator errands. The system worked. It was the division of labor at its finest.

"Are we gonna have Christmas on Christmas Eve—or on Christmas?" I asked without preamble.

"Why, on Christmas, like we always do!" said my grandmother, who refilled my milk-glass and gave me a little hug. I pointed to the glass for her to top it off. She thought that cute.

"Don't ask stupid questions," suggested my father, who had under-dressed that morning. When he was in breakfast *déshabille*, I was reminded of all the hair on his body and was aghast. I sure didn't want *that* when I grew up.

"He's not," said my mother, coming to the rescue. "Some people do open gifts on Christmas Eve. Some of my friends did, in fact. You remember Arlene Thomas, mother?"

"Oh, yes. A very nice girl who lived with her mother near the high school."

"I wouldn't know. We didn't have Christmas where I came from. Not as we understand it today."

My father was lying. There was *a* Christmas. It was his family who had failed to adopt its more consumer-oriented rituals. He was the child who could have gotten coal in his stocking because he was from a smoky little village some twenty miles outside of Pittsburgh. He was the only person in his family ever to go to college, but he carried the ethos and expectations of his boyhood with him at all times. To hear him tell of it, he didn't even get the coal, which was not as plentiful there as it was in nicer places. His childhood deprivations were something everybody did their best to hear out, but not help along. He didn't overdo them as much as many histrionics-crazy people do. It wasn't in him to become the sort of saturnine monologist who'd want you to experience his suffering vicariously, and at a word-count rivaled only by Dickens himself. No, he could suffer in silence if he could punctuate it with a troublesome reflection now and then, or highlight its majestic alienation with a devastating aside. We reacted to these reflections in the same way: we all stopped to listen, but did not provide any window of opportunity through which he could slip on his way to global expansion. "Too bad," I would say, "but you lived during the Depression and nobody had any money then." That was a satisfactory response that left him with nothing except the bare facts. My mother gave him a little squeeze on the shoulder and left it at that. He'd bent her ear with those stories already.

"I want to go to the parade this year. Down Front Street? Do they still have it, Mom?" asked my mother.

"Oh, yes. I don't like it as much as we all did when you were here."

"Nope. We didn't celebrate Christmas. It made no sense, considering," said my father, lost in a Christmas-deprived Pennsylvania.

"But Santa's nice. Off in the North Pole. With all those reindeer. Yes, it's plenty nice."

My grandmother was disappointed past description, but didn't want to put a dampener on it for others.

"Doesn't Amblin's sponsor it anymore?"

"Oh, yes," said my grandmother.

"Oh! Well, it should be pretty good then."

"Oh, it is," said my grandmother, with a combination of cheerfulness and inconsolability that was her own special creation. My mother wasn't bad at it, but she, my grandmother, had many years to perfect its nuanced message; foster the deeply penetrating gloom that enveloped you once the smile that offered it was gone; and keep topping herself again and again. My mother's family had to overcome tragedy and hardship so long that the cheerful façade they'd developed back in the Thirties had cracked a little bit by the mid-Sixties. My granddad—who'd dispensed with such play-acting—could be openly cranky, willfully obtuse. On this day, however, he was feeling droll.

He entered the kitchen some minutes after my grandmother had cryptically pronounced the parade absolutely worthless even as she endorsed it on the surface completely. To understand these people, you had to dig deep. They sure as hell weren't giving anything away.

"I think I'll have some coffee this morning," Granddad announced in self-parody.

"Yes," said my mother, "I think you should have some coffee for once."

"Not too much, though. I'm on a diet."

My mother smirked, as if to say: *he's at it again*!

"Dad, would you go to the parade with us?" asked my mother.

"How's that?"

"The parade downtown? Would you come with us?"

"I don't know. That Santa last year...he was a real doozy. It is my belief that he had tippled a tad. Yes, tippled a tad before jumping into his breeches."

My grandfather was an amateur poet and took a lip-smacking pleasure in certain words. Repetition was his forte.

"Yes, I think he tippled a tad last year."

"Oh, Daddy, stop it!"

"I wouldn't lie about a thing like that," he said, a stern fellow now. Nobody drank around there, so drinking and drinkers were on peoples' minds quite a lot.

"I'm sure they have a new one," said my mother.

"Santa was not present in my life," said my father, whose self-pity had temporarily ruined his posture. He wouldn't have let *me* sit like that!

"No, they do not," insisted my granddad, ignoring the angst. "It is the same Santa this year as all the others. And I believe he *is* one to take liquid refreshment before the event. Do not judge, lest ye be judged—or is that 'lest *you* be judged'?"

To my granddad's interrogative look, my mother shrugged along with her mother. Love him or not, the old man was irrepressible. To bolster that reputation, he recited a poem he'd either written himself or stolen from another amateur.

"'If you take a drink now and then/You belong full well to the world of men. But if you become, by degrees, a dreadful sot/A drunk you are and a man you're not!'"

"Now, hush up and have your coffee," said my grandmother, placing a cup far in front of him. He gestured broadly and was likely to knock a too-near one over.

"I'd like to take the boys. They've never been."

"Well, if you do so, they'll likely witness a public nuisance of the first order. This may not be a lesson we'd care for them to see."

My mother was a patient woman; she had spent years rolling her eyes at such puritanical backwardness.

"Could we see him, Mom?" I asked. "Could we?"

My brother nodded from his chair, which occasionally trapped him when it was pushed too close and he couldn't get his arms through enough to push it away from the table.

"I don't see why not. I'm sure your grandfather is exaggerating."

"No, he's not," said my grandmother, who'd wiped down all the counters and was in the process of dumping the coffee-grounds into a little foot-operated garbage pail I'd been after my parents to get for our house. We didn't have anything like that at all. A foot-operated garbage can might add a touch of the Old World (of, 1957, say) that was lacking in our suburban lifestyle.

My father was, I'm sure, manic depressive. One moment he'd be moping about some irreparable rift between him and a business associate (or about his dismal Christmas past) and the next he'd be doing his famous hyena laugh—at my request, of course—and tickling us. It was the in-between moods that were the hardest to deal with. In the grip of these, he was just plain grumpy, possibly as I am today.

"I'll see Santa drunk or sober," exclaimed my father, startling my grandmother, who stopped cold for a moment.

"Will he fall down?" I asked.

"No, he won't fall down," said my mother.

"Oh, he might," answered my dad, his eyes gleaming with sudden mischief. "I think there's a pretty good chance he'll fall this year. Like this!"

Without bothering to check around him, my dad fell from his chair on to the floor and started to writhe around on the spotless linoleum as a movie madman would. As he did so, he simulated, by means of breathy wails, lunacy's frantic articulation. We burst out in delighted squeals as my mother exchanged horrified glances with her mother. My granddad took it all in his stride as he sipped from a coffee-cup he'd taken from the state-capitol shrine. My grandmother hated for him to visit her credenza for a container he could have found in the kitchen cupboard, but could never get him to stop.

"Oh, I'm drunk and I can't get up!" said my father to a general audience. Then, to me: "Help me, won't you?" His eyes rolled woozily as he appealed to us—a man at the end of his rope.

Mother and daughter shook their heads together.

"Wouldn't put it past him," said my granddad to the writhing body on the floor. Meaning what?

"Oh, my head. It won't stay still. No, it's not my head... it's...it's that person over there. *She* won't stop moving. And he won't either. Lord save me—the whole world is in motion and it won't stop. It won't stop...no, it won't...it won't...it won't!"

My father had a nice B-grade horror-movie performance going. We kids loved it, of course. I jumped down on the floor and started tickling. My brother tentatively joined the scrum, jabbing and poking.

"Please...oh, please stop it! For love of mercy, stop what you're doing and help me...heeeeeelp meeeeee!"

Tickle tickle tickle.

If you had an adult drooling away on the floor, you played it for everything it was worth. I'd never known artistic families, who probably did this sort of thing all the time. I believed that inspired loopiness was something to hold onto. I'd never seen other fathers act like this, but maybe they all did when they were in a comfortable setting surrounded by a family that would never tell. My father's spontaneous hi-jinks were, however, strangely in keeping with his sour moods, in that both were preposterously overdone. Only my mother could out-sulk him. When they were both sulking, it was absolutely miserable. A double-sulk knocked out my concentration like a street-light. It was one of the many reasons I did so poorly in school. My brother's intellectual powers were proof against it. I'd watch them and have to start mowing the grass.

When my father wearied of his uproarious creation, he got up and poured himself half a cup from the electric percolator whose glass top bubbled crazily. When he sat down, he was his old self again—whoever that was.

"You'll find he is not exaggerating. If you go."

My grandmother liked to inject ominous notes. Her sense of drama, though understated, was also excellent.

The rest of the day was spent arranging pre-Santa gifts, such as were already out under the tree, a perfectly symmetrical baby spruce. A downy cushion swirled around its base, which was enhanced with a pretty little manger-scene, complete with ox, ass, and wise men who'd been off their feet all year and were hurting. When lights were low, its bejeweled surface threw iridescent colors around the room. The tree itself was, like the rest of the house, immaculately trimmed, with gingerbread men you could eat surreptitiously and paper-thin ornaments that broke at our house, but managed to survive year after year in this one. We shook various boxes, speculated on their contents, and attempted to crack adult impassivity with probing questions. "I know what this is," I'd say. Always the magpie, my brother said: "I do too!" The adults had to sit there and assume a sphinx-like demeanor—which was much harder to do than it looked.

When idle speculation was done, we went back to the all-consuming subject of a drunken Santa. There wasn't a lot of drinking around the house, or at any of the other houses I would visit, so drunkenness had a peculiar sort of savor to me. It was not forbidden exactly; it just wasn't done. What did a drunken person, let alone a drunken Santa, look like? Perhaps my dad's impersonation of a person caught up in the snares of intoxication was more accurate than we knew? Perhaps your typical drunken person fell to the ground and ranted; rolled his eyes; searched heaven and earth for another bottle. Then what? He didn't do all that just to fade away when it was over.

Toward the end of the day, my mother and father went out to do some shopping. I never knew where my grandmother was till she just popped out of somewhere and asked what we little boys were doing. With an astonishing knack for repartee, I told her that I didn't know. She stood there hoping I would add something interesting to that, but in vain.

Yet my uninspired summation did bear fruit. Whenever my brother and I were by ourselves, she saw our entertainment as her personal mission. Losing no time, she went into our room and set us up in front of an old pinball game whose command-center had a huge leering face that was perhaps unintentionally misanthropic.

"This is an old, old game I've saved since I was a child," she said of it as she pulled it out of a linen closet.

"That's neat," I said, riveted to the blubber-lips.

"Yeah," affirmed my brother, following.

"You don't have to shoot it hard. Just pull it back like this and let the ball meander in its own way."

She shot a small silver ball and watched it meander.

"What if you miss?"

"You get lots of chances."

"How do we keep score?"

"Just add up all your points when you've finished."

"What if somebody doesn't get anything?" I asked, with a nod toward my brother.

"He'll get something. And the more you practice, the more points you'll get."

She handed over the game to us and left for more dust-busting.

Rather than play the game, however, we talked about a drunken Santa.

"I really wanna see him," I said.

"I do too."

"What if he falls off?"

"That would be funny."

I was about to agree, but you don't agree with your brother. I switched points of view.

"No, it wouldn't. It might even kill him if he's drunk enough."

"Oh."

"I don't think it's funny to be drunk, Chad."

"No, it's not."

"I'm not sure we should go see him if he's going to be drunk."

"Maybe he won't be this year."

"It's possible that he's changed his ways and is different now."

"He could be different."

"I think he might surprise us."

"He *will* surprise us."

With a strangler's spirit, I switched again. My brother and I were way too much in agreement.

"But probably not. He'll be drunk and he'll fall off and it'll be terrible. Might have to call off the parade."

"Terrible," said my brother, feeling his way into this new thought-universe.

"Maybe it'll kill him. Maybe it'll kill him dead and we won't get any presents." Another thought-universe: "He's just warming up with the parade. He has a whole night to go after that."

I was going off on a tangent enough to engage my brother's morbid imagination. My brother was the real artist in the family; unlike me, he could concentrate on a thought or feeling and let it do its work on him. He was so immersed in the fearful possibility of a dead Santa that he couldn't suppress the tears I had been attempting to nurture. Then the crying, which couldn't be stopped once the tears started in.

"What's wrong?"

My brother's crying brought my grandmother, who, even before entering the room, was saying "Now you children play nice. I don't want any fussing and fighting. Just play nice and everything will be fine."

"We were playing nice. He's just sad about Santa."

"About Santa?"

"Yes. What if he falls and kills himself?"

"He won't fall and kill himself. Whatever got that idea into your head?"

"I don't know. I was just thinking that he drinks a lot. He's way up there. What if he trips or something?"

"He won't be doing that. He's a good Santa and will stick to his post."

"Post," said my brother, for whom this word seemed to have soothing powers.

"Maybe we shouldn't go to the parade if that's what we're going to think about."

We both cried "Nooooo!" as I assured her that we had all sorts of other topics we could be thinking about.

"All right, then," she said, disposing of the topic, as she thought, for all time.

"I suppose you didn't have much time for this," she then said, removing the pinball game from our sight with a good sense of the anticlimactic. We were obviously incapable of taking an interest in things that didn't revolve around failure and humiliation. In this regard, we were our father's children.

Obsessions took hold of me in those days. After a certain point, I couldn't stop thinking about the drunken Santa Claus we were going to see later on that night. There appeared to be some difference in opinion, not as to the possibility of him being drunk, but of the nature and extent of the catastrophe his drunken behavior might cause. The possibilities of him falling down; or falling down and hurting himself; or falling down and allowing his mortal coil to unwind on the spot—I couldn't get these richly tantalizing scenarios out of my mind. During dinner, we were offered—because it was a holiday—egg-nog with just a touch of bourbon, but my brother and I downed it quickly and went to our room where we discussed a drunken Santa with all of its infinite permutations. Having never downed anything other than a soft-drink before, I thought nothing of it. Yet it was immediately, if only momentarily, felt, as I settled down on a bed that had been seamlessly re-spread as well as spotlessly laundered. While there, I noticed whorls that had not been visible to me before and patterns that may have been lost to me if the egg-nog had not been alcoholically tainted. Yet almost as soon as these insights and sensations appeared, they vanished as if they'd never happened. Is the superior metabolism of youth the best possible crusade against incipient alcoholism? Or couldn't I hold a thought, drunk or sober, longer than it took me, albeit accidentally, to have another. The bourbon didn't seem to affect my brother at all. Chances are, however, he was given less—or was merely told that his egg-nog had been spiked in order to share a special event with his brother.

When my favorite aunt came over the following day, the first thing I asked her was whether she thought the drunken Santa would fall down. Her answer was cryptic, but reassuring. "I guess if he's drunk, he has a good chance of falling now, doesn't he?"

I was the only person who appreciated this answer.

Unfortunately, my aunt had to beg off because of other commitments, but she said she'd look forward to hearing whether he stayed up on that float. If I were a little older, some sort of betting might have provided additional intrigue.

We couldn't go the parade until late in the afternoon, so when all the other aunts and uncles descended upon the house that day, we considered ourselves lucky. These old coots were time-wasters in the very best, and most productive, sense of that word. And there were lots and lots of them.

Because they'd come to see us, we had to pay attention to them as they chucked our chins or asked us questions about what we might be wanting for Christmas this year.

Aunt Beulah came in first, with her husband, a soft-spoken fellow who wore bottle-thick glasses and whose hand shook when it shook yours. His was the shaking hand that made the experience of shaking hands rather awkward. When his hand took mine, I withdrew it as quickly as politeness would allow. My brother seemed to appreciate the massaging action of a hand that vibrated electrically inside of one's own. The old man had to withdraw *his* hand from my brother's.

"You remember your Aunt Beulah. She and Uncle Ovid drove in today from the country."

I knew that. Didn't she, my mother, remember that I'd visited them out at their farm—the genesis of my lockjaw terrors? No. Because they were so terrifying to me that I refused to mention them. Lockjaw was part of a personal mythology. Of one. Case closed. *Finita la commedia.*

"Merry Christmas!" I said, smiling. My brother followed suit. We were some cute little boys.

"They look so adorable."

"Yes," said my mother in cautious affirmation.

"We're all going to the parade this afternoon," put in my grandmother.

"With that Santa?" stage-whispered Aunt Beulah.

"I'm sure he'll be all right this year," said my mother, whose taste for the subject had waned considerably.

"I don't believe I've met your brother," said Uncle Ovid to me, hoping I'd learned manners enough to introduce them.

"This is Chad," I told him by rote. "My brother." To my brother, I said: "This is Uncle Ovid."

"I'm Uncle Ovid," said he, relishing a little joke. He looked around to my mother for recognition and didn't get any. She'd probably seen him do the same thing a hundred times.

"Haven't they grown?" said my grandmother to her brother.

"My, they sure have!" said Aunt Beulah, who mussed my hair. I hated it when people did that, though I realized that some people couldn't resist. I, who needed Sensitivity Training in all sorts of other ways, understood the profound adult urge to muss the wildly proliferating hair of young people.

"How's his...injury?" whispered Beulah to my mother about my brother's ear.

"He's a lot better now. The ear doctor saved his hearing."

"He a specialist?" asked Uncle Ovid.

"Yes. Eye, ear, nose and throat."

"They're all connected," averred my grandmother. "Just don't ask me how."

"The things they can do nowadays," whistled Uncle Ovid. "The things they can do!"

The weirdest among these sub-relatives had to be Uncle Cyril. He was very tall, with a senior undertaker's demeanor, but an impossibly goofy look about him, led by a pair of ears that drooped horribly; huge, flaring nostrils; and intense, buggy eyeballs. When he looked at you, he seemed to be under a magnifying glass. When he bent over, I fought the urge to swoop back.

"Hey there, you two!" said he to the both of us. He was the only Inclusivist among the great avuncular tribe. The rest of the aunts and uncles addressed us separately, though, as the oldest, the spokesman's role fell most often to me.

We nodded our hello.

"Going to see Santa this afternoon, huh?"

"Yessir."

"Seems like he's been here already," he said, looking with the slightest tinge of disapproval toward the immaculately trimmed new tree.

"They're for Grandma and Granddad."

"Well, aren't *they* lucky!" said the old man with an envious eyelid. The "they" made me retreat a little. Uncle Cyril's face seemed to get bigger when a word was emphasized, or when he laughed.

"Want to hear a little joke?"

God, he *was* going to laugh! I braced myself against the possibility of him smothering me with flapping tissue, backed up with extraordinarily prolific facial hair. My grandmother encouraged me to listen with a slight nudge from the eyebrows. Yet her eyes said that I could do anything I needed to in order to survive.

"Don't bother those little boys with your jokes," she said because it was expected.

"No, this is a new one. Just heard it the other day."

"Listen, boys. Your Uncle Cyril's going to tell you a joke," said my mother, perhaps aware of an Historic Moment. She was always telling me that I never knew how long these people were going to live, which I interpreted to mean that any and all of them might die at any moment. This not only scared me half to death, but made me almost supernaturally alert. At the slightest twinge of mortality, I'd make a bee-line for the out-of-doors.

Cyril began a tale I not only failed to relish, but to hear altogether. For him, the better the tale, the more up-close and personal he wanted to get. In the midst of a good yarn, there were no social boundaries. His face against mine was a drooping and flaring universe of age-elasticized flesh degraded with the prodigality of human hair. As he told his joke, the earlobes bounced and dribbled; huge nose-hairs kinked from inside of enormous, Deep Space-dark cavities; great, red-rimmed eyeballs seemed to sneak out of their sockets and hang suspended in front of me. If he'd been somebody my age, I would have said: "If you don't get this kid away from me, I'm gonna hit him."

When his tale was over he laughed quite obstreperously, exhibiting another anatomical feature that shook and bobbled: his astonishing uvula, which was three times as big as any I had ever seen. When my father did his hyena laugh, I sometimes saw his. It was surprisingly small—almost miniature—compared to this one.

I tried to laugh with him; my brother just gaped, humor-impaired. My mother seemed to think I'd made effort enough and thanked Uncle Cyril for his trouble. My grandmother just shook her head; *she'd* certainly heard the joke, or others like it.

So many of the other aunts and uncles just sat down and didn't get up till it was time to go. Fine with me. These were high-maintenance people.

As the day wore on, I could hardly contain my excitement at the prospect of watching this drunken Santa possibly embarrass himself as the float—with its tinsel and trimming, its small reindeer and enormous, cardboard-re-enforced candy-canes, its one waving beauty got up in a Santa suit that did not provide (as it did among male Santas) for her legs—radiated Christmas cheer.

"What'll you bet he's drunk?" I said to my brother as we got our coats on.

"Don't you think he will be?"

"I don't know," I said, somewhat cruelly.

"I hope he will be."

"You shouldn't hope things like that," I said as my mother came into the room and asked if we were ready.

You could get a lot of people into the downtown area of a small city like Owensboro, Kentucky. Its main street was four lanes wide, with sidewalks that could stand six deep if need be. There wasn't so much parking in those days because a lot of people still walked to such events. The cars you saw were generally in the parade, or part of a small security-detail that was there, not for rampaging criminals, but for crowd control and supervision. The city fathers didn't want people getting hurt. Children might also get lost and have to be held until parents came and got them. There wasn't any thought of kidnapping or sabotage—let alone terrorism. In this regard, it was a much simpler time—though, if you looked closely enough, you noticed people who had physical problems that would probably get worse. A small number of pre-medication era people might burst into tears for no apparent reason. Kids our age came in threadbare coats and shoes that were short, not only on style, but on fabric and leather.

We managed to find a good place on the first row nearest the street and dug right in. My mother and father had made room for us between them while grandmother and granddad stood on either side. No aunt or uncle had cared to join us.

"You boys ready for this?" asked my father irrelevantly. Hadn't he been paying attention?

It took a while for Santa's float to get close enough for us to make out the big fellow in the snowy-red hat, surrounded on this particular vessel with oversized elves and apathetic helpers. It wasn't a cold night—not for December—but these supernumeraries were dressed even more skimpily than the beauty queen, who waved, from a float entirely her own, at lubricious husbands and disapproving wives. It was mild for somebody who could stay mobile, but probably a little uncomfortable for the human statuary perceived to be essential to a Santa-centered universe.

"Look, there he comes!" shouted my mother.

"There he is all right," said my dad, who seemed to know something we didn't.

I punched my brother to make sure he was looking in the right direction. In those days, I found all sorts of excellent excuses for brother-on-brother assault.

He suppressed the "Owwww!" and funneled his energy into jumping up and down. This is what he did when overexcited. I probably would have too if he hadn't trademarked it for himself.

"Uh-oh," said my dad. "I think something might be wrong."

"Don't say that!" said my mother to him.

"I don't know. What do you guys think?"

He was asking our opinion about a phenomenon that was highly personal. But he probably didn't ask to get a correct answer.

"I dunno," I said judiciously. "Maybe."

"Maybe nothing! He's fine. Look at him up there. He's the picture of sobriety," said my mother, shooting a look to her mother, who didn't want to get involved.

"I believe I can discern signs of tipsiness," said my granddad instead.

"What's tipsy, Mom?"

It obviously meant drunk; I just wanted to hear her say it.

"It's when...never mind."

"Does it mean drunk?"

"I didn't say drunk; I said tipsy. There's a profound difference between the two," explained my granddad, whose hearing seemed to improve or deteriorate according to the content of a conversation.

"Hush up!" These were my grandmother's only words that evening.

As Santa's float approached underneath the ribbon-decorated street-lights and the sleigh-bell jangling soundtrack produced by people shaking handy little bells, I studied the man as carefully as I could. He posed underneath a banner that spelled out Amblin's, the name of the parade's department store sponsor. To my chagrin, he seemed perfectly all right. As the float got closer and closer, his "Ho-ho-ho's" became audible and sounded heartily sober. I watched the elves and helpers' smiles fade in and out as they tried their damnedest to stay in character in their paper-thin little frocks and wispy leotards. I saw them, for the first time, as people who might not necessarily want to be there. But Santa was the crowning marvel and, as he continued to approach, kids' voices started to say his name in unison, some requesting certain toys, others trying to get a rise out of him with absurd requests ("Hey, I want Elvis!") and impossible timetables ("Another turkey before breakfast, please!") Santa seemed to be keeping up as he "ho-ho-hoed", waved high and low, backwards and forwards. But then something peculiar happened; and it happened very, very slowly. I remember it one section at a time, as if its choreography could be parsed and divided. First came the wobble, which he was able to right; but the next wobble made him lurch forward, which he attempted to right by jerking himself back. But he jerked with just a little bit too much force and started to wobble again. Then, saw-blade style, the wobbling fanned out and slammed him forward. Before you knew it, a full-blown tumble was in progress. I was mesmerized at first. ("Look at that old man go!") Then, horror-struck by this huge man's inglorious descent into limb-flailing, beard-pulling chaos, I tried to coach him back. ("Stayupstayupstayup!") As he tumbled, he took out an elf, who did an elegant nosedive down the snowy bank that supported both of them and came to a bone-jarring stop against a little igloo that formed a barrier between the North Pole and the temperate zone that surrounded it.

"Oh, no!" said my mother, who was seconded by all the adults except my granddad, who seemed to know this was coming and said: "I thought as much."

The crowd shared my mother's sense of "Can-this-be-happening?" and made a gulping sound that echoed off the bright-lit storefronts and seemed to bounce around in space long after the man was down.

But a malignant universe hadn't finished. Once Santa had established a downward course, he picked up a momentum denied to the elf, who couldn't have had more than ten percent body-fat. People who were as thin as that landed without a lot of impact. If a whole group of people could pick themselves up and dust themselves off, it was the elves. But Santa wasn't built that way and crashed down through the snowy slalom with a dead weight's implacable momentum. Equally sickening was his reverberating cry, a cross between "Noooooo!" and "Eeeeeee!"—a strangely pre-cognitive sound that seemed to capture both the nasty surprise and dawning terror of a hard fall.

"Somebody catch him!" shouted my mother. To whom? Anybody who might have caught this man-missile was on the float itself. And when Santa hit a second elf, everybody knew he, Santa, was not going to stop until he hit something that would stop *him*. This second elf was projected by Santa's momentum off the float and onto a trailer that was strewn with holly. His unanticipated journey stopped there. Santa lofted over him and onto the side of the holly-float, down which he started sliding. He crash-landed against the snow-backed mountain that formed the next float's external architecture. And flopped out onto the holly like a dead man.

The parade kept on moving, but the crowd had been shocked into a ghastly silence. "Jingle Bells" blared into the night through loudspeakers clustered at the top of utility poles. This overbearing hymn to Yuletide adventure provided the soundtrack for a disaster I had eagerly visualized, but never dreamed would actually occur.

We looked at each other, not believing our eyes.

"My suspicion has been confirmed. Beyond a shadow of a doubt," said my grandfather, who lit a cigar. He was not a smoker.

The rest of the evening was appropriately solemn, as befits a world that had seen the worst possible thing that could happen. A beloved pastor plummeting stark naked into the laps of his congregation couldn't have been more shocking. I began to feel guilty, as if, by means of a single thought process, I had willed the thing to happen. I sought comfort and solace in my parent's room. I expected them both to be there, but only my father was. My brother had gone quiet, as befits the contemplation of a skewed holiday. For once, I let him be. He was a little kid who'd seen something he couldn't quite understand, for all the preparation he'd had for it. When you still trust, your world can be shattered easily.

When I saw that my father was alone, I assumed that everybody else was in the kitchen drinking coffee and rehashing the events of the evening among themselves. Seemed like he, of all people, would want to be in there doing that.

"Dad?"

He turned halfway toward me, as he often did when his attention was divided between something he was already doing and this question mark that had materialized before him.

"Did you see it?" I asked irrelevantly.

"Yes, I did."

"Dad...could we have done that to him?"

That got his attention.

"What was that?"

"Just by thinking of something...can you make it happen?"

"Oh, I see what you're saying." He was a man for whom this notion was not brand-new—even if he was having a hard time applying it to the present.

"It's possible, but in this case...I'll have to think about it."

I began to feel panicky. If it *was* my fault, what hell was in store for me?

"You don't know?"

"Frankly I don't, son."

"Is he going to be all right?"

"He'll be all right," he said, as a way of letting a conversation that could get to be as somber as the event that precipitated it, die off for a little while. I didn't believe what he said; nor, in all likelihood, did he. We both wanted, I think, some breathing space and, for the time being, we got it.

The parade had been allowed to continue after The Fall, but in that its heart and spirit had been eviscerated, interest waned very quickly. Within half-an-hour people were going home, tramping down the sidewalks three or four abreast, or walking in the street, which hadn't yet been cleared for traffic. It was the first mass exodus I had ever seen.

"You know, we didn't have this kind of stuff when I was growing up."

Uh-oh. A Depression story. I girded my loins for a bout of uneasy listening.

But he took a different angle with it.

"Seems like whenever you get something, something else gets taken away."

"Huh?" I said, not completely understanding the thought, but recognizing its fatalism.

"Maybe it wasn't so bad having so little because, when you don't have very much, you can't lose it. Look at what just happened. A big parade. All sorts of floats. Everybody lined up waiting for them to pass. And then...this. Maybe I didn't have it so bad after all."

"Guess not."

"Yeah, I did. We had it real bad, but I can't remember

anybody getting hurt except when we took turns riding this sleigh down a steep hill that just happened to have enough snow on it that year. Everybody got to do their rides, but I remember one of the guys getting a little too cocky and crashing against a tree. Knocked him out. Had to get stitches. Has 'em to this day. Want to see?"

I told him, yeah, I wanted to see even though I didn't—not at the moment anyway. But he wanted me to and I guess it was the least I could do for somebody who'd driven us so far and had so many lousy Christmases. We all had something to look forward to. All we had to do was settle down and get to sleep. In the morning, we would have our Christmas— which meant the riotous opening of presents we had every good reason to believe we'd get. And if all Santa had was a throbbing headache, he'd still be able to do his job.

Unless Santa was dead and everybody had been lying.

PD and AD

There are certain words that, when you hear them first, occasion a sort of pleasant shock, a species of personal wonderment and satisfaction you, the hearer, have never experienced before. With me, it was the word "damn." Not a particularly profane word, I know, but it had a certain dark authority to it. When you said "Damn!" it was to finalize something. It was not a thought-break; it ended thought completely.

The first time I heard it, I had just finished my first year at school. There I had learned to show up at places and events that were not necessarily to my liking. When you're so very young, temporary salvation is the only kind you know and you can only pursue it seriously when you lack a larger perspective. And no larger perspective can be known unless a smaller one is mastered first. My path was clear: go to school because, for now, there is nothing else you can do.

During the summer that followed that first year of school, I did not venture much outside of my own little yard, in which the grass never grew tall enough for hiding and the two water-oaks were just finding their way and could neither be climbed nor used as shelter. In the backyard you could spread out, but I remember getting lost there and panicking. If you looked at the yard today, you'd wonder how anyone could lose his way in it—even a clueless seven-year old. The focus of the disheartened can be extremely narrow.

One day in July, I was near my small, ivy-covered house doing something I remember taking spirited pleasure in: taking a small stone and trying to break the sidewalk with it. It seemed a possible thing to do. It was just a matter of extremely dedicated repetition. More committed than capable, I could do a thing longer than most people, and could wear out almost anybody; only the completely undistractable ever outlasted me.

To hear the small stone ping off of the hard sidewalk calmed me. A peace that passeth understanding descended upon the world and everything in it: and upon me, a feeling of oneness with concrete, with stone, and with the power of throwing. The stone *pinged* when it hit and went flying off somewhere. Unable to understand the concept of a world in which a plenitude of stones existed, I went running off after the same stone, found it just about every time, and threw it, again and again and again, at the concrete sidewalk. I had a found a sense of permanence there and that's important to a child of seven. You can rattle some children by suggesting that they leave the room they're in. And you can kill them by taking them to another.

I would use different parts or phases of the sidewalk in order, I think, to leave my scent and widen my scope a little. When I passed certain yard-long areas and knew I hadn't done any pinging there, I'd resolve to revisit these places with my one stone and muck around. The stone did not disable the concrete, as I hoped it eventually could, but it did create a sort of surface texture that was appealing to the senses—more in keeping with what an artist might do. A well-hurled stone could make streaks and striations; dents and doo-hickeys; nose-hair sized nicks and bottle-cap style bruises. You could read all kinds of things into these marks—things people might ask you about some years later. Gyrating movements and swirling escape-patterns disabled spatial perception. Which is to say, you could get drunk on them if you looked long enough. You could feel with your hand millimeter-sized grooves, like the ones you could feel on a penny. You could get lost down there in your handiwork and not know where the time went. Nor did parents who let you out in the morning and somehow got you back before flocks of birds began to cry overhead and a sun that had been roasting the pavement during the day's more thrilling phases set without a murmur.

I didn't mind keeping to myself, but when you have the entire summer to work with, you like to break it up with a word or two, preferably spoken to a real person and not the imaginary friend who will eventually become the stuff of adult psychiatry. I had no such imaginary friend at the time, but deep social yearnings no comforting repetition could satisfy. Unfortunately, this was the time of year when everybody seemed to be on vacation. The people next door had gone on theirs and were going on another in July. I had a crush on Vicki, an older girl of seven-and-a-half. She was the first little girl I played doctor with. She lived there with her mother and father during the school year and then vanished. My heart ached for her when I thought about her in our little doctor's office on the grass: she sitting there with me hovering around her with a diagnosis. My best friends, two brothers who lived across the street in a rambling house with a big den in back, were going to camp and were always out buying things for it. Rick, he younger one, would come over and show me his latest acquisition and, if it was wearable, let me try it on. One day he showed up with an ascot. He modeled it for me and suggested I model it for him. I said *that's okay, you can keep it, it looks better on you*. He seemed not to regret my aversion and kept wearing it. He looked like a child actor. If you saw a picture of him in his ascot, you might imagine him talking like Freddie Bartholomew. "I say, I do look rather charming now, don't I!" I wondered about Rick sometimes. He liked to do the same kind of stuff I did, but I felt he was interested in clothes and accessories just a bit too much.

On another occasion, he showed me some rings that were gaudily stamped and signatured. He asked me to try them on and, this time, I complied. But I didn't care for them either. They made the hand feel too *conscious*. If you did something, you'd have to take the ring off and then maybe you'd lose it. How would it feel, to lose something so irreplaceable? How could you possibly live that down, let alone pay for it? Rick said I could keep one of them for a while, but I told him that was all right, I didn't need a ring at the time. This seemed to upset him. He hadn't come by with anything in a couple of weeks, so maybe he was mad at me and would stay mad all summer. Rick and his older brother, Tommy, were inseparable, so if Rick was mad at me, Tommy would be too. It was funny, the way those two stuck together. My own brother and I were not nearly so close, but I was told that had something to do with his ear problem, which had made a different person of him—a person who enjoyed his own company and could read comic books for hours at a time. My hyperactive sensibilities were endlessly provoked by his reading. How had he, fully a year younger than I was, learned to read so well on his own? My own reading had an interesting quality to it. I was very good at the parts whose sound intrigued me, but could barely get through the stuff that fell flat on the ear. I was thought to be precocious because I once took the teacher's manual and read it out loud without a mistake. They couldn't know that I'd studied it and planted it there so I could do that. It had a lot of big words and convoluted paragraphs, which were my specialty. Show me a meat-and-potatoes sentence and I'd just barely walk through the thing with my shirt on. Such minuscule words and pitiful phrases just didn't seem worth the effort. My first-grade teacher had despaired of my backwardness until I showed her that I could read an entire book—one I'd committed to memory—without a hitch. After this performance, she called my parents in for a conference. Words like "idiot savant" and "pre-cognitive genius" were, in all likelihood, passed around, but no definitive conclusions were reached. The teacher had decided, with my parents' blessing, "to study' my progress. The crisis fizzled out after a time and nothing else was said about it. Meanwhile, I made an effort—with Dick and Jane at my side—to master the duller phases of the English language.

I realized after his operation that my brother and I were very, very different people. When your curiosity has developed, this is not a bad thing at all. But in that pre-curiosity part of life, you only care for things that jibe with your own limited experience. If somebody's not like you, you can't understand it. A stubborn mentality might even refuse to acknowledge the difference and go on treating this person as if he were you. I did that to my brother, with an unhappy result: he withdrew, he read, and he got a whole lot smarter. He didn't understand my pinging either; nor would he even go out there and try it. "Come on," I'd say to him, "you'll like it. It's... fun." Aghast at such under-developed persuasive powers, my brother shook his head and stuck it back into The Count of Monte Cristo, which had come out as a comic book. At the time, the pre-adolescent world read the world's great literature. The comic-book format made it palatable to the small, but inquiring mind that could live more easily on pictures than on prose. By the time my brother had outgrown them and graduated to the un-illustrated texts that characterized most adult reading, I had found them for myself and couldn't get enough of them. The big books out of which they came still intimidated me—even after I'd memorized parts of them. For most of our growing-up, I was one year ahead chronologically and light years behind in most other ways. It's hard to be the older brother.

There were a lot of nice people on the block, even if they weren't around much in the summer. Those who weren't nice kept to themselves and rarely consorted with the nice people. There weren't any loners at all. They must've known that this was a sociable place and not to move into it. But because people are sometimes dedicated to interests other than what might be interpreted as their very best, these people did anyway.

But there was a loner *family* who lived three houses down from the end of the block, where I would go and stare off into reams of space I dared not enter until I had to go back to school. They would drive up and seem to run into the house, as if somebody was chasing them. Then the mother would look back for a moment, in an apparent effort to establish that she and her family were clear of *them.*

She seemed to be the leader, if that's the word. I'm not even sure what the husband looked like. He was just a some-what larger person who dashed into the house before her. She did the looking back and that's all I really saw of her or anybody else for a long time.

She worked in a little garden that was ingeniously planned. She planted tomatoes and cucumbers in the front yard and had everything shipshape by the time you could tell something was growing there. She went out and staked the tomatoes, clipping the areas where weeds might grow. I watched her watch her emerging plenty with an unconscious fascination. She got right down on everything and studied it with a pure and righteous sense of wonder. Her devotion to those plants was absolute. She got right down on them in order to understand them better and to be close to them. It was a closer bond that a lot of people might enjoy with their families. I'd seen it in mothers who'd just gotten their babies from the hospital, and in people who had old dogs and would gauge their steps to match them.

I was watching her one morning and noticed a little boy at the door. He was about my age and was dressed much too warmly for the summer. He seemed to hover in the gloom of the carport like the *spirit* of a child—a wraithy thing that had no more physical substance than a wind-chime. I felt badly about the little boy and wanted to tell his mother that he was just standing there. With nothing to do. Please help him. Maybe he had to go to the bathroom. Perhaps he was there to say they were out of something indoors—something only she knew how to find.

"Ma'am," I said without realizing it.

She turned around with her entire body. I'd never seen a person do anything like that before. It was my first encounter with a yoga position.

"Yes?" she said.

"Uh...is that your little boy?"

She turned around to look, again with her entire body.

"What do you want, Clarence?" she said to him. He, Clarence, shrugged.

"If you don't want anything, Clarence, I think you should go back inside."

"Yes, ma'am," he said, startling me with the clarity of his small, but resonant voice. If a boy could be a high school principal, that is what he would sound like.

"He's all right. He just doesn't like to be inside all the time."

"I could play with him," I said, blurting out a suggestion I might possibly regret.

"No, you wouldn't want to do that."

"Why not?" I asked her prone figure, which had turned back to the garden.

"He's a sick little boy. He can't stay outside for very long."

"Oh," I said, unconvinced.

As if she understood my very thoughts, she said: "He's got a rare illness and can't be in the sunlight."

"I'm sorry."

"I am too sometimes."

She propped herself up on her haunches and looked at me.

"Are you from around here?"

"Yes. I live down the block."

She looked relieved, but disappointed.

"I know you now. You're the little boy who's always throwing things. My Clarence watches you."

"Clarence?"

"The little boy you just saw."

"Clarence."

"I'm afraid he...he doesn't do the things most children can do."

"Can't he come out...for just a minute?"

At this reasonable, but no doubt insensitive, question, the woman rose up to her full height and evaluated me. I began to have a self-conscious sense of my own height and weight, a feeling of having my entrails studied, a notion of nakedness such as I hadn't known before. This woman's eyes were powerful spirit-guns that could unlock closeted things—the potent and terrifying stuff that's balled up in a person's psyche. But her reply was bland.

"Maybe sometime...but not now. Why don't you run along for the time being and do your little exercises? Rest assured, Clarence will be watching."

I did as asked, but had this odd feeling all day: that

whatever I did—even if it couldn't possibly be observed by Clarence—I was being closely and thoroughly scrutinized. I was, if not the apple, then the perennial bouncing ball, in somebody else's eye. Under such scrutiny, I couldn't get my groove with the stone. When I threw it, I felt awkward. I suddenly didn't care for my throwing form. But what was *that*? I hadn't thought about the balletics of throwing any more than a squirrel would. I threw my little stone in order to hear it ping on the sidewalk, after which I ran and got it. There were no other niceties or nuances. I just threw and ran, threw and ran, and that had always been enough. But I couldn't do it without looking up toward a possible perch from which Clarence might be watching me. She'd said it. Why would a boy's own mother lie about her child?

After about thirty minutes of feckless hurling, I vacated my position and went down the block toward my house. There I noticed that some other kid had started throwing. I stepped around him as inconspicuously as I could and walked home, where I could maybe rustle up a sandwich. But I couldn't walk easily because I was noticing how I walked. Was Clarence's vision such that he could see me all the way down here? And, if so, what was so interesting about it?

I decided to go inside and lay low for a while. Perhaps Clarence would get tired of watching. Or I'd just forget and re-establish my old ways without any of this strange and biting self-consciousness.

I had the house to myself that day. My little brother was at the clinic with my mother for a checkup. My father was on another business trip.

When you experience such spatial volume, you feel dizzy almost. The places other people generally occupy are vacant and look that way. A table isn't a table anymore; it's a desolate spot from which humanity has been sucked entirely. The bathroom is a dangerous heap of hard appliances that will crack your skull if you happen to slip on the floor. Appeal for help and nobody will come get you. You'll just bleed to death on the floor, amidst the shiny porcelain and the silver knobs and the calamity-reddened tiles. It's not even safe in your parent's bedroom, where the great mirror on the wall opposite the big bed might somehow lose its moorings and come crashing down on you. Yet the enormous crawl-space underneath a two-person bed is something that while initially terrifying, is ultimately enticing. If you're rash enough to explore it, it'll enrich you immeasurably. Why a bed's nether chamber could hold fewer terrors than the outwardly visible and ostensibly challenging, I cannot say. But this one was, as so many others would be in the future. They gave the lie to dawning terrors and *horror vacui*. Rather than a source of compression, they were oases at which the spirit drank as deeply as it could and might, if it could not withdraw, become sated. Such a space is always supplied with objects that can be culled out and investigated. Like the boxes full of college memorabilia, cast-off appliances, and personal items only the person who'd put them there might quantify. These were companionable-feeling and made any temporary occupancy a source of pleasure.

Because of other restrictions I don't to want to get into, I didn't manage to lay low for very long in the house and went back outside without the sandwich I thought I'd wanted when I was on the street. Better to be out, just as it was better for that strange child, that Clarence, to be in.

The next day I went over to the third house from the end of the block and found nobody. The little garden, however, couldn't have been tidier. She'd done some new things with stake and string. Everything was tightly wound and stood up at textbook angles. Even the shadows fell evenly, as if she were directing them from a little control panel inside the house. Here, in this lyric dirt-patch, framed by crab-grass that felt scrunchy underneath one's shoes, was one person's private vision of what a garden should be. I couldn't resist the impulse to walk underneath the eaves of the carport, a semi-dark place where it was possible to list for a while, and touch the warm ground which smelled of the sunlight the wide eaves had kept at bay. The earth was finer here, with a bluish cast and a soothing presence. I let it sift through my fingers, which it caressed with a feathery sort of feeling. I kept on doing it just for the sake of doing it when I noticed that there wasn't any sun above me. I looked upward to where the sun should have been and saw the lady, who'd come out in something that covered about 27 percent of her body. She was the first nearly naked adult I had ever seen. I adjusted quickly to the sight, as children do, and waited for somebody to say something.

"You like my garden?" she asked me without much friendliness.

"Yes, I do."

My voice froze and produced a discreetly muffled verbal salad. As the conversation went on, I let it do what it wanted to. I had temporarily lost control. Small wonder, considering my sudden nemesis.

"You must know that you shouldn't be playing in it."

"Yes, I know that."

"Are you aware that there are property-rights on this block?"

"Uh...I...I think so."

"And that you are trespassing on mine?"

"Uh, no, I didn't."

"But you just said as much. Are you always so contradictory?"

The lady bent down, way down, to put her face into mine. It was a sharp face from a distance, but a round face close up.

It held no fear because it didn't look like a face anymore. It was just a huge fleshy expanse punctuated with openings and small dark holes from which sound issued with a somewhat disorienting audibility. This enormous face that faced me was an absolutely infinite sort of thing. My mother rarely put her face up to mine like that—and certainly not for any great length of time. And when my father pretended that he was burning me with his whiskers, the contact was glancing and not head-on. It left me with a feeling, not an image. But this... this woman's face was an all-encompassing phenomenon. If I could have expressed my feelings, I would have said: *Stay right here, face. Stay close and surround me.*

"There are not," she began, "very many things in life we can call our own. We buy things, but we trade them in. We make things, but they often break. We might even steal things, but it feels bad to steal them so we can't take any comfort in owning the things we steal. Do you understand?"

I didn't. Nor could I say that I didn't. Her mouth was much too big, and her ears too small, to be able to hear anything I would say.

"When people have few things, they are very particular about them. You do understand that."

"Yes, I do," I said, as the automaton I had willingly, and necessarily, become.

"And when they do, they want to be able to enjoy them just as they are. They don't want people messing them up. You understand that, don't you?"

I said I did.

"So what do you think I'm feeling at this moment?"

"Uh...bad?"

"No, not bad. The word is...violated. What if I took your rock and wouldn't give it back to you?"

"You wouldn't do that."

"But what if I did? You wouldn't like it, would you?"

There was some kindness here, or enough psychological wiggle-room to allow me to imagine it. Which prompted me to say what I'd say to any authority-figure who expected politeness rather than paralysis.

"No, ma'am."

"But look what you've done with my garden. You've taken it and you've displaced some of it, for the sheer pleasure of taking something somebody else did and doing that."

I suddenly noticed, out of the tiny peripheral vision I had left, that Clarence was hovering in that almost pitch-dark space between door and steps. He was there and he was watching me—watching us: me and his mother there in the dirt.

"So what are you going to do now?" she, Clarence's mother, asked.

"Me? I don't know. "

"Don't you feel you should apologize?"

Having never been asked to weigh in on something that I had done automatically when scared and grudgingly the rest of the time, I couldn't say. Rather than render such an unsatisfactory reply, I shook my head for a moment, as if to say I didn't feel apologetic, but decided, in the interest of playing to a draw, that I ought to be at least a little sorry and found the words that would express those pesky nuances that hovered between resistance and surrender.

Uh...I'm sorry about your dirt."

"Soil. I prefer the word soil."

I repeated the word for no good reason: "Soil."

"Soil is the foundation of everything that's real. You see that big tree over there? It couldn't grow without the soil that's underneath it. Soil is everywhere. Even when you're not thinking about it, it's underneath you. Always underneath you. Besides the ocean, there's more soil on the earth than any other element."

She paused to let the thought sink in, and continued:

"Now, I want you to turn around and go away from here and not come back. Clarence cannot come out and play with you, do you understand? Clarence has a sickness that keeps him inside of the house. You don't want to play with a little boy like that, do you? No, you don't. Not you: you like to throw rocks at things and Clarence could never learn to do that. He's a very sick child and I don't think you'd understand that. No, I don't think you would."

I did as I was told and, when I'd gotten to the next yard, I started running. While my block was no longer than any other block in the neighborhood, it had an exceptional length compared to Brooklyn blocks, for example, and most certainly blocks that ran along Manhattan's Upper West Side. You're on and off of them before you know it. I seemed to run into the next day before I got to my house, where I paused and wondered whether what had just happened *had* happened. Perhaps it had not. These were some *very* odd people! They never visited anybody and popped into their house so quickly, you could never believe you'd actually seen them. The father seemed to be around, but he was somehow unwilling to establish his presence as the mother had. The boy, Clarence, had an awful disease that kept him indoors. Yet with her huge hat, her perfect garden, and her clipped, dialogue-coach way of speaking, the mother had brought me to the heights of pre-adolescent pleasure: she'd introduced me to the sense-surrounding wonder of a face that could expand and contract at will. And when she was ready, she flung me homewards with a pack of bewildering admonitions whose dark majesty and plummy sound I would not encounter until I saw Moses shriek out the Ten Commandments on a movie-screen downtown.

In the interest of re-establishing my old life again, I picked a section of new sidewalk and started throwing a choice little stone at it. It pinged and I ran after it. It pinged a second time and I ran after it again. When it pinged off in a wild direction, I chased the stone down with an unerring sense of its serpentine movement. The artistic patterns I studied after the fact were beginning to enlarge my thinking and I felt free and alive: my own boss; a little lord out among the sticker-bushes and the Johnson grass. As I flung the stone, however, the kid I'd seen pinging his stone against an adjacent sidewalk settled near me and started an exercise of his own. It involved throwing multiple stones and *not* chasing after them. I felt he was cheating, but I couldn't tell him that because I couldn't really think of what to say to him. I also felt I couldn't vacate my spot lest he grab it. So whenever I threw, I leapt toward the stone I'd just pinged as it caromed off the sidewalk. I caught it in midair a few times; others I had to run and get it so I could get back to *my* spot before *he* could. But the inevitable finally occurred: after I'd hit the sidewalk with a bad throw, it pinged weakly and shot off away from me toward the street, where a nice, late-model Chevrolet was crawling along at a pace that suited a car everybody could admire in passing if they had a mind to. Unfortunately, I didn't notice the car until I was right up in front of it. The driver saw me, but couldn't stop in enough time to avoid hitting me, so he jerked the wheel and swerved without unnecessary finesse away from my person. The car's right front wheel jammed up against the curb, stopping it cold. The driver exited the car and came up to me where I was watching him from the middle of the street.

"Do you realize what you've done?"

Here was another large face pressed into mine. It did not, however, have the same spiritual repercussions. It was a snarling sort of face whose ganglia appeared distended while its various openings smoked somewhat. Its sun-sharpened contours were jagged and tinged with red.

I said I did.

"What are you going to do about it?"

I shrugged. What kind of question was that? I was neither a mechanic nor an insurance adjustor and he should have known that.

"I want to know where you live, who you are, and…would you please get out of the middle of the street and come here to me!"

Then he said it: the word that still resonates in my memory. He said the word that seemed to clear the air like no other. The word that would separate one era—PD—from the next—AD—forever.

"Damn you, little kid. Damndamndamn!"

I flinched as if hit, but was also encouraged. If this was the worst, I could bear it.

"Do you know what you just did here? You don't. Dammit, would you look at this wheel? Just look at that wheel, dammit!"

Then I tried the word out myself: "Damn!" I said. It felt good to say it. I understood immediately how useful such a word could be. When you said it, you didn't need to say anything else. No need at all.

The man said that I shouldn't say that word, but he really didn't put much heart into it. His job was not to be the language policeman for other people's children—even if he had introduced a probable cause. His job was to show me the consequences of my pinging and to perhaps break me of a habit I might not have outgrown, if left to my own devices, for years and years. Then he went back to his car, straightened himself out a little, and asked me some questions. Were my parents at home? If they weren't, when would they be, and could he have a telephone number?

After he got it all sorted out with my mom and dad, I didn't throw stones anymore, partly on their suggestion, but partly because the Era of the Small Stones had ended some-how. I could surely could do more constructive things than hit other cars and have my parents deal with the owners. I was left with only one pastime: to go sneak a look at that lady's garden.

As it got well into the summer, the tomatoes came out, then the cucumbers. The tomatoes were blood-red and burst-ing on the vines, which were double-staked and tied with some sort of heavy-duty string. The cucumbers were subma-rine-length and almost black. Whatever her shortcomings as a neighbor, the lady was a gardener to reckon with. She knew what soil did and was possibly justified in ragging me out for touching it.

I was never tempted to steal anything, but I couldn't keep myself from going over there and watching. I thought I felt those same piercing eyes upon me as I watched, but they didn't bother me as much anymore. Yet what if the little shut-in boy decided to reveal what I was doing? I didn't want another scene with his mother, so I stopped coming over for a while. It was at this time that we went on *our* vacation, up to my grandmother's house in Kentucky, where all sorts of people—including my grandmother—had gardens whose good warm dirt you could sift through your fingers all you wanted to. You could also ramble about the countryside, which didn't exist where we were. Our part of town—which was the newest part at the time—had been paved over and gridded off to the point where, if somebody had told you this was so-and-so's farm, you'd think he was kidding. When I ran into some-body new, however, I'd tell him or her that the very block we were on had been farmland and that there were pigs and cows here just a few years ago. I got so confident in the story that I embellished it with exact locations and sad-but-true incidents involving livestock and farmhands. I'm sure this new person passed it all on to the next person. There came a time when nobody seemed to be surprised that moo-cows and chickens had occupied the land before them; besides, it was an excellent little ice-breaker, which got people talking easily about other things. It pleased most people to know something interesting about the neighborhood. It pleased me to have helped create a luminous fiction other people might pass along. More importantly: telling made-up stories got me up to speed as a reader; it also gave me a sense of greater horizons. The pinging of stones would never quite hold my attention again.

When we came back in August, it was time to get ready for school again, so I didn't think about the lady or her frail son or the small, sun-warmed garden in the front yard until the wait was over and I was inside the school building every day. When I saw the garden for the last time, there was nothing left but the patch of dirt and a few stakes leaning crossways over it. In disuse, the garden was unlike its creator: mussed-up and out-of-kilter. She had bent over me there when it was going strong and had given me a sense that there would be unanswered questions and paradoxes in life and perhaps not to get bent out of shape wondering about them. I had a sense that there was this moment and there was the future—and there was no turning back. That lady's face and the car hitting the curb were definitely PD, and everything afterwards AD. Thus was my private Caesarian calendar born and it's served me pretty well ever since.

One River's Enough

uber stood six-foot two inches tall and his flesh was marbled with the sort of adipose tissue acquired, in one's early years, by a fanatical regime based largely on a single food group. In Huber's case, that food group was sugar. He did not eat the lunch his mother made him, but removed a secret cache of Mars bars, individually wrapped Chunky clusters, and however many ice cream sandwiches the conscientious nutritionists at the lunch-line would allow him to sneak away with. I don't remember him arriving at his table with less than three or four. Then as now, Purchasing Power is Everything.

At first, I did not care much for Huber. He was large and ungainly and a natural unifier-*against*—which is almost as good as an argument *for*. If you could find somebody to pick on, you had something to talk about with everyone else. You were also temporarily out of the line of fire yourself. Yet because I had been on the receiving end of juvenile ridicule, I wasn't about to become unified against anybody even if they were patently ridiculous, as Huber undoubtedly was. I acknowledged the cautionary tale he represented. But for the grace of an apple or banana, anybody might become the sort of prodigy Mom and Dad never think about when they see that violin and say, "Now, why can't our little Phil learn to play that?"

At first, I avoided Huber. His excesses revolted me, his gargantuan proportions disturbed my sense of classic form, his lack of couth was a source of acute embarrassment. Yet his nature was gentle and his temperament, like his padded flesh, was yielding, even sentimental. He would extricate flies from spider-webs with the equanimity of a born rescuer. He would escort frailer children across the street after the cross-walk guards had pocketed their police-whistles and scooted away. He would give other kids lunch money, mostly for the sort of treats that were his dietary staples. When Mrs. Fuseli persecuted him, he found an ally in me—and, to a certain extent, in Sam, who was never eager to run to any-body's rescue in public, preferring to work for justice in more devious ways. When, on the first day in class, Mrs. Fuseli made Huber stand up and announce his height and weight, Sam and I followed suit, inflating the figures somewhat in order to make a point that seemed to escape everybody but ourselves and the teacher. "I'm a hundred and seventy-five pounds soaking wet," averred Sam. I quoted a more modest, but thoroughly outrageous, figure, considering my skinny wrists and fine-boned features. All Ms. Fuseli could do was thank us and ask us to sit down. Sam emphasized his point by sitting down real hard and spilling some of the lesser con-tents on top of his desk. The class tittered. A minor victory, but a victory still.

After prying more information of a personal nature out of Huber, Mrs. Fuseli asked us to go out in the hall and wait for her. When she came toward us, she seemed to be brandishing a waffle-iron, when, in fact, it was just a piece of chalk she wished to dangle our way as if to keep us at arm's length.

"So you're defending him," she managed to say to both of us. The head-swivel that allowed her such full range was quite arresting. It would be used to great effect in a movie made many years later. When I saw the movie, I was impressed with its fidelity to the Fuseli style.

"Uh...no, ma'am," I said, hoping to buy time.

"No, we weren't defending him," stated Sam, who had obviously come up with an Idea. A born litigator/rabble-rouser/standup comedian, he could think on his toes divinely.

"What's that?" she said, bearing down on him. Sam was cool and stepped back against the wall, against which he scratched himself momentarily.

"Just thought we'd share sizes. I thought that's what you wanted and were warming up with him."

I said: "Yeah, we were sharing sizes."

When Sam got going, I was good for an affirmative cheer, a culminating burp or comma.

"And why were you doing that?"

"Because...I thought that's what you wanted us to do. Why would you want to know just *his* size? I thought you were going to go around the room and ask everybody."

"That's ridiculous. You don't do that to girls. It's indecent."

It was here that Mrs. Fuseli bared her teeth against a statistical indecency that would threaten All Mankind.

"You're right, Mrs. Fuseli. Girls excepted."

"What do you have to say?" asked Mrs. Fuseli of me.

"I thought so too. I thought, why just him? That's what I thought."

"Yes, I'm sure you did," said she. A sidekick's lackluster mind, said the tone she had selected, should add discretion to its repertoire of cliches.

"If you must know," she announced, spreading her legs apart and thrusting arms that settled gelatinously into her chest, "I wanted the class to see that Huber didn't belong here with us. He's already flunked out of two grades."

I gasped, as if the infamy of the ages had been revealed.

Though academic excellence was not admired, failing to pass was a notion unendurable. I'd had nightmares about it: nightmares in which I woke up mutely screaming. Scholastic excellence was regarded as marginally desirable; a little went a very long way. None, however, made you the absolute scum of the earth. When I made my first F, I moped around for weeks, dreaming of the C I would absolutely have to get the next time. As in all things, moderation is key.

"Some people learn at different rates," said Sam, startling the both of us. He was a collector of random knowledge and could score very big with it when he wanted to. He also understood the subversive nature of Good Timing.

"Yes, that's so, but I think Huber is just a little dumber than most of you kids and I wanted to…I wanted him to be able to shine in this other way."

An outright lie, of course. Mrs. Fuseli wanted to fire a salvo of humiliation from which an oversized underachiever would not recover. And, indeed, as Huber fumbled for the correct answer, his face had turned beet-red. When he began to fight off the tears that were to become a sullen triumph for our teacher, Sam's moral sensitivity was enraged. He was damned if she was going to break another person. While he did not bother to illustrate the process, he drew a line in the sand, which only the iniquitous might cross.

"Why don't you boys go back into the room and stay quiet? I think I want to talk to little Huber in private."

In this way we became Huber's champion and protector. We knew, once she wanted the rest of the class to think in a certain way, it would. Children generally wish to please, the better to purchase immunity against some future transgression for which they too might be called before the class and "outed." It was a lesson in group behavior, which vacillates between cowardice and cooperation.

As I said, I didn't take to Huber readily and, because of his psychological makeup, Sam had "issues" as well. He didn't like taking sides and here he'd gone and done it. Now that it was done, he wanted to let time and the tide of forgetfulness envelop his partisanship and wipe it clean before he made any other moves in this direction. Luckily, Mrs. Fuseli ceased her persecution for a little while and allowed a sort of nervous democracy to settle over the class. She was, after all, a teacher who had to start on page one just like everybody else. And get through all the books she would assign us by the end of the year. There was a sense of trepidation among a certain number of our classmates whose worst nightmare was to get too far behind. And sixth grade was just one grade back of seventh, which was said to be so hard, it was held in junior high school—and at a completely different location! As it had done to so many of our predecessors, junior high would eat half of us up and not even bother to spit wide. Words like "individualism" would not leap off the page and had to be spelled one letter at a time; geography would be structured on a spool of strange-sounding names and ridiculous customs—none of which could be had by merely spinning the globe. And math would be incomprehensible, as numbers were split into fractions and multiplication tables ran into triple digits. This was no time for any of us to be splitting our focus.

And yet *we* had to: a higher moral purpose was at stake.

We'd taken to walking with Huber all the way to this house, which was in a part of town we knew only in passing. Huber lived on stately Pontius Street, a stretch of pavement that crawled a few blocks east of my brick and wattles. The houses in Huber's area were distinguished, not only by size, but by "extras": multi-acre yards, good high fences, and lordly trees through which the light filtered down onto stunning vistas. The houses were big too—almost as big as the ones our doctor, whose blood-stained clinic was within walking distance of my house, lived in. You could almost visualize the safe deposit boxes through which a lucky owner rummaged for the wads of cash that had purchased them. With its complement of post-WWII suburbans that had beckoned inner-city kids out to the East side of town, our side of Pontius was more modest. The houses were not mean, but hardly ornate. With their nearly identical floor-plans and cute little weedy yards, they spoke of homebuilding on a budget. They spoke of fast-working crews who could hammer a frame together in a matter of days. They spoke of haste and efficiency working hand in hand to create an illusion that would attract first-time homebuyers by the dozen. Huber's house had been enlarged over a period of time that stretched from horse-and-buggy days up to the present. It was intriguingly layered with spry Victorian curlicues subsequent generations had attempted to iron out, but had failed to eliminate altogether. Looking at it was like studying a face with big eyebrows, a small mouth, and a head of hair that was neatly combed on one side and weedily vigorous on the other. Nothing was in proportion—which was what made it so interesting. My dad never missed an opportunity to make a Jerry Lewis-type face whenever we passed it. "See?" he would say. "I'm the house." As time went on, he took more pleasure in performing the impersonation than we did in appreciating it.

It was at Huber's house that I saw, and then used, a refrigerator whose ice-maker spit out perfectly sculpted cubes into a glass. It was at Huber's house that I saw a humidor for the first time. "What's that?" I asked. Huber's answer came in the form of a moist cigar, which he laid before me as a cat might lay a squirrel at his master's feet. I didn't know what to do with it, so I put it in my pocket and took it home with me. When it was found, I was the center of attention for a while. It was also at Huber's house that my skin felt cool without becoming clammy. Huber's far-seeing parents had installed peculiar vents and arcane passages that made the air flow around continuously. Its stimulating force had not, alas, seeped into Huber's mind, which was not easily awakened by subjects on a page. Yet Sam and I were convinced that some inner strength there, waiting to be tapped, would sooner or later show itself. If there wasn't, Huber's IQ did not arise from the mingling of parental genes, but of flawed sensibilities that were his and his alone. In a brief ceremony during which we stared at a poster of W. C. Fields, Sam and I aimed to find out.

"I vow to help Huber find the source of his brainpower," said Sam.

"I do too," said I, uninspiringly.

"Huber is our friend now and we must protect him. But because the world can be harsh, he must also fend for himself."

"Amen," said I, content to function as a sort of human chime.

"We cannot make his mistakes for him. He must learn to do that himself."

Sam looked to me for an appropriate ending and, after watching me choke for a while, supplied it himself.

"This is a cliché and I wouldn't normally use it, but I think it's appropriate here."

"What's that?"

"We're all he's got."

Huber *was* genetically primed for an acute intelligence he did not, or cared not, to show. His father was in finance while his working mother helped found an agency that brought "largesse"—whatever that was—to the poor. She was featured in the newspaper for having brought this largesse to an underserved population that had developed all kinds of social problems because it had apparently lacked it. There she was, handing out food to a scrawny-looking colored kid while looking dreamily at the camera. She looked pretty enough, but she was the type of woman who wore her idealism on her sleeve and not up it. "Nobody lasts in a job like that," my father was heard to say.

After having visited Huber a number of times, I became conscious of a double plight: that of him not measuring up to the glittering accomplishments of his parents while also being a kind of stooge among us. Yet he'd been trying to make better grades and exercise somewhat. We felt we should help accelerate the possibly thankless process of expanding his mind while trimming down his body. We studied him one day before a mirror like scientists attempting to crack a Major Enigma.

"Stand up straight, Hubie," suggested Sam.

Huber followed suit, increasing his height while making no appreciable dent in his *avoirdupois.*

"Maybe you've got a thyroid problem," Sam observed, glandularly erudite.

"What's that?" I asked.

"It's when the thyroid gland is inactive, which keeps the body weight high," he said to me. Then to Huber: "Has that ever been a problem?"

Huber shook his head, uncomfortable with diagnostic thinking. His parents had been coming at him from various angles, all intent on nurturing. Having been denied as children, they were lavish in material splendor while less than rigorous in the way of discipline. They were austerely conscious of food choices during the holidays, but cheerfully oblivious other times of the year. Throw open the cupboard and you'd find every sugary cereal in the book. There were always bags of things you could tear open and empty into any number of large ceramic bowls, which they had purchased from real artists who'd sat at a wheel to make them.

"If it isn't that," suggested Sam, "maybe we can exercise weight control by means of old-fashioned calisthenics."

On that cue, Huber reached into something I didn't see and extracted a candy bar, which he ingested as a king snake would a rat. This quick-and-do-it technique was astoundingly sophisticated—something Huber had developed and refined during whatever free time he had away from the larder. Until that moment, neither I nor Sam had ever seen him eat anything. I was tempted to say "Do that again!" in order to witness a sort of process that was not only unfamiliar, but might possibly change my thinking about what people choose to learn in life. Huber's hand-to-eye coordination might be taken to task in other areas, but in the way of food-delivery it was absolutely superb. His was a human potential that had not been overlooked, but misapplied. Perhaps if it could be made to do something else, other faculties might start to develop around it. If nothing else, we realized that Huber's gluttony was not surreptitious, merely super-fast. Perhaps we could get him to slow down. If he could learn to savor, perhaps he'd slim down that way. Didn't Sam's own mother emphasize this very concept when she adjured him to "Chew your food, don't swallow it!" (Having acquired the habit of emphasizing Big Picture concepts, she took out part of that equation. Most people would have said "Chew your food *before* your swallow it." Not she. A purist at heart, she fastened on Major Functions and let the rest take care of themselves.)

In the interest of scientific accuracy, Sam had Huber bolt down another candy bar.

"Very interesting," said Sam, stroking his chin and pacing around like scientists used to do in B-movies. "Could you get me one of those too?"

Sam—who believed in a sort of constructive sadism—posited

an initial strategy of hard physical exercise supplemented by fewer spontaneous ingestions. He would come to enjoy putting Huber through his paces; contests of heart and stamina had in a special place in his psyche.

We went out to a place near the high school, which had been divided up into field (for track meets and such) and forest (for whatever the prurient might devise after three p.m.) The air was fresh, as it used to be in the fall, and there was an apple-smelling aroma that came from the great heart of the earth exhaling. Huber couldn't have chosen a more invigorating moment to begin afresh. We'd dressed him in an outfit whose clashy quality suited him very well: a tight crew sweater over a pair of gym shorts that would have showed off a smaller man's legs. Huber's over-padded stumps distended them almost audibly. If seams could talk, they would have been yowling like cats up a tree. All in all, however, he cut a sporty figure and seemed eager to start.

"Should I warm up?" he asked.

Good question. I didn't know. I just slammed my way through things, nursing wounds as they occurred, while taking a general sense of immunity for granted. Huber seemed to sense his vulnerability. Sam wasn't, however, interested in easing Huber into the process.

"Nah, just start running. But don't start too fast. You've got to pace yourself or you'll tire out."

Huber surprised us by disappearing into a glen whose primeval aspect carried uncomfortable associations: of wild animals stalking and maiming one another; of erring man about to step into a booby-trap that would break and smother him; of the wildly unpredictable nature of...nature. It was into this screeching serenity that Huber ran, without a care in the world and a song he didn't know he was singing.

"Hmmm. He may have found his ideal occupation," said Sam, who was impressed in spite of himself.

"Occupation?" I asked.

"That elephantine carcass of his may be ideally suited to foraging."

Nurtured by the humor of W. C. Fields, Sam had just made a statement that was too polysyllabic for me to follow. I nodded, as I had done in classes that were emphatically numerical.

"Which is to say: he might do okay out there."

We waited, at the verge of the forest, for what appeared to be some hours, after which time we started to discuss alibis Huber might not be able to make, having been devoured by some free-roaming creature of the veldt or plain—some free-roaming creature who'd stumbled upon the most astonishingly delectable meal of his entire career. We hadn't thought of Huber from a purely animalistic point of view. To us, his flesh was unattractively inordinate; to a predator, it might mean an extra day or two of mouth-watering joy.

I kicked off the topic with the obvious: "What if he doesn't come back?"

"Nature. Chalk it up to nature."

"Is that all?"

"No. But it's what we'll say to anybody should they ask."

"We can't just say that nature did it. What do you mean by nature anyway?"

As Sam explained to me his highly personal concept of Creation, the Western sky began to dimple garishly as previously unostentatious clouds danced and whirled like tipsy chorines and everything below them began to insidiously darken. In minutes, Huber was going to be swallowed in a primeval forest, from which he would not return a human entity, but a big bag of bones or a room-filling cloud of dust.

He finally materialized, a sweating hulk, curiously triumphant. He was the worse for wear only in his outward accoutrements, which were stained with iron oxides and brambled with the fruits of a teeming wilderness.

"Huber!" I exclaimed, running toward him. "I...we...were getting worried."

"It was great out there," he said. "I saw some big animals like...no, not like a dog or a cat but...big animals that swoop down and get whatever they can get. And if they don't get it, they don't give up. They keep on coming. See this cut? Some bird kept diving at me, but I kept on running. I like running. Running...you can cover a lot of ground that way. I don't know how far I went. You guys have any candy?"

One thing at a time. We could deal with the candy-eater if the nascent runner could return.

Because Sam was a miracle-worker, he produced a morsel that would sustain Huber till we got him back home. As we walked, he was full of plans for his next run.

"I think I want to go someplace different next time. You guys need to find a place for me that...well, it has to be different. How about the ocean?"

Sam told him that any ocean was out of the question. Why would he even think of such a thing, since it was the wrong element to be running in.

"I should learn to swim. I think I'd be able to float, don't you?"

"Odds are for it. How 'bout the Mississippi? Think you could stay on top of that?"

Huber nonchalantly affirmed his capacity as he started to run away from us. Self-guided movement down trail or road offered Huber the sort of pure delight that had obviously been denied him. And while no marvel of grace and coordination, he was surprisingly fast. We didn't catch up with him until he reached Pontius, where he slackened a bit, but did not stop. Though we kept this sentiment to ourselves, we were bursting with pride. Here was somebody who not only took instruction, but could run with it as well.

Having held back for reasons that would strike any coach as sound, Sam threw himself into his role as trainer. He conceived of schedules Huber might be able to meet within two months, then three, then half a year. He made sketches of Huber the way he was now *vis-a-vis* the Heroic Huber of the future. Sam drew his pupil bending and stretching; running and hurling; turning 'round and going wide. Finally, he came up with a test that, should Huber acquire the physical prowess for which Sam and, to a lesser extent, I would dedicate ourselves heart and soul, he might, should conditions favor him, be able to pass on his own. Not only would Huber thrive with his running, he would distinguish himself in an activity very few odds-making people had ever, or would ever, attempt: floating down the Mississippi River.

"I think he would be able to do that," said Sam to me as we loped behind. "Let's go see."

Meanwhile, Mrs. Fuseli had devised other plans to torture and humiliate our poor, bloated minion.

"Now that we've made our way through the fundaments of spelling, I think we ought to have an informal spelling bee. Why don't you, Amanda, come up here? And you, Huber, I think you would make a worthy opponent, having been in class so much longer than the rest of us."

Huber eagerly joined Amanda up in the front of the class and was bombarded with words such as his mother and father might use routinely, but from whose syntactical hinterlands he, Huber, would be forever banished.

"Spell the word 'internecine' for us, Huber. Just listen. It's spelled just as it sounds."

Huber fumbled gamely, yet he couldn't try all those s-sounds out in his head without them coming directly out of his mouth. It was the sort of comic relief people of a certain age relish more than any other kind and appreciation was expressed readily and categorically. Amanda Greystoke missed the word too, but only because she'd gotten nervous and transposed vowels.

"Here's another, Huber. Spell 'quotient.'"

"That's easy," said Huber, with a spirit of bravado he had not exhibited before. Unfortunately, bravado has never substituted for hard-earned knowledge. After fumbling with various clicking sounds, he made a spirited hash of a word that doesn't begin in "k" in any dictionary.

"Let's turn 'quotient' over to Amanda," said Mrs. Fuseli without seeming particularly eager to do so. In front of class, Amanda was not the whiz she was on the page.

This time Amanda scored and thus began a rout that befuddled and, ultimately, hurt a strangely defiant Huber to the soul. When the round was over, he returned to his seat and slumped way down into it, as if to hide himself there.

"Sit up," enjoined Mrs. Fuseli. "You'll get curvature of the spine."

Huber moved not a whit.

"I said sit up. You don't want a medical condition, do you?"

For once, Huber was not about to be subjected to any kind of preferential malignity. Mrs. Fuseli saw curvature of the spine everywhere she looked. In Mrs. Fuseli's eyes, everybody who sat down was angling for it.

In defeat, Huber was casually accepting; he clearly didn't give a rat's ass about curvature of the spine.

"Curvature of the spine is a grave physical deformity that ravages one and all, regardless of race, color, or creed. Or *size*."

Huber kept his slouch throughout this harangue and wouldn't budge the rest of the day. He'd won a round, in spite of his drubbing in orthography.

We congratulated him as we walked him home.

"I'm going to the ocean," he said. "If you won't help, I'll get there on my own."

Sam and I had a conference in his room, which was our personal hideout and a place that was perfectly suited for exchanges of sensitive information. If we got rowdy only his father, Aldro, could hear us. Being stoic in character because he was raised in the Midwest, he didn't much care what we did as long as we shut all the doors and didn't pee on the bathroom floor—or any other, for that matter. Volatile Southerners were masters of exaggeration. If something started out as a scratch, it would widen as the day went on and have to be operated on at dusk. Should a typical Southerner fall from a ladder, he hoped that something was broken so that he could go on about it. And if a cornbread-eating driver crashed into a curb or some other minuscule object, he'd leap out of his car, show the world his wounds, and insist that he be treated with something nice to eat, preferably with some "sweet tea" to wash it down with. If a Midwesterner got hurt, he was told to walk it off. Aldro took it a bit further and denied there was any hurt in the first place. Sam's mother was a different story, but she was hardly ever home, being addicted to shopping at a time when such addictions went happily undiagnosed. Sam's sister, Leah, was present in an abstract sort of way. She was the sort of person who couldn't accept things as they were and had *questions*. The first time I saw her, she asked me whether I was happy inside of my own skin. I said the first thing that came to my mind. "Yeah," I said, without realizing the power of subtext. "I wouldn't be too sure," she said challengingly. "Underneath our skin is where we really live. In spite of all of the superficial damage for which we appeal to puppet saviors and charlatans with scalpels, our lives really happen where we can't see what's going on." My interest in her was largely prurient. Underneath the sack-like creations she wore around the house, I discerned breasts of a prematurely abundant character. She was "developing" and while Sam respected—at least in theory—the privacy of a sister to whom such physical changes might be traumatizing, he was not averse to the practice of spying, so long as I carried most of the water myself. "How would you describe her titties?" he would ask of me after I had looked through a little hole at a blurry body that could have been blandly undistinguished or ruefully spectacular. I knew what kind of body she had, but held my tongue. I did not wish to be assigned Leah Duty if I could help it. Such things always backfired.

"They're average," I told him, pretending to have seen them—or something like them—in the murk. There were all sorts of inorganic things that might look like "titties" through a crack in the door. I didn't understand Sam's reluctance to explore this ready-to-appreciate phenomenon himself. Which is to say, I thought he should consider Leah's anatomical splendor more of an open road. Given the keyhole situation, titty-identification would remain forever dicey—like trying to make out an obscure planet, or planets, from the wrong side of a telescope.

Why *couldn't* he have gone and looked at them himself? In all other situations, he just forged ahead. It is possible that Aldro had forbidden him to do so. You didn't want to mess with Aldro. It was the stoic people who went crazy on you.

"I seriously doubt it," he said of my observation. "They swell magnificently under her bathrobe. Ah! Perhaps she's wearing falsies. Next time you look, would you keep an eye out for them?"

Sam's approach to my surveillance was so casual that I couldn't do anything but nod. He made it seem like a sort of class project for which a gold or silver star might be available when it was satisfactorily done.

Sam finally wearied of Leah's developmental attributes, or their rumored abundance, and wanted to get to the Great Adventure he had been contemplating for some time.

"Let's take him down to the river," said Sam, who, in his own element, could make executive decisions.

"How? When?"

"After school sometime. We'll take him down there and, if he drowns, we'll know. It being the Mississippi, they won't find him for a while."

"Drowns?"

"Of course. Anyone who runs the gauntlet of the river must face drowning."

"Why not start him out on something easier?"

"He wants an ocean. We should at least give him a river."

Sam's perverse imagination didn't care a whit for Huber's safety; it just wanted us to go out on the river with a single human's potential sort of balled up in our fists and see what would happen. I bridled. I couldn't get my mind around Huber drowning.

"I still say we should let him learn in a smaller place."

"Like a wading pool? He wants an ocean. An ocean! You would insult him if you suggested a pool. We start him out in the river and that's that!"

On the day we decided to go out, Huber had just undergone another trial in class. Mrs. Fuseli wanted to know how much bigger he'd gotten since the year began. And, guilelessly, Huber produced the evidence: which is to say NONE! In her wicked heart, Mrs. Fuseli had been expecting him to bear fruit and multiply, but our austere regime had actually trimmed him down. For that indignity, she asked him things about Ecuador and Columbia, and, finally: Louisiana.

"Louisiana," said Huber, "is the poorest state in the union. It has the lowest poor-capita income and a literacy rate that is only matched by Alabama and Mississippi. Its major source of income is tourism, but it is in dire need of a more viable and enduring economic base."

The collective mouth of the class dropped as Mrs. Fuseli totted up Huber's observations on the bulletin board. She wrote in a good, old-fashioned script, which lent credibility to this sudden savant's pronouncements.

"Where did you learn that?"

"I take an interest in the economy of my home state."

And there it was! Huber had come from an exotic wasteland whose only hope was in its *joie de vivre*, its Mardi Gras, its po' boys. We had studied its casual corruption and historic *bonhomie*, but were not as well-versed as this! The class was stunned.

"Class. Here's something you probably wouldn't have learned for some time, but now that it's come up, we might as well deal with it."

The entire class sat forward. It was rarely asked to *deal* with anything and was intrigued by the challenge.

"Smart people acquire information as it's needed. That is to say, they know what they need to know. But there are other people into whom information seeps. They can't help what they learn because it either gets into their heads or it doesn't. We call them idiot savants. Our friend Huber's command of spelling seems to reflect his IQ. But look. He can quote from the great Guide to New Orleans without taking a breath. In some people, this would be genius. But in Huber, it's clearly a case of idiot savantism."

That was the gauntlet she should have never thrown! We *had* to take him out on the river then.

Sam was the first to speak up.

"Should it matter how knowledge is delivered, just so long as it shows up, like the proverbial newspaper, at one's front door? I think our C-student *extraordinaire* has something to tell us, class. Let's listen because we'll want to emulate his scholarship and grasp of intellectual subtlety."

Titters followed, largely because Mrs. Fuseli waited for, and expected, them. I observed the toadies in my midst and felt strangely knowing. Perhaps I'd be able to catch them at something and save myself in the future. If not, I'd at least had an insight about them. That had to be something.

Sam decided to face the class, which included me. I didn't like for him to preach to me this way, even if I wasn't the only person getting the sermon.

"Yes, I do have something to tell you, though it may be too complicated for y'all to grasp. Nonetheless, however, I am committed to the dissemination of knowledge, howsoever it be...disseminated."

"Listen, class. I think we have another idiot savant in our midst."

Mrs. Fuseli was telling an outright lie that nonetheless showed her willingness to gamble. If a teacher says something, a certain number of people will always believe.

Luckily, Sam understood the essential gravity of The Pause. It drew people in. By the time he was ready to speak, the whole class was leaning in his direction. If some believed Mrs. Fuseli, they all wanted to hear him.

"Huber has a very original mind. He doesn't seem bright to you, but he can go out into the wilderness for hours on end and come back. And if he asks for candy after he tells it, why should we deny him? I have learned a lot from my association with Huber, who isn't just a big kid. He's got everything you should have if you see life as a great adventure. If he doesn't measure up in spelling, who cares? If he can't tell you what Costa Rica exports every quarter or how much sugar cane we get from Cuba each year, it doesn't matter because other people know that already. I propose that we honor Huber for the unique individual that he is and forget about his spelling. It's been proven time and time again that there is no correlation between a good speller and natural intelligence. Or a capacity to live life to its fullest."

Sam didn't wait for an answer. He was out the door after he was done talking, which led to a voluntary stint in the principal's office. As far as I know, he was the only person who had ever checked himself in. He understood the value of being absent once the content of your message starts to sink in.

We were out on the Mississippi River next Friday afternoon. We took the bus downtown and chased boxcars over to the Memphis-Arkansas Bridge, which we walked across. Child of Destiny, Huber did not complain. He felt like Marco Polo, Christopher Columbus, and Vasco da Gama, whose name Sam had famously corrupted into "Ask Fo' Yo' Mama." After crooning it a little, Sam was paraded before class in an embarrassingly unsuccessful attempt to shame him. He was good for five minutes on the value of wordplay, not to mention the vaunted blues tradition, which every Memphian should know. Certain classmates began to call him "nigger-lover." After he made a bobble-head of the biggest and dumbest, the epithet was withdrawn.

Huber was so elated that he did not feel the heft and roll of the bridge as we did. I would look down every once in a while and shudder. Huber didn't seem to care that we were suspended by antique engineering over one of the rudest forms of nature in the Western Hemisphere. Sam was telling the truth about Huber's spirit of adventure, which apparently needed the proper medium to wake up and thrive. Pathfinder Sam studied the great steel girders that formed a massive web-work around us.

"Bridges," said Sam, "have to accommodate stress. Life

accommodates stress by making itself available to it and getting used to it over time."

"Oh," said Huber, looking down into the water, which would surely—as he attempted to accommodate it in his own way—drown him. His unexpected courage made me jittery for him.

"There are all sorts of ways you can be dragged under," I said.

"I know."

"Do you?"

"I don't care," affirmed Huber. "I want to do this."

I'm sure, as we walked across the bridge, that all sorts of motorists were wondering why in hell we were there. Few would have guessed the serious, and possibly life-threatening, mission we were on.

Sam was, of course, cool as a cucumber. The outcome of the experiment was, to his mind, fore-ordained: Huber would drown, but achieve a kind of immortality doing so. When Sam explained it all to me, all I could think of was passing by that great big house and realizing that he, Huber, was no longer in it. This particular aspect of losing him seemed unbearably poignant. His parents moping along the wainscot; the refrigerator door opening hardly at all; and the sound of tinkling ice-cubes extinct as the Passenger Pigeon. (It did not occur to me that adults might enjoy a cool drink themselves.) I did not, however, believe that either Sam or Huber would consider turning back. I watched Huber lumber along the sidewalk, possibly for the last time. Yet it wasn't a bad image; his step was lively and he'd shed pounds from calf and thigh. He looked nearly credible as the adventurer/explorer he would have to become. As he was in his heart already.

In those days, and perhaps in our own, you got down to the Arkansas side of the river—if you were on foot—by being patient. Once off the bridge, you were not necessarily going to make it to the river. It was merely a prerequisite. A lot of people got tired and went home. But we found, in Huber, an unusually motivated person. He seemed, after a time of stress, and in the midst of outlandish expectations, to have found a source of peace and serenity. But he had to prove something—which worried me. I don't believe Sam ever worried about anything, except the dire consequences of spying on a naked sister. Which is why he turned the job over to me. I never figured out why he wanted to do it at all. Except that he might have been inspired by the enigma of a once-gangly physique turning into a pin-up girl. Because, however, it was his sister, nobody would understand the scientific curiosity that drove him, through me, to look in on her now and then. For the majority of mankind—which at least pretended to be looking out for the other half of humanity—it was a moral splinter that, once lodged, could not be removed without tremendous suffering. Unlike his bravery in other things, his voyeurism—which, because it happened through me, might be regarded a voyeurism-twice-removed—made him hesitate and assign the dirty-work, as it were, to me. In retrospect, I think he wanted me to become hopelessly fascinated so that he might have tried out some sort of cure—as he had done with Huber, though with potentially tragic repercussions—on me. Unlike anyone else I had ever known, he seemed to be motivated by only one thing: the sometimes-reckless pursuit of knowledge for its own sake. Yet, as in the tale of Icarus, I think he was flying, in Huber's case if not my own, a little too close to an inferno. Yet, when he was attempting to get at something, Sam was as irresistible as a spider who had chosen his fly, subdued it, and spun hoops of silken steel around its wings. In spite of the possibility that Huber might drown—which seemed to awaken Sam to a higher purpose—I was going along. Just goes to show you how, when we're mesmerized, cherished principles as well as conventional moralities have no more effect than a drop of water in a rainstorm.

Sam and I had no plan except to launch him and hope he'd wind up somewhere downriver, tuckered out, but not much the worse for wear. We'd done it, but that wasn't much help to him. But Huber wasn't oriented so much to the consequences of things as to experiencing them one blissful moment at a time. When he emerged from those wild acres only the sexually precocious knew well enough to get in and out of, he was a different person than the one who'd gone in. Did he know that in advance? Or was he a born adventurer whose deeper calling had been awakened by having seen, if not conquered; experienced, if not understood? He wanted to do this thing and that was all he could see. The obstacles and conundrums other people worried about didn't concern him. In this regard, he *was* the idiot savant Mrs. Fuseli accused him of being.

We had laid in a Styrofoam raft for him, and felt, like all skinny people before pneumatic flesh, that, in a jam, he would become exceptionally buoyant. We'd been nearly drowned several times and were somewhat wary of the river's force. On the other hand, the Mississippi River was *supposed* to drown you. But perhaps it would spare somebody with a floating capacity denied the rest of us and was therefore more suitable to the work at hand.

When we found the river-bank—and the raft we'd set aside—we gravely steered Huber toward a shoal that was atypically roilsome. Yet it was the right time to go: the sun was out, man's toils and troubles did not, temporarily, concern us, and we were embarked on a collaborative effort we would, no doubt, remember the rest of our lives. I thought of Huber's ice-maker. *He's not going to make it. The ice-maker knows.*

"The cubes just come right out when you want them to—and you don't have to wait for them. You just put your

glass underneath the chute and they're there. They're there."
I stammered, acknowledging one of Huber's signal contributions to a life that was going, because of our presence here,
to last decades longer than his. Ready ice made a lukewarm
existence tolerable. Ready ice was one of the unheralded triumphs of civilization. Ready ice made you feel in control, as
if you needed nothing outside of it. Ready ice...with it, you
were cool. Without it, something was missing. Without it...
you had fewer friends in a world that managed friendships
poorly. *Huber, don't go in there! The ice-maker knows.*

"I'm sicka that thing," said Huber, affirming his native
dignity. This hero needed no frills.

 Before you go," said Sam, who hadn't said much, "you
need to know you're on your own."

"I know," said Huber.

"Do you?" asked Sam, as if scripted.

"Yes," said Huber, with a similar consciousness of style
and effect.

"If anything happens..." said Sam, drifting off, just so he
could be drifting off. None of us had any idea of what would
happen should "anything happen."

"Yes, I know," said Huber, with a sense of drama that was
maturing with every syllable. It was as if Sam and Huber were
carrying scripts around and going through motions some
director had plotted out for them.

"But first: are you really from New Orleans?"

"No. I just have this little book about it."

"I was thinking that you have a chance of getting down
there right now."

"I know," said Huber with a faraway look.

"Okay, then. Let's get you on this raft and make history."

As it turned out, Huber was ideally suited to floating on
the river, which had, of course, claimed far more nimble

floaters who were equally survival-driven. But he didn't seem to care whether he'd fall off or not, which attitude provided him with a lackadaisical stability. As the sun declined, and the sandy beach lit up with a light that was too good to be merely golden, we watched Huber as he breasted the back of the river like an old pro and vanished quickly. We speculated on the length of his journey. Depending on how far downriver he made it, he might not be able to find us—nor we him. In that nightfall was approaching, he'd have the added challenge of a nocturnal river—which couldn't be much different than any other kind except that it wasn't visible.

We both had the same thought: we've murdered him.

A family that had installed sophisticated air-conditioning would give no quarter to the likes of us. We'd be skewered under the glare of logic, cut to pieces with cunning sophistries, neutralized by nuances we could not think of ourselves and spend the rest of our lives attempting to understand. His folks would outspend and out-argue us. I began to see myself as a transgressor and not an activist. Sam was fatalistic, knowing that what one does cannot be undone—even if it might be explained in such a way that perception might swing in one's favor.

And it was fun camping out there on the Arkansas side, with no adults to provide structure and none of the usual claptrap about curfews and schedules clouding up our minds. If need be, we'd stay the night—something I had never done before. There was a parental conundrum: if we didn't show up when we were supposed to, calls would be made, curfews would be discussed, and we might even be the subject—or victims—of a minor manhunt.

"We could get arrested, couldn't we?"

Sam was always one to feed paranoia and not, as the normally humane person would do, minimize it.

"Should he run into something downriver, yes. Hey, maybe we should float down and join him! Come on."

As casual as that, we launched another Styrofoam pad and were out in it, like two hunters without a dog. Sam knew that I got panicky if we started to roll too much to one side or the other, so he did most of the paddling.

"Just hold on," he said to me, as he had said all the other times we'd done the same thing.

"He'll be all right," I thought aloud. "He has a built-in life preserver."

"It's a fallacy to think that fat people float better than skinny ones."

"I thought they did."

"No. We all drown equally."

"That can't be. I thought...why didn't you tell me?"

"He *needs* to do this. It's connected to all sorts of things. Drowning could be the best thing that ever happened to him."

"What?" I spluttered, spitting out half a mouthful of water that tasted warm and yellowy.

"Surely you knew that."

"No, I didn't," I said with a sort of wounded simplicity. Sam never let you in on the joke—if there was one; and if there was a deeper meaning, he waited for time and circumstance to reveal it.

"I shouldn't have expected you to," he said, paddling us out of a shivery spot where the water seemed to bank up against something.

The river was pretty wide from where we were, though it was not the open channel it was said to be farther down. Nor were we casually afloat. We were still in the shallow water, which had a rollicking life of its own. For a moment, however, the raft seemed to pull itself along. I stopped paddling as Sam twisted this way and that to keep it steady. I was invariably responsible for scuttling us and knew, this time, to keep still as I held onto the bow. We'd learned that the best way to control it was to lay flat and steer gently. If you over-steered, it would tip over. As usual, Sam knew what was too little and, more importantly, too much.

"Any sight of him?"

"Nope."

"Do you think we'll find him?"

"Dunno."

"Me neither."

"In this case, we should probably get used to..."

"To what?"

Sam did not deign to answer, as he kept us afloat through eddy and shoal; along creepy passages that rippled very strangely and calm-looking spots that were swirly toward the bottom. We'd been scuttled at this point before, and could easily swim back. For once, however, my mind was not on self-preservation, but on the larger issues prompted by fate and circumstance.

"If he dies, we're responsible," I said.

"He won't. I have instincts."

"He's never done this before."

"Doesn't matter. He's got a feeling."

"He'll die!"

"He will not die, but he will be changed. That's why I wanted him to come out here. He likes challenges, but he's been protected and hasn't had the opportunity. We're giving him that opportunity. Just watch what happens. You'll see what I'm talking about."

I stayed silent until the river presented us with an immediate challenge we were obliged to ride out, if we could. As usual, I panicked, the raft overturned, and he, Sam, swam it back to shore as I trailed him languishingly. I flopped on the beach trying to catch my breath as Sam—who seemed to lack breathing limitations—calculated the distance we'd traveled and hit upon a good way to get back. He did not mention Huber.

"He's still out there, you know."

"Yes, I do. Come on."

"We can't leave him."

"How you do suggest we stick by him now? "

I had always found Sam unorthodox, but rarely callous.

"But we *have* to find him!"

Looking toward where Huber might, at the moment, be struggling with a current that had bested us—or me anyway—Sam said: "He's lost, but not gone."

"I wish you'd stop saying things like that. You can't see him anymore than I can. God, we've killed him. I know we have. I just know!"

Rather than argue with me, Sam made one of those welcoming gestures with which movie-butlers had provided head-tilt and elbow-room and invited me to join him.

"Come on. If we hurry, we can get back before dinner."

And so we left: without our man.

Dinner was being served as we got to the front door. If anyone has ever doubted the soul-comforting nature of good—or even bad—cooking, all one has to do is encounter it after some sort of stressful activity and it's just as good as any unexpected panacea. It works its magic right away and, no matter how unendurable life, at that moment, appears to be, it irons out all wrinkles, smooths furrowed brows, and rocks every cradle. I didn't let on, but I felt as if we had been given, by steam and vapor, a second chance. By Huberian standards, it was hardly overwhelming. But Huber didn't care for anything other than snack food anyway and wouldn't have cared how much, or how little, comfort was suddenly available to us.

"You boys wash up," said Sam's mother, as if she'd been expecting us that very moment. She was dolled up in a way I found initially comical. Sam said it was for Aldro—who was not conspicuously captivated. Perhaps it was not stoical to be oversexed.

"Where have you all been?" she asked. "You reek of something very...original."

"You mean *ab*original," put in Aldro.

"Do I?" asked she, consulting a thought-bubble that was ever-rising. Her breasts were magnificently restrained behind a bright, button-down shirt that was tied at the waist and aromatically laundered. There was no ambiguity to them and therefore no spying. You admired them openly or admired them not at all.

Leah wandered in, looking abstracted. She wore oversized glasses that corrected astigmatism and all sorts of other impairments too esoteric for the layman to understand.

"Hello," she said to me, failing to aim her face in the right direction. I said hello back, aiming my own face somewhat more accurately. Her breasts were well-hidden behind a sheaf of terry-cloth. She liked studying in a robe, and since studying was just about all she did, she had a robe on most of the time she wasn't in school, or at the eye doctor's.

"Leah's going to test out of the sixth grade," said the mother.

Expected to react, Aldro looked up from his newspaper and said something I couldn't quite catch. Sam was already tearing into his food. Unlike Huber, Sam's appetite was best activated by a full plate, which it engulfed with joyous abandon. I was more timid, preferring to spear a discreet little portion of the dish and hold it up to my nose. I was there to make a case for standard etiquette.

"Shall we say grace first? Sam?"

Sam obliged with a rather heady sermon on the fruits

of the tree and the bounty of nature. He concluded with an overall hosannah to a godlike creator that existed everywhere, and in lower case. Then he proceeded to make up for lost time.

"Sam doesn't believe in God," said Leah, expressing a truth that was fairly controversial.

Sam shook his head in agreement.

"Let's not get into that right now," said his mother, with a noggin-twist that was so delightfully undignified, I was hoping she'd do another. Or outdo it with something even better. Yet, whenever I saw her, I could never make myself pay much attention to anything other than those breasts of hers, which lacked the motherly graces of near-invisibility and gravitational surrender. Unlike my own mother, and, it seemed, most women, her center of gravity was at the chest, which prompted forward momentum as well as overall stability. I found myself watching this chest as you'd watch a well-coordinated crew that knew its place under every possible circumstance. Pitching forward, drawing back, it was always riveting, always fascinating. I think she liked me staring at her; she obliged by providing me, albeit discreetly, with every conceivable opportunity to observe and appreciate. Aldro was, at best, a neutral spectator, lifting up his head from time to time as if to ascertain his whereabouts. His appetite for breast-sightings had possibly been quenched long ago—or perhaps his stoicism wouldn't let him do it quite so openly as I was.

"I don't believe in anything I can't see," affirmed Sam, who was already on his second plate.

"Let's change the subject, if you don't mind," suggested Aldro, who didn't look up.

"You heard what your father said," added his mother, as if to The Deaf.

"I'll be gone someday, so it doesn't matter."

"Don't say that," whispered his mother, as if to a blaspheming saint.

"So will I," said Leah, who had not, thus far, contributed Abstract Thought to the discussion. I was under the vaguely narcissistic illusion that she had a minor crush on me. I occasionally fantasized about her offering me her breasts one day as I came in from out of the cold or just any old time I happened to be around. I wasn't quite sure what to do with them, but I appreciated the gesture and said so. In this fantasy, I let her go on about the nature of breasts and why they were so conspicuous. "You see," she adumbrated, "they are nature's way of tantalizing males, who are so differently made that, because of the benignly antagonistic nature of attraction, they are compelled to touch them. You want to touch my breasts, not because they are beautiful unto themselves, but because of a primordial urge with which nature endows you." In this fantasy, I touched them as a sort of neutral party who can't understand nature's role in something I seemed to be doing all by myself. And because it was a fantasy, she didn't say "You're so stupid!" and flounce off.

"I think we've heard quite enough about that," said Sam's mother. "You're much too young to have morbid fixations. Besides, you're here now and we have a guest so I want us to all come together like a family and be cheerful."

"I am always cheerful," said Sam, whose mouth drooped into a frown. I laughed because Sam had segued so exquisitely from one expression to the next.

"It isn't always wise to be cheerful," chirped Leah, who picked at her food, possibly because picking ensured that she was participating in the meal without having to aim bits and pieces of it at her mouth. Her glasses were supernaturally large and made her eyes bug out. They were crude magnifiers that were helping her skip a grade, but had limited practical value beyond the fine print of things.

"My, my!" said Sam's mother. "She'll be in college before we know it!"

"Hmmm," said Aldro, flexing his newspaper.

"College: the royal road that leads to knowledge."

"I'm going to get a Ph.D," said Leah, who regarded life as a series of increasingly daunting academic challenges. For these, she would not necessarily need breasts. They would just be along for the ride. I had a picture of them bouncing alongside of a great, book-filled caravan. Just as that vision faded, her mother's center of gravity intruded with a plate-full of green peas.

"If nothing else, Sam eats his vegetables," said her breasts to me.

"He eats everything," observed Leah, who didn't seem to be able to distinguish between food groups until they found their way to her mouth. Everything she ate was therefore surprising. Sometimes she demanded to know what something was before she tucked it, a thing at long last identified, into a mouth she would only half-open. She'd been in braces the year before and hadn't quite adjusted to their absence.

Her mother's breasts assured her that everything was fresh and worth eating. After slamming down some droopy vegetables, she, Leah, went back to her usual routine, which consisted of staring dreamily at something which had no material existence because Abstract Thought would not permit it.

When Sam finished, he always shot up from his chair and wafted out of the room—a gesture with a limited, but site-specific outcome, since he always exited to his room. I was expected to follow him at some point. Before I was able to, the mother, and not the breasts, asked me where we'd really been that evening.

"I know you go places you're not supposed to. But a mother likes to know where her children are. They grow up so fast you hardly ever see them."

"I'm growing up faster than anyone," challenged Leah, who had begun to lash herself back into her robe against the chore of rising. While tantalizingly present, her own breasts were regrettably protected and out of sight, if not mind.

"Yes, we know."

"What's that supposed to mean?" shouted Leah, suddenly out of control.

"That you are, that's all. Sam doesn't seem to need to grow up. Which worries me sometimes."

"Well, I'll be in college soon enough and it won't matter," said Leah, who had risen and was tacking away.

"Did she excuse herself?" grunted Aldro.

"Yes, she did, husband," Sam's mother replied, with a look toward me. Her breasts were adrift on a sea of discord. A son had absconded, a daughter had stormed off, and she was interrogating an unreliable friend who'd probably tell her a pack of lies.

"Tell me where you two went this evening," she demanded, as if to let no small edge slip away from her.

"To the river," I replied obligingly. It seemed far-fetched enough to elicit surprise, then incredulity, then relief over my having committed a charming outrage against truth and dignity.

"I remember, in a college course I took about the novel, where a protagonist extricates himself from a bad situation by means of a colorful story. Could you be doing that!"

Having ceased to listen to her after the word novel, I couldn't, in truth or no, answer such a question and, in the interest of incriminating no one, I remained silent. I always looked to Sam for either silent corroboration or...a colorful story. I couldn't discern whether he wanted me to tell the truth or not.

Having, in light of what his mother had just said, re-considered his hasty exit, Sam occupied a portion of the dining-room that was given over to his mother's art-work: great splashy expanses of flat color alternating with fuzzy charcoal lines. These were the abstract paintings she'd learned to do in a class. They were a perfect counterpoint to her breasts, which stuck out disconcertingly in form as these journeymen efforts stuck out in color.

"We went to the river in order to initiate a good friend of ours into its myriad dangers."

"Where's this friend?"

"Went home."

"Oh," said his mother, radiating satisfaction at her son, brother to all men who didn't worry their families.

"You could drown there, son," was Aldro's piquant observation.

"If you couldn't, it wouldn't be any fun."

"Listen to him! You boys didn't swim, did you?"

"Why go to such a place and not swim?"

"What did the other boy do?"

"Swam with us."

"I don't want you boys doing that anymore," warned Aldro, who was going through the motions. He understood his son to be unreachable, as his mother could not. But he had to express timely concerns and familial attitudes. As far as Aldro was concerned, Sam was not the result of his teeming loins, but a kind of extraterrestrial phenomenon that had displaced his seed and inserted something he would never like nor understand. Unlike a conventional parent, who might prefer to sire his own children, he seemed oddly comfortable with the idea.

"You heard your father. Don't swim."

"All right, all right," agreed Sam as you'd agree to any absurd notion you're too fastidious to oppose.

As I left the table, daubing my face with an oversized handkerchief whose ulcerous discolorations kept the daubing at a minimum, I thanked them both for the excellent meal.

"He's so polite. I wish Sam could be that way sometimes."

After having made our exit, we were off for the night. I had already cleared an entire evening away from home with my parents, who were no doubt relieved that I'd be spending time with Sam, because if I was with Sam, I'd be away from them. It's not that they didn't want me around. When, however, I wasn't, my personal dramas could be displaced by the relatively placid ones my little brother—who was a mostly unoffending soul—brought to the table. He was the sort of ideal person for whose creation parents-in-waiting—who get stressed out by all of the anticipatory angst—dream. He did his homework, he was an excellent little student—mostly because he wasn't big enough yet to be called anything else—and he was polite to his elders, which encompassed a swath of humanity who could grant favors and provide a sense of ease as life's growing pains rattled one's bones and distracted one's attention. They sorta liked having me around, but they felt guilty about granting me so much attention when I wasn't the stellar performer my brother was. We want people to be low-maintenance, but we don't pay as much attention to them as their more unpredictable counterparts. Among the inequalities of youth, this might well be—particularly to those who are capable of doing the right thing—one of the tragedies that lead, later in life, to therapeutic sessions that end in tears, or start that way and wind down without any sort of favorable outcome. There was also this: whenever we stayed at my house, the place was—given the conflicting chemistries Sam and I brought to an equation that, with my brother alone, wasn't uproarious at all—in an uproar well past everybody's bedtime. Sam's parents weren't any more adaptable than mine were. With Sam's mother leading the pack, however, they could be as high-strung as we were and didn't notice our temperamental peculiarities as much as mine did. My younger brother raised the bar, I took it down, and that was our dynamic. At Sam's house, you weren't always sure who'd raise it—or whether it would be raised at all. With Aldro as referee, however, things never quite got out of hand. Yet they were never, not exclusively because of all of the breasts that could be viewed openly or clandestinely, unexciting.

"If he drowns...they'll know."

"You don't seem to understand the nature of this mission," he said, crowding into me as if to make a huddle.

"What do you mean?"

"Whatever happens, *has* to happen. It's out of our hands. We guided him there because that was our function. But after we did that, we had to stand aside and let everything run its course."

"But...do you think he's drowned?"

"No, I don't."

"I don't understand why we didn't just go after him."

"We couldn't. This was his journey."

I'd never heard such talk in my life.

"Did you see him at all?"

"He's already come back."

"WHAT!"

"I know he has. I can sense it."

With this pronouncement, Sam acquired the faraway look that was Leah's absolute stock-in-trade. Who was borrowing from whom?

"What do you see exactly?"

"His homecoming."

I caved.

"Really?"

"Yes. He's home already and is being embraced like a prodigal."

"I...so he's okay?"

"He's not only okay. He feels better now than he has ever felt before."

Perhaps Sam didn't know he was paraphrasing a character in a movie who makes the ultimate sacrifice to save another man—and scores points with a woman he loves, but who will be denied an opportunity to savor and appreciate this love.

"Okay, if that's so, why don't we go over there?"

"We could. I would personally enjoy seeing him."

"Really?"

"Yes."

The walk was fairly long, through hundreds of undistinguished properties very much like our own; along streets from which traffic was eerily absent; past lanes and alcoves late-night developers had carved out of forest and farmland. Most of the streets were named after English villages. Memphis was big on old-world nostalgia, particularly if it spoke in a recognizable tongue and was just polysyllabic enough to add class and cachet.

Hoisting myself up between Sam's inter-threaded hands, I banged on Huber's bedroom window. Huber presently appeared, an enormous face looking down upon us. Its studied languor charmed me infinitely. No, it gave me pause. No, it summed up the unspeakable delights ordinary things can have for those who could have lost them. I was a survivor of my own dreadful feelings, which had consigned Huber to the bottom of a river that was infamously hard on newcomers and punished every mistake without mercy.

"Let us in!" instructed Sam, who pantomimed a possible progress between bedroom, kitchen, and front door.

The face we saw was enormously impassive. We could have been old friends, distant relatives, or speck-like things who might be worth coming out to crush.

But Huber opened the window and began to speak.

"You'll never know...how it was out there. I can't believe I did it. I never tipped over. I just decided to pull in and come back. I think I want to do the whole thing. All of it."

"That's great, Hubie."

"I thought, when you left me, that you were playing a trick on me. But I don't think you knew what was going to happen. Did you?"

"Just let us in," pleaded Sam.

"No, I'm too tired. But thanks for coming. We can talk in class."

And with that, Hubie pulled the curtains and was gone.

As we walked back home, we were gripped by a sullen urge to revisit Huber and force him to tell us at least a little more than he had. For once, Sam was out of humor.

"He should have told us something," said he, trying to understand an independence he had helped, by letting him go his own way, foster. It was as if we were a necessary first act that moved the main character forward, after which we could be conveniently ignored. Sam visibly struggled with something that was way beyond my understanding, but had assumed a palpable presence under streetlights that completed, rather than minimized, the darkness all around.

"Come with me," he said.

In order to find out what was bothering him, I would have followed him anywhere, provided comfortable seating was around.

Between Huber's glitzier neighborhood and ours was a shopping center keen-eyed developers had put up to serve a population they had put into starter-homes and prefabricated ranchers. Whenever we went there after dark, it was to have a sort of home base from which we might consider an elegant break-in or rambling adventure. The place was nearly

pitch-dark as we walked briskly along an arcade that protected—and provided access to—a barbershop, a hobby-store,
and a dry-cleaning establishment whose punctual service my
father called glumly into question every week or so. (He was
a traveling salesman whose need for reliability was superseded
by that of military people, for whom special coordinates and
exact arrival times were paramount.) I stopped at the hobby
store's window and looked in. My collecting mania had been
most recently captivated by ancient coinage. It was to this
place, and another several miles into town, that I would come
when I was loaded down with a few extra dollars. Sam had
no need of such places. If he wanted something, all he had
to do was visualize it. It made me helplessly envious to think
of his large-cent collection, come by at an antique shop along
a country road.

"They don't have anything. Come on."

We ascended to the roof of the small grocery store by
means of a slippery series of pipes and footholds Sam utilized
with gymnastic skill. I clambered up them gingerly, afraid
not only of falling, but of appearing as graceless, in Sam's
eyes, as I no doubt was. But superior people are sometimes
compassionate. Whenever I got to the roof's jagged rim, Sam
was always there to help me up it.

"I think," said Sam to an astronomical backdrop that was
somewhat disorienting, "I understand. I think...he went to
the ocean this afternoon."

And with that pronouncement, Sam went gravely silent
while I searched the roof for small stones I might hurl into
the darkness.

Sam's prescient moment bore immediate fruit. For one
thing, Huber was late for class. His mother generally drove
him to the western entrance of the school, there to deposit
him, with a mother's kisses, onto the narrow concrete lane

that led to a comic portico, over which the school fathers had set, in concrete bas-relief, a severed head that seemed to wink at you from one angle and roll its eyes from another. The crueler kids liked to watch Huber shamble up the lane with his schoolbooks riding along his hips and stomach, which accommodated them very nicely. They suggested, with helpful insight, that he might consider balancing them on his head. Or rolling them along in a chuck-wagon. Or just leaving them at home for all the good they did him.

On this occasion, Huber ran the gauntlet of low-grade ridicule; his dignified condescension was not only magnificent, it seemed pre-ordained. Because he seemed immune to it, the raillery that accompanied him faded before he finished his progress down the lane. There he threw back his head, ignoring one and all, and went in. I witnessed this peculiar ritual with a kind of mentor's pride, taking credit where I thought it was due, while saving some up for Sam, who didn't mention Huber that whole weekend. It was as if he, Sam, was done with Huber and couldn't think of anything more climactic than to exile him from his consciousness. I was still dying to hear what had happened to Huber on the raft. He'd obviously made it—but how? Where did he end up and how had he gotten home? Did these particulars have anything to do with the way he was acting—with the way he acted when he paid him that surprise visit?

Huber distinguished himself in class by shambling in late and occupying his seat in the back row. The class felt, with the instinct of a homogeneous organism, something different about him and waited for him, albeit unconsciously, to reveal it.

Mrs. Fuseli came in angrily, opening and shutting the top drawer of her desk. It was there that she kept the spool-bound notebook in which she recorded test scores and individual grades. It was a powerful location and she enjoyed reminding us of its presence.

"Stand up, please, and recite the Pledge of Allegiance," she snapped as we all snapped to. Huber took his sweet time and didn't start mumbling the words until we'd come to "...one nation, under God, indivisible, with liberty and justice for all." While he dawdled, Mrs. Fuseli studied him with a pinchy look. As the study deepened, the pinchy look morphed into something dark and moody. A fundamentalist might have interpreted it as The Devil's Wrath taking hold of a person's face before it ravaged his or her body. I tried to get Sam's attention, but he seemed absorbed in re-establishing his loyalty to The Republic. It was strange to watch Sam perform a ritual he ordinarily disliked, but, because it was Sam, it had to be accepted. Sam was always whoever he was at the moment and therefore impossible to pin down. He would, however, explain his metamorphosis in such a way that it appeared not only inevitable from a psychological standpoint, but somehow heroic, as if he were re-inventing himself as freewheelingly as one could. But my focus was chiefly on Huber, whose behavior was casually insolent, not to say self-destructive.

When the mumbling was over and everybody crash-landed into their desks, Mrs. Fuseli darted her eyes around the room as if to exercise them. They played malignantly around somebody's forehead, then darted away to a trembling hand or drumming finger. Of course, she was just biding her time. What she most wanted to execute, and was preparing coolly, was a fresh assault. Huber, whose shambling insolence could not go unchallenged, waited for her to move in for the kill.

"What, Huber, did you do over the weekend?" she asked with what might have passed in a human being as benign curiosity.

"Me? Nothing. Ate a little, walked some. Studied. Nothing."

"Then how am I to interpret your general demeanor?"

"I don't know. Maybe that's your problem and not mine."

"What was that?" she hissed.

Sam was itching to rise, but knew that Huber had to play this one out.

"I did do something over the weekend, Mrs. Fuseli. But I don't want to tell you about it because it was private. It was just for me. I don't want you to know about it. You or anybody."

That hurt. Huber was not excepting us from the high-rolling disdain everybody else was getting. This was a brand-new place: anonymity, a moral vacuum, total exile. If Huber didn't need us—and Sam in particular—we had no purpose beyond that of showing up, squeaking by, and waiting for summer. Sam watched his hands as they folded together on his desk. This was submission and surrender. We were out—and Huber was not yet done.

"I don't think that's an appropriate response, Mr. Huber."

"I do. In fact, if you don't mind, I'm hungry at the moment and am going to have a little something. If you'll excuse me."

After announcing his intentions, Huber took out a Baby Ruth and started chomping.

"Listen, buster, if you don't put that back, you're going straight to the principal's office."

"Fine. I've always wanted to meet him."

Mrs. Fuseli's rage expressed itself in a kind of forward momentum that unfortunately snagged, and, in a bewildering series of little clashes and attempted escapes, forced her downwards. In addition to finding herself facing the baby-shit linoleum the school's dedicated cleaning staff buffed every night, she was partially without her dress, which had bunched-up as she descended. A goodly part of it was dangling on an oak-hard knob while a lesser part managed to hold on. The class's natural reaction was to laugh, but of course, it could not do that unless it wished to be visited by The Devil's Wrath, so the humor of the situation had to be dealt with surreptitiously. As to the means, instinct had provided heaving intakes of breath followed by a kind of coughing that could be muffled somewhat inside of the hand.

At this point, Huber rose and started to leave the room, pausing, with devastating effect, before Mrs. Fuseli without bothering to help her to her feet, or even deigning to acknowledge her distress and discomfort. At his exit, the class couldn't help itself anymore and moaned with the collective relief of a strangled impulse. It moaned with the sheer delight of having found the proper way to express the inexpressible. It moaned out its love of justice, its hatred of a bitter old woman who singled out the weakest in the pack and flung all of her reprehensible energies toward it. It moaned ecstatically and unapologetically until it could no longer produce any sound. Then it fell quiet, only to realize that Mrs. Fuseli was still there on the floor and was as ridiculous as she had been all along.

In striding forward and offering to help Mrs. Fuseli to her feet, Sam broke the force of so much sudden hilarity. It was the sort of courtly gesture that is admired in retrospect, but is rarely mustered while a satisfying humiliation is in progress. It seemed as if Sam was born to it, however, as he grabbed Mrs. Fuseli's hands, hoisted her to a sitting position while pushing down the part of her dress that had gotten tangled and returning it to her as if it were a crisp dollar bill. Then he escorted her out to the hall, where she burst into tears and ran somewhere without him. When he returned, he said: "And now, class, I think we should turn to our spelling."

At which point the class dissolved into a joy that was as completely unrestrained as it is possible to be anywhere and at any time.

As we walked home, Sam explained it all to me.

"As I told you, he doesn't need us anymore. He doesn't need anybody."

"What do you mean?"

"I told you when we were out there. Whatever happened to him out on that river made him different. Better. More alive."

"Huh."

"Remember when he said he wanted the ocean? That indicated that his dreams were big. All we could offer him was the river, but remember how he took it?"

"Uh...okay," trying to remember Huber there. All I could remember was my own despair. And something about the ice-cube maker at Huber's house.

"He went somewhere on that river. He went somewhere and we can't follow him."

I was a little annoyed.

"You mean because he found something out there, he doesn't need us?"

"Yes, in a word. You know what he found out there on that river?"

"Uh..."

Sam edged close to me and took my shoulders. In movies, this is the point at which somebody is taught a lesson—a life lesson in general, a lesson in decorum or morality, or a lesson in how to do something better without trying to show off about it. In any case, it's a climactic moment and it changes everything.

"He found...he found himself. Now let's go over to his house and eat something."

Because Sam never met a door he couldn't break into, we were inside of the big house within minutes. The news was on in a distant room, but when I started to point in that direction, Sam merely shook his head and led me to the fridge, which could make ice all by itself and set you up for a course of lifelong addictions.

"Somebody's here," I observed with my usual grasp of the obvious.

"I know. Hey, look! They've got shrimp!"

As Sam started to chow down on the pinkish delicacies he extracted from a bowl that looked ages old, but was, in reality, signed on the back by a local artisan, Huber came in, noticed us, and said, "Go ahead. I'm not hungry now" and went to the distant room where the TV was on. We kept on eating. It was the first time I'd had cocktail shrimp and they were even tastier than I thought they would be.

Acknowledgments

Abundant thanks to Leslie Weisman, whose understanding of *le mot juste* is supported and enriched by the Big Picture mentality miniaturists often lack. To my brother, Bryan, who's been "there" all the way. To Scott White, who considered individual stories and was circumspectly admiring. To David Ross, a man who grew up in a rather different place and is probably more glad of it—having read these stories—than he ever was. To Harvey Huddleston, who chose to leave, but never will. And to Peter Bowman, whose unbridled imagination could not be hobbled by garden hoses or second gears.

www.ingramcontent.com/pod-product-compliance
Lightning Source LLC
Chambersburg PA
CBHW031215260626
47169CB00007B/2063